In memory of my mother,
Michelle LeMay Doran

In memory of my mother,
Michelle LeMay Doran

The voice of the sea speaks to the soul.

—KATE CHOPIN

Don't be afraid. It won't hurt you.

*D*on't be afraid. It won't hurt you.

Nora shrieks and darts up the beach, the waves inches behind. She is laughing. The water can't get her. Her mother won't let it.

Take my hand.

Her mother's fingers are warm. Nora only reaches her waist. *I'll never be big enough. I'll never be like you.*

Her mother laughs. Her voice is as sparkling as light on water. The folds of her skirt cling to her legs. She'd dived in, fully clothed. She isn't like the other mothers with their rules and careful ways. *Of course you will, in time. You are a part of me. You always will be.*

Why?

That's the way it is with mothers and daughters. She touches a finger to Nora's freckled nose and smiles. There is no other smile like hers. No one else who looks at her like this.

Nora giggles and runs away. *Catch me! Catch me if you can!* She hears the *shush* of sand shifting beneath footsteps, the sound of breathing, close at first, then receding. She ducks between the rocks, rife with mussels and barnacles, limpets and periwinkles, the stones wetted, dark. Her mother can't follow. She isn't small enough. Only a child could pass through here. Nora seldom wins the games they play. Today will be different. She hides, waiting to be found, for her mother to say she gives up.

Minutes pass. A red-shelled crab salutes with a claw, before vanishing into a crevice. A gooseneck barnacle clicks closed like the aperture of her father's camera. The creatures of the ocean are locking themselves up tight, as if they sense something coming. At first, Nora doesn't think to wonder why.

And then she realizes: the tide is coming in. She shouldn't have gone this way. She doesn't know how to breathe underwater.

Nora! Her mother calls. *Nora! Where are you?*

Here. I'm here.

Her foot is caught, the sole of her sandal wedged tight, as if the rocks have reached out and grabbed her.

She tugs at the straps. Her mother always helps her with the buckles, and now that the leather is wet, they are even harder to loosen. The waves are rising, to her ankles, her knees, higher each time. Unless someone finds her soon, she is going under.

Nora opens her eyes, her breath coming in shallow gasps. Light filters into the room along the edge of the window shade. It is 5:30 a.m., Tuesday morning. The digital numerals glow a nagging red, reminding her of how little sleep she managed to get the night before. The newspaper hits the front door with a loud thump that startles her.

It was only a dream. She gazes around the master bedroom, assuring herself of the surroundings, of reality. She didn't think she would be grateful for that, not with the events of the past few weeks. She is alone, but she isn't drowning.

She notices that the letter she received a month ago has fallen off the nightstand and onto the floor. She doesn't know how. The sash isn't open. There is no draft. She must have knocked it over in her sleep. She'd been rereading it the night before—she'd meant to respond sooner, but life, tumultuous as it has proven to be recently, had intervened—weighing her options, deciding what to do.

The letter is from her aunt Maire, summoning her to Burke's Island, the place of her birth and her mother's disappearance, for the first time in decades.

There's no more time to waste. School is out for the summer. She can't bear to stay in the house another day. She has to get away. She'll pack her daughters' things that very morning, and then, they will go.

Chapter One

Someone was watching them that afternoon. Nora was sure of it. She scanned the cove, eyes sweeping over the shingled beach, the dun-colored rocks. Fishing floats bobbed on the surface, faded, disembodied, the water hiding its secrets under a mirrored sheen. The polished glass fragments for which the beach was named glowed in the sunlight, and skeins of seaweed laced patterns on the shore, waiting for the tide to claim them.

"Do you see something?" her daughter Ella asked.

Nora shook her head. She had to remind herself that they didn't have to keep looking over their shoulders, not on Burke's Island. They'd left the scandal and the press behind. Her husband, the source of it all, too.

"Look." Annie pointed to a pile of shells by the back deck. "It's like they knew we were coming." At seven, she still half lived in a world of make-believe.

"Who?" Ella's brow creased with trademark skepticism.

"The shell people," Annie said with a secretive smile.

"Don't be silly. Aunt Maire probably left them there," Ella replied.

"You have no imagination." Annie sniffed.

"Well, at least I have common sense."

"Girls." Nora turned a periwinkle over in her hands. The blue-gray shell twisted in on itself, forming a tight knot, a dash of silver nacre at its center. Her mother had been an inveterate beachcomber, reading the shore, the waves, Nora trailing along in her shadow. She remembered a gauzy sun, wrapped in diaphanous clouds, light seeping through the gaps. A God sky, they called it, as if its source were indeed divine. *Don't look*, someone said, putting their hands over her eyes, shielding her. From what? The voices distorted, as if speaking underwater. The bone-aching cold of the ocean at first touch, the numb acceptance. *Keep moving and you'll stay warm.* The memories flitted, scaled, slippery, before they disappeared into ether once more, swallowed by the murky depths of her subconscious. *Don't let go.*

She sighed. It must have been the long drive, making her feel so fatigued. Three and a half hours north of Boston, then the chartered boat, past Monhegan. That and finally being able to let down her guard after everything that had happened, giving in, to a certain degree—not entirely, she could never do that, not with the children to consider—to exhaustion. And yet standing on that crumbled shore near the cottage gave her such a piercing sense of déjà vu, she felt dizzy.

In the distance a ship steamed eastward across the Atlantic, a pawn in the vast ocean. The wind picked up. High summer on the outer New England coast, the best chance for fair weather.

She returned to the front of the cottage. They'd arrived to find no one home. Not in the cottage, nor the house up the road, where Aunt Maire lived, according to the name on the mailbox at the top of the drive. "Flanagan," it read, her aunt's married name. Nora hadn't expected a ticker-tape parade, but she thought someone would be there to greet them, let them in.

"So this is it, huh?" Ella regarded the cottage doubtfully.

"I like it," Annie said.

"You like everything."

"No, I don't. I don't like black licorice or meat with bones or spiders. But I like this place. It feels like home."

"Boston is home," Ella reminded her.

"It's our home away from home," Nora said. "A summer place."

Built of gray island stone, the cottage was squat and sturdy, with scuffed white trim, a weathered red door, and empty window boxes. Nora made a mental note to purchase flowers—geraniums or herbs perhaps, for a mini kitchen garden—if she could find a shop in town that carried them.

She touched the doorknob, and she was a little girl again, the metal sphere dwarfing her small hand, the lock in its center an unblinking eye. As she suspected, the door was locked. Perhaps there'd been some confusion. She should have written sooner. She hadn't anticipated how long a letter might take to reach the island. It very well might come after them, on the ferry, later that week.

She felt above the doorframe, checked under the mat. No key hidden in the usual places. She jiggled the windows. The sashes held firm. She peered inside, making out only shadows through the lace curtains.

"No one's here," Ella said. "Does that mean we can leave?" At twelve, she had perfected the art of the derisive lip curl, another indication that her adolescence was entering the fullness of its bloom.

"And go where, exactly?" Nora asked.

"Some place with central heating."

She had a point, but Nora wasn't about to give up. They'd come all this way.

It was understandable they'd be tired and prone to snappishness. Ella had always been precocious, but now there was a wariness in her eyes that hadn't been there before.

"So begins my exile," Ella intoned. She'd wanted to make the trip to Burke's Island—until it meant taking sides, until it meant leaving her father behind.

"You've been reading too many books about the Roman Empire," Nora said.

"You can never read too many books about the Roman Empire," Ella said, with a nod toward the car. "The food will go bad, if it hasn't already. Then we'll starve. All that will be left of us, bones—"

"I don't want to die," Annie cried.

"We'll be fine," Nora said. They would be, one way or another. "We definitely won't starve. We have food, and we can buy more in town when we need to." Nora had packed provisions, the bottles and cartons rattling during the journey as if they too were nervous about where she was taking them. She'd been reluctant to stop in Portakinney, the main village, sensing she'd be too weary to exchange the most basic of niceties, assuming the shops were even still open at that hour. The media attention in Boston and the shifting alliances among her friends and acquaintances had made her more cautious of social interaction than she used to be.

Nora took out her cell phone.

"Who are you calling?" Ella had taken to watching her mother's every move.

"I'm tracking down the key."

"We don't know anyone here."

"We know Aunt Maire," Annie piped up.

"We've never met her," Ella said.

"I have—and you will," Nora said. Though it had been years and she hardly remembered her, or much of anything related to the island. The truth was, she wasn't sure who to call. She didn't have Maire's number. Information? Did they have such a service on the island? She imagined an operator, hunkered down in the village, listening in on the inhabitants' calls. "Let me try to get a signal, okay?"

"Good luck with that," Ella said. "Seeing as we're in the middle of fricking nowhere."

"Language," Nora said over her shoulder, not breaking stride.

"It's not even in the dictionary."

"Maybe it will be in the next edition. Anyway, we both know what it means." A stand-in for a four-letter word Nora muttered under her breath (and shouted when the girls weren't home) with greater frequency lately than she'd like to admit. She zipped her rain jacket to her chin. Despite manufacturers' claims otherwise, the material did little to cut the wind. Jagged bits of gravel pressed against the thin soles of her tennis shoes. The roads on this part of the island weren't paved, scattered instead with crushed shell and rock and prone, no doubt, to wash out.

The wind stiffened. Her lips tasted of salt and her curly dark hair streamed behind her in a tangled mess. At least she didn't have to worry about appearances here. That was the point. To be somewhere where she didn't have to be Mrs. Malcolm Cunningham. Where the only sounds she could hear were the voices of her children and the crash of the waves and her own footsteps on that solitary road.

At the top of a bluff, away from the trees, she managed to get a weak signal. She phoned Malcolm to let him know they'd arrived, as promised. (She was more determined than ever to be a person of her word.) She didn't want to make the call in front of the girls. She hoped it went straight to voice mail. Of course, that being the case, it was one of those rare instances when he picked up right away.

"Where are you?" he asked.

"I told you. Burke's Island."

"I thought you might have changed your mind."

"You haven't done anything to change it."

An impatient sigh. "How long will you stay?"

"Like I said, for the summer."

"But the girls—"

"We can arrange something if you'd like to see them. How's your schedule?" Her voice went taut.

There was a dry-leaf rustle of papers on his desk. This great legal mind, giving her the artful dodge again. He hadn't lost his touch. The youngest attorney general–elect in Massachusetts state history, once destined for higher office. A man of the people, one of their own, born in South Boston, achieving the American dream. "I'm in the thick of things," he said. "I'll have to get back to you."

She had a feeling he'd say that. "All right. I have to go," she said. "You're breaking up."

"Bastard," she said to the dial tone. He'd hung up before she got the word out, no doubt thankful for the escape. He knew how sharp her tongue could be, especially now. The expletive could wait for another time. She had plenty stored up, an arsenal.

She thought of how his name began with the French word for "bad." *Mal.* How it was incorporated into a long list of words with negative connotations: *malfunction, malfeasance, malignant, malicious.* There had been a time when she'd associated only complimentary adjectives with him: *magnificent, mellifluous, magical, merry, mesmerizing.*

Those days were gone.

The usual prefixes that might produce results at home yielded nothing. Nora looked down at her cell phone ruefully, considering what to do next. Maybe she should check into getting a room in town for the night.

As she climbed down from the bluff, taking care not to stumble, a car sputtered around the corner. A woman with short, spiky hair rolled down the window, the car, a rust-patched 1960s-era Volvo, shuddering in idle as if it were having a seizure. "Hello, hello. I'm Polly Clennon, your personal welcoming committee. I waved as you drove through the village earlier, but you didn't see me. A lot on your mind, I expect. Maire left me the key. She's up-island today. Haven't kept you waiting too long, have I?" Mrs. Clennon spoke with a slight lilt, a hint of the Irish that lingered in the accents of the islanders, whose ancestors had settled its rocky shores after fleeing the Famine.

"We only just arrived," Nora said as she trailed the juddering vehicle to the front of the cottage.

"Maire should have left the key for you under the mat," Mrs. Clennon continued as she gave the driver's-side door a practiced slam. "Not that we lock doors here much. It's only that no one has lived in the cottage for so long. She must have forgotten in the rush."

"I hope nothing's wrong."

"Oh, no. At least I don't think so. She's the island midwife, bringing babies into the world. Delivered you too, you know."

She didn't. Her father had never said.

"What a to-do that was." Mrs. Clennon rattled on, before Nora could ask what she meant. "Our Nora, all grown up. My goodness, you probably don't remember me. I'd babysit you sometimes. Yes, I did. Maeve was the sort to get out and about. Never liked to stay in one spot for long. You were such a little girl, five, weren't you, when you went away. But now you're back. Don't know why Maire didn't mention you were coming sooner, but then, she's never been much of a talker. I tend to do the talking for both of us, in case you couldn't tell." Indeed, she barely paused for breath. She could have been an auctioneer. "I'm sorry to have kept you waiting out in the cold like this. Distances can't be traveled as quickly as one might think. The roads are, shall we say, narrow and windy."

"It's all right, really. It seems like it's getting warmer," Nora said, hopefully.

"That's the spirit. Though it's not exactly Club Med, is it? I'm guessing you're used to finer."

The banquets and cocktail parties. Little black dresses and ball gowns. The clatter of heels on polished floors, the murmur of gossip, the clinking of champagne flutes rimmed with lipstick traces, the faint jingling of charm bracelets and loose change. Those days seemed like a dream, as if they had happened to someone else. Now she was awake, awake to the sharp stinging air, the sky peeled back to a vertiginous blue. "I'm grateful for the quiet."

Mrs. Clennon shot her a brief, penetrating look, equal parts sharp-eyed speculation and sympathy. For all her prattle, she didn't miss much. "Yes, I suppose you are. Sad business when a man starts thinking himself John F. Kennedy for all the wrong reasons."

"So the news made landfall? I guess it caught the weekly ferry too." Portakinney was a small town, and such gossip probably too juicy too resist.

"Don't worry. I tossed the papers with the headlines. A good few days' worth—they do go on, those news people. I let the islanders think the delivery truck broke down—which it did, though not for as long as they thought. I'm the postmistress, so I get a look at all arrivals and departures, at least of the postal persuasion. Anyway, I remembered you. You look like Maeve. I felt protective of you, and of Maire too, so I took things into my own hands, as it were." Mrs. Clennon put a finger to her lips. "What transpired over there," she said, gesturing to the distant mainland, "will be our secret."

Nora wondered if that were possible, though she appreciated her discretion. The islanders, or at least some of them, must have Internet, after all. "You knew my mother?" she asked.

"Not well," the older woman said, perhaps too quickly. "I was barely a teenager at the time. Didn't run with the same crowd, being three years younger, although my sister did, God bless her. Passed on. Two years ago, last April. Lung cancer."

"I'm sorry." Nora touched her arm.

"She's in a better place now."

Ella and Annie emerged from the rocks, where they'd been pretending to be spies. "What darling girls. They have the McGann look about them." They gathered around as Mrs. Clennon slipped the key in the lock and gave it an expert jiggle. "I've told Maire to change the locks, but she's fond of the old keys."

Skeleton keys, apparently, Nora thought, considering the shape.

"So you must have passed Maire's place, Cliff House, on the way in. That's the main residence your great-grandfather built once the family was more established.

They lived here in the cottage at first. And there's a fishing shack farther up the point, past Maire's." She gestured to the north. "*Shack* being the operative word." She grunted as she attempted to persuade the door to yield. "Funny how you need to be a locksmith to get into the place."

"Or a cat burglar," Annie chimed in.

"True!" Mrs. Clennon laughed. "Here we are."

Nora sneezed as she crossed the threshold, a hint of dust lingering in the air, despite what must have been a recent cleaning. The whitewashed interior was simple and bright, the view of the ocean through the large picture window in the main room stunning as ever. She remembered standing there as a little girl, resting her arms on the sill, staring at the waves on stormy afternoons, imprinting the glass with her fingertips, with the fog of her breath.

Mrs. Clennon bustled about, throwing open curtains, testing taps, peering into the fireplace flue. "The first tenants in thirty-five years, and family to boot. What a happy coincidence. I think Maire had the sweep in not long ago. Wouldn't want you to have a chimney fire the first night and burn the place down, would we?"

"There's no TV." Ella took in the contents of the room and clearly found them lacking, dismay registering on her face.

"Maire has one," Mrs. Clennon said. "You could always go over there. No cable though. I don't like to miss *Sex and the City* reruns on Sunday nights myself. I made my husband get a satellite dish, so he has his football and I have my dramedies."

"What are we supposed to do without a TV?" Ella hissed when Mrs. Clennon was out of earshot.

"Use your imagination," Nora said.

"She doesn't have an imagination," Annie said. "She has common sense. That's what she's always telling me."

"Well, maybe it's time to get one," Nora replied.

Mrs. Clennon flitted through the rooms, testing the lights. "Everything seems to be in working order, fingers crossed. Could do with some new bulbs. Mind, the electricity's not very reliable. One of those realities of island life, I'm afraid."

Nora fingered the doorframe near the kitchen, the height marks Maeve had ledgered there visible in ink.

"Were you really that little, Mama?" Annie asked, reading Nora's name repeated at intervals, along with dates and measurements.

"I was," Nora said. "Hard to believe, isn't it?" The last time she'd been inside the cottage, she'd seen everything from a child's point of view. The interior appeared more modest to her adult eye, reduced, at once familiar and strange.

"At least the pipes haven't burst," Mrs. Clennon went on. "You never know, after a long winter. Doesn't warm up some years until May. Maire set traps on account of the mice—and Flotsam and Jetsam will be on patrol."

Nora gave her a puzzled look.

"The cats. Half wild, they are. If you bribe them with fish tails and kibble, they should do a fine job controlling the resident rodent population. Don't spoil them too much; they'll take advantage if you do, sly creatures that they are. There's driftwood for the fire. The nights can get chilly, even in summer." She laid sets of quilts and sheets on the bare mattresses before heading to the living room to light a fire in the hearth.

There were two bedrooms. Nora's old room, the one the girls would share, looked out over the grassed meadow and stands of spruce and fir to the north, the roof of Maire's house visible over the needled spires. A teddy bear sat on the bed, as he had in the old days. "That's Siggy," Nora told Annie, surprised at how quickly the name came to her. "I bet he's glad to see you." He must have fallen out of the bag her father packed hastily the day they left. She thought he'd been lost for good. Her father had bought another bear, once they settled in Boston, but it hadn't been the same. She'd pined for Siggy for months afterward.

"And look at this." Annie pulled a book from the nightstand, Siggy on her hip. "It's a book of fairy tales."

Irish fairy tales. "Your grandmother used to read them to me before bed," Nora said, startled by the sight of the faded red cover after all that time. She'd begged Patrick to let her bring the book to Boston, but he refused.

"You'll read to us later, won't you? Like your mother did when you were a little girl?" Annie asked.

Nora nodded, scarcely trusting herself to speak. "Maybe tomorrow. We've had a long day, and we need to settle in." There were groceries to be put away, clothes to be unpacked, Saint Christopher medals tucked in each of their personal bags, a tradition instilled by her paternal grandmother, to ensure safe travels. Books (the Brontës, Wilkie Collins, *Jonathan Strange and Mr. Norrell*), games (Go, backgammon, Scrabble, Jenga, Candy Land, Sorry), sunscreen, bug repellent, Neosporin, foam noodles, boogie boards, and snorkeling equipment. The back of the SUV so crammed she'd barely been able to see out the rear window. She had tried to think of everything, unsure of how well stocked the shops were in town.

Nora took her parents' room, fronting the sea, the queen-size lace bedspread yellowed with age ("A good vinegar bath should set it to rights," Mrs. Clennon said) and the tarnished vanity mirror before which her mother used to sit brushing her hair before bed, Nora watching, until Maeve tucked her in with another fairy tale, a kiss on the cheek. *Sweet dreams.* The room seemed smaller than she remembered. All the rooms seemed smaller, shabbier—lonelier too.

She turned to the main living area with its sag-bellied couch and balding chenille chair, the kitchen ("I think the stove tends to be a bit temperamental," Mrs. C. warned, "don't hesitate to give it a thump"), and the single bathroom with cracked tile. There was a streak of rust in the porcelain tub, a persistent drip from the tap.

They made their way to the deck, two sun-bleached chairs on either side, armrests akimbo, depressions in the split cushions, as if their inhabitants had risen from them moments, rather than decades, before. "Maire talked about getting new ones. Scanlon's might have something that would do. Or you could make your own, if you're so inclined. Your mother, Maeve, had an artistic bent, I seem to recall. Crafty. No, that sounds wrong. Craftsy?"

Nora nodded. She could already feel the island inspiring her with its ever-changing palette of blue, green, gray, and amber.

In what other ways was she like her mother? The waves washed against the shore, sighing briny whispers, reaching for her, as if to say, *You are here at last, you are home. Come closer. . . .*

"Are you all right?" Mrs. C. asked. "You look pale."

"A bit tired," Nora confessed.

"Is it as you remember? The cottage and all?"

"I was so young then." Nora ran her fingertips along the windowsill. Yes, it was real enough, and yet it also seemed like a mirage, as if it might disappear any second.

"You were," Mrs. Clennon agreed.

Annie exclaimed over the purple and orange starfish that clung to the newly exposed rocks, the tide at its ebb. She scrambled across the headlands, Ella not far behind.

"Be careful!" Nora called after them, almost reflexively. "The ocean is stronger than you think."

"Look, Mama," Annie cried. "A seal!"

Indeed, a shiny head bobbed in the eddies that curled toward the shore, indigo depths between. The creature met Nora's gaze directly, its dark eyes wide and oddly human, before the children's laughter drew its attention once more.

"Every seal has his harbor," Mrs. Clennon said. "The resident colony lives on Little Burke." She gestured toward the faint outline of an island in the distance. "You might want to paddle over, when the tides and weather are right, though the currents can be tricky." The wind nearly plucked the scarf from her neck. "Maire should be back tomorrow. Don't hesitate to call me if you need anything, anything at all. " She handed Nora a slip of paper with her number written on it. "Civilization can be as near or far as you need it to be."

That evening, as the girls played Go Fish before the fire, Nora walked down to the beach. It was after sunset, the day fading in the coolness of twilight. Malcolm was somewhere on the other side of that body of water, far south, out of sight, but not out of mind. A spiraled piece of shell lay at her feet, bone white, split open to its inner workings. She fingered the edge, worn smooth by the waves.

The beach's uneven surface made it difficult to find the proper footing, a goose-necked barnacle here, an angled rock there, a slick of kelp and seaweed, large pieces of driftwood tossed high during a storm, as if they weighed nothing at all. The tide pulled back from the shore with a mesmerizing rhythm, carrying rock and shell fragments as it went. It seemed as if she and the girls had been on the island for weeks, not hours, her life in Boston, her life with Malcolm, receding with the tide. And yet the problems had stowed away on the journey; they refused to be left behind. She sighed, trying to clear her mind, to no avail.

The girls' voices rang across the bluffs through the open window as they played another round of cards. Sound carried near the water, when the wind was still. "You cheated. Cheater! Cheater!" Annie cried.

Nora pressed her fingers to her temples.

Cheater. Cheater.

She should go in. She should tell them to stop.

But she stayed there a moment longer, drawing long breaths in tandem with the waves that crept closer, closer still. One tear after another ran down her cheeks and fell into the ocean, small and insignificant in that great body of water, yet a part of it too, salt-tinged and grieving, finding their way home.

Chapter Two

Maire noticed the SUV with Massachusetts plates as she passed the cottage the next morning. At first, she thought her eyes were playing tricks on her. It was early, before dawn, a time of shifting shapes and shadows. She'd been up all night for the birth of Sheila O'Brien's first child. A twenty-four-hour labor, exhausting for everyone, and yet the baby, a boy, was healthy—Bevan, seven pounds, five ounces, with one of the strongest sets of lungs she'd ever heard. Maire was getting on in years for this sort of thing, sixty that spring, but she couldn't think about retiring. The islanders needed her, and she needed the work.

Though Burke's Island wasn't exactly having a baby boom, a birth here and there kept her busy, not only with deliveries but with prenatal care. Most island women opted for home births, given the difficulty of traveling to the hospital on the mainland, and Maire was the person they turned to, as they had to her mother, grandmother, and great grandmother before her, generations of women at Cliff House, bringing new life into the world. With Joe and Jamie gone, she was the only one left at the point. She wasn't sure if she'd ever get used to it, this afterlife filled with interminable hours and silences. She'd been a good wife and mother in that house, and now, given the opportunity, she would be a good aunt too.

Her heart quickened at the thought of what the presence of the SUV meant: her niece, Nora, had returned to the island. Maire was surprised and relieved. Nora must have received her letter. Polly had seen Patrick's obituary in the Boston paper, and Maire had decided to try writing to Nora again. Previous attempts at communication had gone through Patrick, and, she supposed, had never reached their intended recipient. Years of birthday, Saint Patrick's Day, and Christmas cards, a few bills tucked inside. Who knew what he'd done with them? She didn't blame him. She knew that by writing, she revived memories he wanted to forget, and yet there was Nora to consider. There had always been Nora to consider. Nora, who deserved to know the truth, such as it was.

No lights shone in the cottage at that early hour, and yet they would later that day, and hopefully, for days to come. It had stood vacant too long.

Her great-grandparents had been part of the first wave of settlers that had put down roots on Burke's Island after a stint in the Massachusetts quarries. They'd brought little with them on the coffin ships, except the few possessions they could carry and the stories and myths of that patch of Donegal they were from. The deep knowledge, they called it. The dreaming. They'd constructed the cottage in the style of the crofts back home, of hewn granite, now grayed with age. They knew how to cut and shape the rock. Hard, bloodying work, it was. But the place was theirs. The first property they'd ever owned, free and clear. The cottage sheltered them until they had enough resources to build Cliff House years later, and yet the cottage remained a touchstone. The modest home held its own through storm after storm, its squat frame withstanding the worst gales, a Celtic sea dragon carved into the wood over the door hinting at its inhabitants' steady fire and endurance.

The roof was shingle now, rather than turf, the dragon weathered to near invisibility. One had to know it was there. After Maeve and Patrick moved into the cottage, he upgraded the interior, crafting the cabinets and other woodwork by hand, an ever-present level on his belt in those days, which Maire thought appropriate somehow, because he balanced her volatile sister so well, their differences not yet driving them apart. Maire visited regularly, being unattached in those days, a little sister, two years younger, bringing baskets of vegetables and fruit from the Cliff House garden, for even then she had the greenest thumb in the family. She remembered Patrick's hands, strong, yet sensitive and slender-fingered, working with measured certainty as he sanded and planed, joining edges and corners, polishing the grain until it gleamed.

No one stirred at the cottage this morning. Nora was still sleeping, she supposed, the curtains closed, only larks awake, flitting through the predawn meadow in search of seeds and grasses. It was nesting season, her niece too, coming home to roost. Maire had seen a picture of her in the papers. (Polly had shown them to her and pledged to keep the contents confidential, ever the good friend, despite her gossipy nature.) The image caught Nora half shielding her face from the cameras. The affair had apparently been going on for months before it came to light. How long had Nora known about it? This thing that should have been a private matter, but became public because of her husband's position and his status as a rising star in the party. Maire couldn't imagine what Nora must have gone through—continued to go through. She wondered if Malcolm had come with Nora to repair the damage. And the children. She supposed there were children; she didn't know for certain. The articles hadn't mentioned any. They only referred to Nora, Malcolm, and the other woman, a trinity of infidelity and betrayal.

Maire had intended to get a few hours' rest that morning after the birth, but the excitement over her guests' arrival made sleep impossible. She headed home, the tires of her truck churning over the shell road, scattering a hail of broken fragments behind her. First, she'd make a batch of rhubarb muffins. She'd leave them on the porch for her niece, tucked in a basket with a jar of island honey from the hives she tended in the orchard at the eastern edge of the property. The rhubarb plants grew on the south side of the house, against the stone foundation, past the main garden. Maire selected the choice stalks after giving them a firm but gentle tug, taking only those that yielded easily to her touch. She twisted off the leaves with a firm flick of the wrist and tossed them into the compost pile. There. She had what she needed. Some brown sugar, oil, flour, eggs, buttermilk, and baking soda, and voilà. If only everything were so simple.

She heard a splash near the dock as she opened the kitchen door. A seal, most likely, what type, she couldn't tell. She could have sworn she saw a flash of silver. There hadn't been silver seals in the waters surrounding the island for as long as she could remember, though people spoke of them, sometimes, with awe. But then it was nearly midsummer, and in midsummer along that coast, anything was possible.

Midsummer, the season of her sister's disappearance.

Nora looked like her. Maeve. With perhaps less of the flirt factor, which Maeve had in spades, even after she married. She couldn't help herself. It was an essential part of her personality, that irrepressible spirit. She couldn't resist charming any man in the room. It was as if Maeve cast a spell, the village women said, wishing she'd leave some for the rest of them, wishing they knew her secret.

All three had the McGann curly hair, Nora's dark, like Maeve's, the girls' lighter, like their father's, perhaps. A sprinkling of freckles across their noses. The high cheekbones, the eyes tilted downward, ever so slightly, at the corners.

"Aunt Maire?" Nora took her hands, her expression warm yet searching, her two daughters beside her not so different from Maire and Maeve when they were young, Maeve taller, bolder. Nora's older one too. A feisty thing. Oh, you could see it in her eyes, flint-dark and sparking. She seemed ready to bolt any minute, held only by the force of her mother's will. And yet the other one had something of Maeve in her too, with her liveliness, her charm.

Her niece and grandnieces regarded her with curiosity and a palpable mixture of anticipation and uncertainty. She had summoned them, after all. She had started it, opened the wound. She'd imagined this moment for so long, and now that it was here, she didn't quite know what to do or say.

"Nora." She opened her arms, pulled this girl—no, she corrected herself, this woman—close.

Nora gave Maire an extra hug before introducing her daughters. Her eyes flitted around the room. Did she recall being there? Did she remember sleeping in Maeve's old room, upstairs, when her parents needed a night to themselves? When her father was reeling after Maeve vanished?

"Come in by the fire," Maire said. "I made muffins and tea. I was going to leave them on the doorstep of the cottage, but you beat me to it."

Come in by the fire. The same words she'd uttered when she found Nora wandering the beach as a child. Many days she was alone, barefoot, shivering. Did she remember? Maeve diving into the ocean, galli-vanting across the island, near or far, Patrick search-ing for her by boat or car, too many steps behind. Bewildered at first, then angry, and, she supposed, in the end bereft, as Maire herself was after he and Nora went away.

"I can't believe we're here," Nora said, as her daugh-ters fell on the muffins. She took in the sitting room, the pictures of her ancestors on the mantel, the jars of sea glass, the shells and rocks in a bowl on the coffee table, its top a spiraled mosaic of smooth beach stones.

"It's been too long," Maire agreed. She adjusted a fold of her madras shirt, crisp, rolled to the elbows. Her jeans were cuffed to the ankle, and she'd retied her Keds with twine, because it was handiest when the laces broke.

"I thought you were gone. That everyone was gone." Nora's eyes shone with tears, swiftly blinked away with an apologetic smile.

"They are. Except me."

"My father said—"

"I know. I wrote, but he—"

"Yes."

There was danger in the half-completed thought. The way the two women could fill in the blanks, sense what was left unsaid.

"You must find things very changed," Maire said. "The cottage wasn't in such rough condition then. Your father spent weeks getting it right. He made the cabinets by hand. I'm not sure they can be salvaged. I've been meaning to have a carpenter look at them."

Nora clasped her hands in her lap. "It's so strange, so jumbled in my memory."

"I'd meant to fix the place up before you arrived," Maire said, "but I wasn't sure you'd come."

"I'm sorry I didn't give you more notice. That was thoughtless of me."

"No, really, I didn't mean—," Maire hastened to assure her.

"There was so much going on." That wry smile again.

"I understand," Maire said. She wanted to ask Nora more about what had happened in Boston, but now wasn't the time. She didn't know her niece well enough, and the children were there, no doubt already far more familiar with the situation than they ought to have been. There would be time enough for that later. "You don't have to explain."

"This is exactly what we need." Nora spoke with almost too much conviction, as if she had to convince herself she'd made the right decision coming here.

Ella mouthed the words, *As if.* That age, so difficult to navigate, even without the present complications.

"I have an idea. Why don't we give the cottage a makeover?" Maire proposed. She'd draw Ella in like a fish on a line, a tug here and there, not too much at once. She was good at that. "We could start by picking out new paint colors at the hardware store in the village. The place could use some spiffing up."

"That's not necessary," Nora said.

"It needs a going-over anyway. Too many chips and cracks."

"Blue!" said Annie. "Like the ocean."

"Gray," Ella said. "Like the clouds."

"Gray's depressing," Annie said.

"Exactly."

"El," Nora said, a warning note in her voice.

"I like gray," Maire said, taking the diplomatic route. "It's the color of heaven."

"Where the angels are." Annie moved toward the window. "Come on, El, let's explore. We haven't seen this part of the beach."

"Good idea," Nora said before Ella could object.

Ella sighed to register the inconvenience and accompanied Annie outdoors.

"I was wondering why you sent this." Nora took a compass, scarcely the size of a dime, from her pocket.

Maire had enclosed it with the letter. "Is it from the family?"

"Yes. Your great-grandfather brought it over from Ireland. He said it kept him on the right path on his trip halfway around the world, into the unknown," she said. "I sent it to you, because it's rightfully yours."

"Mine?" She turned the compass over in her hands.

"You were clutching it in your hand. Your mother must have given it to you to hold."

"I don't understand. When?"

"When they found you, on the beach at Little Burke. You kept the compass with you constantly after that. You even slept with it. You wouldn't let it out of your sight. Not until I found it on the nightstand of your room, the morning after your father took you away."

"And you held on to it all this time."

"I thought you might need it someday."

Nora stared at the compass, the needle pointing north, magnetic, not true. It spurred her onward, but to what? *This way*, it seemed to say, because she still hadn't arrived at her appointed destination. It was as if she'd been destined to return to Burke's Island, the details of her past coming together, one piece at a time, with the intricacy of a fisherman's net, a journey that had only just begun.

Outside, Annie hopped from stone to stone. The rocks on that part of the shore resembled bowling balls, round and smooth with a few thumb-size holes in the top, regular and deep as if they'd been bored. The locals called that section of the coast the Alley. "Let's play," she said, jumping up and down as if her legs were springs.

"I'm too old to play." Ella kicked at a pebble, sending it skittering across the beach.

"No one's too old to play."

"Think again. If you can."

"What's your problem, anyway?" Annie stamped her foot, nearly slipping off her perch. "You go around acting superior, casting aspersions—"

" 'Casting aspersions'—big words for a little girl."

"I'm not that little—and you're not the only one who's smart. I just don't make a big deal out of it like you do."

Ella smirked. "Score one for you. All right. I'll play, but I get to choose."

"Fine." Annie ran ahead.

"Where are you going?"

"I see something. Over there." She raced toward a pile of driftwood at the base of the bluff. Annie was a fast runner, the fastest in her class, even faster than the boys. The low tide allowed relatively easy passage.

"Look at the birds." She indicated the colonies of puffins nesting in the outer rocks, bright-beaked and comical. "They could be in a cartoon."

"I wouldn't get too close if I were you," Ella warned. "You'll get pecked—or swept out to sea."

"There you go, thinking the worst again." Annie balanced on a log. "I'm Sir Francis Drake—"

"He killed people, you know."

"I'm Christopher Columbus—"

"Do you have a multiple personality disorder or something?" Ella leaned against a granite boulder, hoping Annie would tire of playing the great explorer, that something truly interesting would happen. She wasn't holding her breath.

"Ha!" Annie spotted something tucked among the rocks and driftwood. "Behold: a boat!"

"Thank you, Captain Obvious."

"Don't you see? It's waiting for us." She pulled aside the piles of twigs and netting that half concealed the find, heedless of the scratches she sustained in the process.

"I doubt that very much. It looks like it's been there a long time, judging from the barnacles on its bow."

"There's nothing wrong with a few barnacles. Whales have barnacles. I might too, if we stay here long enough, like the sea people."

"Would you stop talking about the sea people? There's no such thing."

"That's what you think." Annie climbed inside. The boat wobbled slightly as she settled her weight. "There. I'm on a voyage. I'm the captain." She held her chin high. "You're supposed to salute me."

Ella got in across from her. "You can't be the captain. You're too little. Captains have to be at least twelve."

"Who made that rule?"

"Article three of the Mariner's Code. Everyone knows that." Ella thought for a moment. "You can be a cabin boy."

"I want to be a captain too. And besides, I'm a girl."

"Even if we decided not to honor the code—risking the prospect of being charged with treason—there can't be two captains. You'll be the first mate."

"All right," Annie said grudgingly. "Where are we going?"

"To the end of the earth." Ella lowered her voice. She relished opportunities to give her little sister a good scare, like the time she'd put on a Halloween mask and hidden in her room in the dark, one of those instances when getting in trouble was well worth the consequences.

Annie wasn't deterred this time. "We should go to Little Burke." She gestured toward the island. "It could be our great adventure."

"You're still thinking you're Mr. Columbus, aren't you?"

"That's Sir Columbus to you."

Ella laughed.

"What's so funny?"

"Thinking of you as sir anything." Ella gazed across the channel. The water seemed calm enough for the journey, but she knew they weren't ready. "One problem with your idea. No paddles."

They heard Nora's voice in the distance. "Come on, girls," she called. "We're going to town."

"Oh, joy." Ella alighted from the craft and brushed the sand from the seat of her shorts.

"Didn't you hear? We can get paint—for our room."

"Big deal. It will smell bad and poison us with toxins and fumes."

"You're the one who poisons people with fumes."

"Ha-ha. You're so funny, I forgot to laugh."

"And paint for the boat." Annie continued, falling into step beside her. "It doesn't have a name. We can name it anything we want."

"The *Ella*."

"We are *not* naming it after you. I was the one who found it."

The *Endeavor.*

The *Leaky Kon Tiki.*

The *Mermaid.*

The *Sea Maiden.*

They retraced their steps, arguing the whole way, Ella looking back over her shoulder, sensing that someone was watching them from behind an opening in the southern rocks.

Chapter Three

"This is the main village, Portakinney. You must have passed by on your way in," Maire said as they headed into town in her brown truck, a rosary hanging from the rearview mirror. The village buildings, mostly stone, occasionally clapboard, huddled together against the elements. Nets were draped across fences, festooned with colorful floats, drying in the sun, and crab pots and rubber boots sat on front steps.

"Portapotty, more like it," Ella said.

Annie laughed.

"I wasn't being funny." Ella wore her combat boots that day, ready for battle. They were her preferred footwear, along with a pair of black high-top Converses. Nora had done little to discourage her daughter. There was a part of her that secretly reveled in Ella's challenging the narrow strictures of the dress code at St. Ignatius (St. Iggie's, they called it), where the girls had finished first and sixth grades, respectively.

It had been a bumpy few weeks for Ella. She'd withdrawn from friends, locked herself in her room, iPod earbuds blocking external sound. (She kept the device at the ready on the island too, when she felt the need to tune them out.) The scandal hadn't been quite as hard on Annie. Younger children had a short attention span for such things, if they paid much mind at all, and Annie's generally sunny disposition kept any negativity at bay. Some of Ella's friends, unfortunately, distanced themselves from her with a chill factor bordering on arctic—whether from standard mean-girl behavior, change of interest, or parental example—as many of Nora's acquaintances, even those whom she'd thought close, had done; and Ella's analytical, reserved nature did little to remedy the situation.

"Portapotty," Maire mused. "Some of the local kids call it that. Teenagers often get restless, wanting to see more of the world, be somewhere else. Small towns get too small for them, islands too."

Four representatives of the island's teen population slalomed down a side road on skateboards at breakneck speed, not a helmet or kneepad in sight, narrowly missing the front bumper of the truck. Maire tapped the brake calmly, as if she expected them to be there. Nora caught Ella watching them, particularly two boys whose scruffy good looks, knit hats, and flannel shirts wouldn't have been out of place in Boston. She guessed them to be about fifteen years old.

"Saw you look," Annie said.

"Shut up," Ella hissed. Before they'd left Boston, she'd taken to spending long sessions in the bathroom, primping in front of the mirror and practicing the muscle isolations required for raising a single eyebrow.

Polly Clennon beeped from her postal van, a bright red boxy affair square as a postage stamp (apparently she handled the deliveries as well), as she roared out of town. "She's a speedy one," Maire said indulgently. "Never been in an accident though. There's no one more capable behind the wheel. She could have been a race car driver." Maire offered a running commentary on the other villagers they passed—a fisherman clomping down the road in waders, a duffel bag in hand ("That's Duff Creehan, setting out to crew on one of the trawlers," she said, tapping the horn in greeting); an elderly woman, her bent back echoing the shape of the pines nearest town ("Meera Dooley— she's nearly ninety-eight now; walks into Portakinney every day"), who offered a wave—and a double take, as she noticed Nora and the girls in the cab. The island didn't receive a great deal of visitors, being far enough off the tourist trail and somewhat deficient in amenities. Counting the latest birth, the population numbered 201, on a piece of land measuring three miles at its longest point.

Maire steered down the steep main street, the truck bouncing. "Doesn't have the smoothest ride," she apologized, "but it gets us where we need to go. The roads have a lot of character, and it's useful to have the high clearance." She pulled into an angled parking space near Scanlon's Mercantile. "Here we are."

The village was quiet except for clangs and shouts at the docks, where fishermen unloaded their catch. Longliners, trawlers, and purse seiners crowded the modest harbor. Their captains and crews, dressed in flannels and T-shirts stained with fish blood, shouted instructions to each other, while petrels, shearwaters, skuas, and terns circled for scraps. No news vans. No cameras. No questions Nora didn't want to answer.

A message board outside Scanlon's bristled with pushpinned announcements and advertisements:

Spare tires for sale—the automotive variety, not
the ones around your waist.
Don't miss the Saturday Market. The Docks,
Portakinney.

Bodhrán lessons. Reasonable rates.
Irish dancing workshop, the week of June 12.
     Contact Rena McGlone for details.

A bell jangled as Maire pushed open the door, announcing their arrival. Eighties music played on the sound system, taking Nora back to her youth, when both her hair and her ideas had been big, her face unlined and relatively innocent, her boots and skirts short; not long before she'd met Malcolm in law school and they'd become inseparable. "*Lies, lies, lies, yeah,*" the Thompson Twins sang.

"Do you know this one, Mama?" Annie asked.

Nora nodded. Yes, she did.

A golden retriever sprawled inside the entry. "That's Mortimer," said Maire, as he thumped his tail. "He's a lazy, friendly fellow, especially if you give him treats or a pat on the head."

"Sounds like others I know, animal and human," Nora said with a smile.

"Humans are animals," Ella pointed out.

Nora stopped just short of rolling her eyes. Ella could be such a know-it-all.

Mortimer licked Ella's hand. She squatted down beside him, his head in her lap within seconds. "Can we get a dog, Mom?"

Nora had seen that coming. "We're only staying the summer, honey."

"I know. I meant, after we get back to Boston."

Nora had been avoiding thinking about their eventual return and what exactly it might involve. "We'll see."

"You always say that," Annie said.

Nora didn't feel like discussing the matter further. She selected a flat of red geraniums from the rack of plants by the front door.

"Your mother used to grow those in the window boxes at the cottage," Maire said. "She liked the way they brightened up the place."

Nora felt a prickling sensation on the nape of her neck. Had she known that?

"No need to bring them in. Just let Alison or Liam know at the counter, and they'll add it to the bill."

Annie begged for a treat from the candy and toy machines, their prizes encased in plastic capsules, things easily broken and lost, a coin in the slot the price of their release. *Please. Please.*

"This way," Maire said, her rubber boots, the ubiquitous island footwear, squeaking across the sloped linoleum floor. Nora and the girls picked boots from a display at the end of aisle 1. The navy and forest green footwear had an L.L.Bean appeal at half the price.

The shop sold everything from rope to fishing nets, oilcloth to embroidery thread. Maire directed them to the east wall, where paint samples were displayed. Annie selected cerulean, as promised, Ella dove gray (at least it was a pretty shade; Nora thought she might have gone for something called "scowl," if such a hue existed), and Nora pale eggshell, with a warm white for the trim. They proceeded to the rear of the store, skirting stacks of crab pots and waders, to have the colors mixed by a pale, monosyllabic young woman— Nora guessed her to be in her early twenties—in black skinny jeans and a holey T-shirt, a snake tattooed around her left wrist. As she flipped through a graphic novel, she blinked at them through a curtain of shaggy dark bangs.

"She looks like a vampire," Annie whispered.

"Careful. We have extra-sensitive hearing." There was a flicker of amusement in the girl's gray eyes. "Like bats."

"She's kidding, right?" Annie asked Ella. She continued to study the girl, her lips moving as she counted the piercings in her ears (six), on the lookout for any sudden diabolical moves.

"I wouldn't count on it," Ella said.

Nora shushed them. They must have been watching *Dark Shadows* reruns before they left Boston—Ella, in particular, couldn't get enough of them—though Nora had explicitly said not to. Annie was susceptible to nightmares.

"How goes it, Alison?" Maire asked.

The girl shrugged. "The usual. Trying not to die of boredom." She glanced at Annie. "Oh, I forgot. I'm one of the undead."

Annie pointed to the bandage on Alison's finger. "You *are* kidding. Vampires don't bleed."

"You're good." Alison cracked a smile. "And you picked my favorite color, cerulean. It's worth liking for the sound of its name alone."

As the mixer shook the cans with a near-deafening rumble, a woman bundled in an oversize army green slicker and fisherman's sweater shuffled through the back door. Her short neck craned forward from the shell of her coat, giving her the appearance of a large, disgruntled tortoise, lips bent into a perfect upside-down U. Her eyes, dull at first, sparked when they locked on Nora. "What are you doing here?" she demanded.

Nora stammered. "I'm sorry. Do I know you?"

"Maggie, this is my niece," Maire began.

Maggie ignored her, her attention fixed on Nora. "You have some gall coming here."

"Mom, what's going on?" Ella asked.

"It's okay, honey—"

"Gran—" Alison attempted to calm Maggie. "I'll take care of the customers. Why don't you—"

"Customers? She's no customer." Maggie Scanlon stabbed a dirty-nailed finger at Nora. "She's—"

"You must have mistaken me for someone else." Nora held her ground. "My name is—"

"I know who you are," Maggie said. "You can't fool me, the sea witch, the whore that you are." She trembled with rage, spittle flying from her lips.

"Gran!" Alison took Maggie's arm as the older woman headed for Nora. "That's enough!"

"Maggie, please." Maire stepped between them.

"There's no call for that kind of talk," Nora said, shielding the girls.

Maggie's voice rose to a shout. "Get out! Get out of my shop!"

"Fine," Nora said. "We'll take our business elsewhere." She hustled the girls out the door.

What was the matter with that lady?" Annie asked from the safety of Maire's truck. "Is she going to come out here and yell at us again?" She scrunched down and peered over the lower edge of the rear passenger window.

"No, honey. She was confused, that's all," Nora said, though she too stole glances at the storefront, wondering if Maggie Scanlon would barrel through the front doors and accost them again.

"I'm sorry," Maire said. "I wouldn't have suggested going there today if I'd known that was going to happen."

"It's not your fault," Nora said.

"I feel responsible. I heard she's been having some issues, but I've never seen her like that before." She dug through her purse, murmuring something about the frequency with which she seemed to misplace her keys.

"I guess I have that effect on people." Nora tried, not quite successfully, to keep her tone light. Her hands trembled as she fastened the seat belt.

"I told you we should go home," Ella said.

"We'll be there in a jiffy," Maire assured her. "I just need to find my keys. That's what I get for carrying such a big purse. There's more room for things to get lost in. Sometimes I feel as if it's a magician's hat. Polly says that one of these days I'll pull out a rabbit."

"I meant our real home. Boston," Ella said.

"We just got here," Annie protested, "though that lady is kind of scary."

"Don't let Maggie frighten you off," Maire said, still rummaging around in her handbag in mounting frustration.

Nora hoped Maire hadn't left the keys in the store. She didn't relish the thought of any of them going back inside.

"I'm not frightened of anything," Ella said, stubborn as ever. "I just don't like her."

"She hasn't been herself lately. Please don't judge her—or the island as a whole—by this unfortunate episode. She'll probably have forgotten about it by tomorrow. Her memory comes and goes, short-term, especially. Happens to me sometimes too. A symptom of age, I suppose." It apparently dawned on her that she'd slipped the keys in her pocket before going into the shop. She selected the proper key and inserted it in the ignition.

"Do you know her well?" Nora asked.

"We islanders all know one another, after a fashion," Maire said, starting the engine and putting the truck in gear at last. "Too much in one another's business. I wouldn't say the families were close, not since—"

They jumped at a knock on the glass. It was Alison. She motioned for Nora to roll down the window. "You forgot your things." She handed Nora the bags and retrieved the flat of flowers from the rack outside the shop as the truck idled. "I'm sorry about what happened in there. Da doesn't want Gran in the shop, but she still acts like she runs the place. Don't pay her any mind. It's dementia. She's got good days and bad. Thursdays are probably the best to come in, for future reference. She's at my aunt's, up-island, so she won't bother you then."

Nora thanked her.

"Come back and see us again," she said, with a note of dry humor that only made Nora like her more. "It's usually not so dramatic."

" 'Bye." Maire pulled out of the parking space and turned in the direction of the main road.

Alison waved from the sidewalk, growing smaller in the rearview mirror as they headed for home. On the outskirts of town, the close-set cottages and buildings gave way to open fields, dotted with flocks of sheep, goats, cows, and an occasional horse, a tranquil scene at odds with what had happened a short time before.

"Who did Maggie Scanlon think I was?" Nora asked as they passed a broken fence, the wood weathered gray.

Maire weighed her words before speaking. "Your mother."

Later, after a dinner of thick clam chowder and homemade bread at Maire's house, the girls played on the deck while the women talked in front of the fire over glasses of wine. Maire figured they could use a glass or two after what they'd been through that afternoon.

They sat on the sea green sofa she'd reupholstered herself, the chenille soft and plush, the cushions deep and inviting. A stack of gardening books by Rosemary Verey and Gertrude Jekyll rested on the end table beneath a silk-shaded lamp, favorite passages marked with Post-it notes, a garden journal open to the current date, with jottings of chores to be done that month and records of plantings. Sun filtered through the curtains, dappling the slate blue walls with spots of light and shadow, the doors and windows open to let in what remained of the day.

"Is there anything I can do to make you more comfortable at the cottage?" Maire asked. "You have enough room? You're welcome to stay here at Cliff House, you know—"

"There's plenty of space, since there's only the three of us," Nora said, more free to talk now that the girls weren't underfoot. "Malcolm, my husband, is staying in Boston."

"It's settled, then?"

"No, not exactly. We both needed space to figure things out. Or at least I do. It's for the best. The media seems to follow him everywhere these days." She fingered a loose thread on her sweater, a green that brought out the color of her eyes. "I wish you could have known us before all this happened. We were good together once."

"I'm sure you were. You might be again."

"Maybe," Nora said. She didn't sound optimistic. "What about your family?" She nodded to the photographs on the mantel.

"Joe and Jamie were lost in a fishing accident three years ago."

"I'm sorry. I didn't realize—"

"We've lived whole lives without each other, haven't we?" There was so much about Nora's life she didn't know.

"Yes, we have." Nora paused. "And after what happened in the shop today, I have a feeling there's a lot I don't know about my mother, too."

Maire swirled the liquid in her glass, contemplating the whirlpool it made, spiraling down the stem. She'd made it a policy not to talk about Maeve much up to then, though she remained ever-present in her thoughts. Anything could spark a memory of her—the color purple (plum, for the sky at evening, the waves too); the sound of the wind chimes, which she loved to touch as she came in the back door, announcing her arrival; sweet scallops on the half shell . . .

"What was she like?" Nora asked. "You were her sister."

Sister. A word freighted with shades of meaning. "Maeve had a special way about her. A light."

"Was she beautiful?"

"She was lovely, yes. But it was more than that. There was something special that came from within. You must have seen pictures. Your father took so many. He was a talented photographer."

Nora shook her head. "There weren't any. I didn't know he even had a camera until I cleaned out the attic after he passed away last year. It was as if she'd been erased."

"Oh," Maire said, startled. "Well, then. I guess that gives us a place to start." She pulled a photo album from the built-in bookcase and sat next to Nora on the couch. The album had a scarlet cover, worn down at the corners, the images within black and white. "Here are your grandparents with your mother and me on the beach, when we were girls." The family resemblance was remarkable. Her mother faced the camera, a hand on her hip. "Bold as brass, as your grandmother used to say. Maeve wanted to be a pirate queen when we were little, until she realized it wasn't as romantic a profession as it seemed, even if it had been possible for her to take up arms and sail away."

Maire flipped the page, the tissued inner leaves crinkling. "This one was taken when she was eighteen." Maeve stood up to her thighs in the water, seemingly heedless of the waves lapping her dress. Her clothes clung to her curves. "She'd gone swimming in her skivvies that day. She couldn't always be compelled to change into a bathing suit. She jumped in whenever she felt like it, heedless of the temperature, clothes and all. She wasn't bothered by the cold like the rest of us." In the photograph, Maeve's eyes were dark, her brows too, skin radiant as pearl. Maire peeked from the edge of the scene, as if hoping to be noticed.

"Was it difficult for you, being her younger sister?" Nora asked. "You were close in age."

Maire paused. "I loved her more than anyone in the world. But yes, I suppose it was hard, sometimes, being in her shadow. She didn't mean to cast it. There it was, all the same, and I probably stood in it too much, when I should have moved and found my own light. That was my own fault, not hers. I was so quiet and hesitant in those years. I didn't have her fire. She made things happen. I waited for them to happen." And yet there were similarities too, as there are with sisters— the same gestures (they both tended to talk with their hands), the same musical laugh (though Maeve's was heartier), the same brown eyes, courtesy of their father.

She turned the page. "Here's a picture of your mother and father, shortly after he came to the island."

"How did they meet? He wouldn't tell me anything."

"Your father arrived by accident," Maire said. "His boat had been crippled in a storm. He sailed into port for repairs. We didn't get many schooners passing through in those days. He was lucky to be alive. Men died that night. I imagine he thought Maeve was an angel, for he never took his eyes off her from the moment he set eyes on her, though there were other women who sought his attention."

"Like Maggie Scanlon?"

"Perhaps."

"And my mother fell in love with him?"

"I believe so. Caused a scandal, her falling for an off-islander. People rarely married anyone from away in those days, now either."

"Were they happy?"

There were no simple answers, not when it came to Maeve. "Maeve was always something of a restless soul, but she settled down with your father, made a home in the cottage you're staying in now, the cottage that is, by rights, yours."

"Mine?"

"You're the last surviving McGann, after me." She hesitated a moment before continuing. "I've never seen

Maeve as content as she was then. She was delighted when she learned she was pregnant with you."

"I was born here?"

"On the beach. Maeve had some odd notions as she got close to term. She insisted on giving birth in the ocean. Very nearly did, but we found her just in time." She'd been pacing in the shallows, talking to herself. Maire hadn't thought much of it at the time—it was a week before the due date, after all—until she heard Maeve cry out.

"She wasn't attempting to—"

"Drown you? Oh, no. It was her peculiar idea of a water birth, I suppose. I doubt she would have considered it if it hadn't been summer. You were a darling little thing. You didn't cry at all. You seemed perfectly at home." A good-size baby, eight pounds, ten ounces, with a full head of black hair and alert dark eyes. Maire recalled how the infant Nora gazed around her with interest—at the faces of the women, and especially at the waves, creating their own cradle song as they shushed against the shore.

"Maybe that's why I've always felt drawn to the ocean."

"Do you like to swim? Your mother did too. She won the annual open water race for her age group every year. They're thinking about holding it again this summer. Perhaps you'd like to sign up? The girls could too, for the shorter distances."

"Maybe we will," Nora said.

"The sea calls to us, doesn't it?" Maire said. "What was it I read? That we contain the sea within us, made, as we are, of salt and water?"

"Yes, I remember hearing that too."

The two women turned toward the open window. The sound of the waves carried across the bluffs, the cool breeze stirring the curtains, mixing with the voices of the girls, laughing and squabbling by turns.

"But something happened, didn't it? To my parents?" Nora pressed on. "Did they grow apart after I arrived?"

"They made their lives here, happily so. Your father became the new harbormaster. He'd worked for a shipping company in Boston; we were fortunate to obtain a man of his experience. And your mother, your mother took to wandering again, as she had before she met your father, before she had you. I don't know what got into her. She had that faraway look in her eye." Maire would come upon her sometimes, arguing with an unseen person behind the rocks, near the point, but when she rounded the corner, there was no one there but Maeve, eyes flashing, revealing nothing.

"Could it have been postpartum depression?"

"It's hard to say," Maire replied. "She wouldn't tell me what was on her mind. She was never much for confidences." Maire closed the album. That was enough for one evening. She hadn't anticipated how draining such discussions could be.

The sun slipped toward the horizon, silhouetting the girls and the distant shore of Little Burke against a gold-and-plum-painted sky.

Maire yawned. "I can't hold my wine the way I used to. I'm afraid I'm a little sleepy."

"You must be tired after such a long night." It was clear Nora wanted to continue the conversation but was too polite to insist.

"Yes, for the very best reason. There are few greater joys than bringing new life into the world. Babies are such a gift." She squeezed Nora's hand, a gentle pressure. *Like you were, too.*

Nora and the girls walked the beach home, twilight inking the waves. The same beach on which Nora had come into the world, on the changing tide, that long-ago evening. Had her mother given birth there, by the tide pools? There, on that soft patch of sand where the rocks curved into a perfect half-moon?

Piano music drifted across the fields from Maire's open window. The crystalline notes stopped abruptly at times, before she began again. She'd said she often played in the evenings, Debussy primarily, the impressionistic passages filled with a passion she didn't readily express in words, which made Nora wonder about the deep well of memories and feeling she stored within her. Her aunt was clearly talented. Nora wondered if she'd ever yearned to pursue a concert career when she was young.

Ella swatted at a mosquito in time with a particularly strong chord. Nora was surprised that they hadn't seen more of them, but Maire told her the bugs were worse in the spring and that the wind and the swallows tended to keep any malingerers at bay; she rarely bothered with repellent at that time of year. Too bad there wasn't a repellent for straying husbands—and the women who would steal them away—Nora thought.

"What are you thinking about?" Ella asked.

"Insects." Her husband the lowest form. "Do you have a bite?"

Ella shook her head. "I got him just in time."

"Her. Biting mosquitoes are female. We learned that in science," said Annie.

"Good for you."

Unperturbed, Annie blew into a piece of kelp, marching along as if she were leading a brass band.

"That sounds like a fart," Ella said.

"Don't be crude, El," Nora said.

"Well, it did. Are you going to swim in that race Aunt Maire was talking about?" Ella asked. "We overheard you talking about it. We could help you train."

"You little eavesdroppers. Maybe I will. She said they have shorter races you girls could enter—or maybe you already heard that too."

Ella was fiercely competitive, whether at cards, academics, or sports. (She'd been known to throw her racquet and stomp off the court after losing at tennis.) "I'm going to swim every day," she said. Both girls enjoyed the activity, Annie a budding diver, Ella, a sprinter. "Do you think I could win?"

"I think you can do anything you set your mind to."

Nora bent down and picked up pieces of sea glass. There was still enough light to see by, though there wouldn't be for long. Green, blue, the rare lavender, white, some pieces frosted, some clear. Mermaids' tears, Maire called them. Maeve collected them too. An image flashed in Nora's mind of jars lined up on the windowsill at the cottage, catching the light, of her father hurling them onto the floor in a rage during a fight with her mother—before she disappeared, it must have been—shards scattering across the floor. "Stay back!" her mother had cried, a slender ribbon of blood circling her toe. Nora huddled in the doorway to her room as her father slammed the door and stalked out into the muggy afternoon, thunder threatening. Then no sound but the *hush-hush* of the broom as Maeve swept up the brokenness and threw it away, even the once-beautiful sea glass, except a single piece Nora rescued from the far corner, hiding it under her pillow for safekeeping.

"Why are you collecting sea glass? To put in jars like Aunt Maire does?" Annie asked.

"I was thinking we could make jewelry." In the Victorian style, perhaps, ornate, not the typical organic creations she'd seen in the beachside shops on the mainland. Designs were already taking shape in her mind. It surprised her, how inspired she felt. After she left her law practice to raise the girls, she'd taken a few art classes at the local institute, and now seemed as good an opportunity as any to put her skills to work again.

"We want to help!" They scooped up handfuls of pieces, some usable, some not. She'd sort through it later.

"Look," Annie said. "The seals are bodysurfing."

The sea glass weighed heavy in Nora's pockets, pulling at the seams of her jacket, and yet she couldn't stop searching, always a greater treasure, a more perfect piece to be found. The task required a meditative focus she found calming, one that distracted her from thoughts of

Malcolm and Boston and what she would do next. She imagined combing the shore daily, swimming, reading, gardening with Maire. Already she sensed the quiet pattern that would shape their days on the island.

"It's nice here, isn't it?" Annie said.

"Is Dad coming too?" Ella asked. "He said he would."

Did he? That was news to Nora, but then, communication hadn't been his strong suit lately.

"We'll see."

That noncommittal sentence again, but really, it was all Nora could say. Because when it came to Malcolm, nothing was certain.

Malcolm had always been unpredictable. It was one of the things she'd loved about him from the moment she met him. Being unreliable, that was new, something different entirely. He had never failed her in this way before, not to her knowledge, constant since they met at Harvard in the early 1990s. She remembered the first time he sought her out, outside of class, as if it were yesterday. Nora had been studying in the law library for hours, her eyes closed and fluttered opened, her head nearly sliding off her hand. Torts were putting her to sleep, but she had a test later that week and she needed to prepare. She'd been in the library carrels the entire evening, the only sounds the occasional cough or turning of pages among the warren of cubicles. Her roommates, who didn't seem to care as deeply about such things—sometimes she wished she didn't either—were having another party at the house they shared off-campus, and she knew she wouldn't be able to concentrate there.

Hands closed over her eyes. She smelled leather and mint and wool. "Guess who?"

It was him. J. Malcolm Cunningham, who sat behind her in class. A guy whose very presence made her excessively inclined to nervous laughter and dropping pencils, she, who was known for being so composed. He appeared to enjoy his effect on her.

"Malcolm, I need to study," she protested. His first name was John, but he went by his middle name.

He reached in front of her and closed the book. "C'mon, milady, the night is young." Within minutes he'd packed up her books and taken her hand. "You're too lovely to be shut up in this tower of academia all evening." He wore a finely cut vintage cashmere coat, jeans, and laced oxfords, a scarf around his neck, creating his own style, boho-prep, Nora called it. He could make anything look good.

He guided her down the steps and out the main doors. She liked watching him walk. He moved with such an easy elegance and grace, tall and sure of himself. Neither of them had to work that night. (Both were scholarship students, Nora nannying for a faculty couple; Malcolm having talked his way into clerkship, due to his powers of persuasion.) It was dark outside. It had been late afternoon when she went in. She could lose hours, cramming information into her head. But now she felt free again, thanks to him. The lights glittered, making Cambridge appear more magical than it ever did during the day. "Close your eyes," he said.

"Why?"

"Trust me."

She felt the softness of his coat against her cheek as he led her forward. At first, it seemed as if she were stepping into a void. She stumbled against him, unsure where to put her feet. She didn't like not knowing where she was headed. His arm tightened around her. "It's all right," he said. "It's hard to get your balance at first. Remember, I'm here for you. I'm not going anywhere."

She felt safe with him. She barely came to his shoulder. He was six-four; she, nearly a foot shorter. As they walked, she became more aware of each sound—footsteps, doors, cars, the hum of neon lights, the wind in the laurels, each smell—Chinese food, aftershave, cinnamon, coffee, exhaust, each touch—his hands, his lips in her hair as he whispered directions: "Step up," "Step down," "Turn left," then "Open your eyes." They traveled from one neighborhood to the next, block after block, the city at their feet.

"Where are we?" she asked when they came to a stop at last. She opened her eyes. It was beginning to snow, flakes sifting down and landing on their hair and shoulders. Soon the world would be transformed into a hushed wintry kingdom, the two of them at the very center. She didn't feel the cold at all, just the warmth of his hands, holding hers.

"Here." He kissed her then, beneath the trees of Oak Street, with its moldering Georgian and Tudor homes. "The place we're going to live someday. You and I, together."

Malcolm had tended to read the bedtime stories when the girls were younger, but it was Nora's turn now. She would be the designated storyteller on Burke's Island. As she tucked the girls in that night, Annie pressed the book of Irish fairy tales into her hands. Siggy was already cradled securely in her arm. "You promised."

Nora curled up next to her daughter. A bookmark tagged the page where she and Maeve might have left off earlier. She hesitated, hand poised over the cover.

"We can't read if you don't open it first," Annie said.

Nora's consciousness seemed to split in two. Was it the wine? The power of suggestion? Maeve's voice echoed in her mind, a melodic contralto. *Once upon a time . . .*

"Mama?" then her own daughter, reminding her of her place in the present.

"Sorry. Here we go." Nora opened the cover, the leather brittle as bark. A silverfish darted from the binding, and a tiny cloud of dust lifted into the air. "Fairy dust," Annie said. "Dirt," Ella said from her side of the room. (She'd drawn a boundary in chalk, a preliminary measure against sisterly encroachment.) The spine crackled and water spots spattered the deckled edges, and yet the illustrations were as enchanting as ever, the paintings and etchings richly detailed and the colors, though somewhat faded, lush. Each story began with the flourish of a Gothic letter, as if to herald the magic to come. "They don't make them like this anymore." Nora ran her fingers over the glossy images of serpents, flowers, waves, and seals.

"Why?"

"Too expensive and time-consuming to produce." Why was her heart pounding like that?

Few believe, but we do, don't we, love? Maeve's voice again, coming to her vividly from the past.

"Then we're even luckier to have it," Annie said.

"Yes," Nora agreed, "we are. It's an old family book. My mother gave it to me."

"What was her name again?"

Nora had barely spoken of her. She'd never been a presence in the girls' lives, barely Nora's either, in the physical sense, though in her absence she hovered about the edges of her consciousness like a ghost. "Maeve."

Annie repeated it. "What does it mean?"

"It was the name of a great Irish faerie queen."

"Did you hear that, El?"

"Hard not to with your chattering away like that," Ella said, turning to Nora. "What happened to your mother, anyway? You never talk about her."

"I scarcely remember her. She disappeared one summer, when I was five years old."

"And they never found her?"

Nora shook her head. "No, they didn't."

"Not even a trace?"

"No, not even a trace."

"You're not going to disappear, are you?" Annie asked.

"I'm staying right here." Nora pulled her close. "Which story do you want to read tonight?"

Annie studied the table of contents at length. "This one," she said finally, "about the boat. We—"

Ella coughed and gave her a pointed look.

"What were you going to say, honey?" Nora tucked a lock of hair behind her ear.

"That we like boats," Annie said quickly. "There are so many here."

"Me too," Nora said. Her father had been an accomplished sailor, but he'd only taken her out a few times on his boat before he sold it, when she was about Annie's age. He said it was too much trouble to maintain. She wondered now if the sale had more to do with memories of her mother and their time together on Burke's Island.

" 'There once were two young brothers who lived in Killaran,' " Nora began. " 'They found a coracle by the sea.' "

"Wait a second," Ella said. "Why do boys get to have all the fun?"

They did, didn't they? Her husband too, in the running for philanderer of the year. Nora cleared her throat. "Good point. Very well, then.

" 'There once were two sisters who lived in Killaran . . .' "

Chapter Four

Annie woke the next morning having dreamed of a coracle on sapphire seas, of gorgeous towering waves, the compass needle spinning, spinning, sea glass falling from the sky like hail, the ocean outside the cottage window a wayward cousin of the one in the book, a body of water that wouldn't be contained. What was it hiding? What would it bring?

"Do you think the boat's still there?" Annie threw back the covers and hopped out of bed.

Ella, always slower to awaken, mumbled a reply and burrowed deeper into the blankets.

Annie didn't wait for her. She pulled on a sweatshirt and a pair of shorts and dashed outside. Wildflowers painted the meadow with strokes of red, blue, and yellow. She raised her face to the sky. A light wind was blowing, pleasantly cool on her cheeks. She spread her arms wide. I'm a kite, she thought. I'm a bird.

It was a Tuesday. Tuesdays at home meant swim team and art class at the museum. They'd been doing a unit on Picasso and cubism, and the instructor, Rodney, had them paint a portrait. She'd done one of Ella. She felt bad about using her for a subject, putting her face in pieces like that, later, when she wasn't mad at her anymore for saying she was stupid. Tuesdays at home meant takeout Chinese, which their dad brought home from Ming's, at least until recently, when he hadn't been coming home much. Annie had asked Nora if he'd migrated, like the geese. They'd been studying migration at school. She'd said no, but Annie wasn't so sure.

There weren't any geese on Burke's Island, at least not at the moment, or fathers who didn't come home. Tuesdays were different here too. There was no schedule to be kept. She could fill Tuesdays—and any other day of the week for that matter—with whatever she chose.

She scrambled down the bluff. The beach was deserted, except for a boy standing at the tide line, the water rushing over his feet, sand huddled between his toes, streaking his legs. He was bare-chested. He wore a pair of tattered brown shorts. He was wet, as if he'd been swimming. His skin was deeply tan. She guessed him to be eight or nine years old.

"Hello," Annie said, happy to meet someone close to her own age. "Do you live around here?"

He nodded. He seemed shy. His eyes were dark, watchful.

"My name is Annie."

"I'm Ronan."

"That sounds like a superhero's name. Do you have special powers? I can fly, see?" She sailed off a rock, at least for a second or two.

He laughed.

"Is it all right if I call you Ronie?"

"If you want to."

She noticed a crab leg in his hand, the shell broken open. "What's that?"

"Breakfast," he said.

"It's like a crab cocktail, without the sauce."

"Fresh is best." He licked his lips. "I'll bring you some next time."

"From where?"

"Out there."

"I've only been on the open sea in the charter boat. We came in a few days ago. There were porpoises running ahead of us. I wanted to stop and watch, but the captain doesn't stop the boat for anything. Mama said it had to be on time. There's so much in the ocean, isn't there, beneath the surface?"

He nodded. "Look." Beyond the rocks, two whales breached, as if on cue, shooting out of the water like rockets, an explosion of spray as they plunged downward once more.

Annie gasped.

He gazed at her expectantly. "Humpbacks, on the move."

She didn't know how she could top whales. "I have a boat," she offered, pointing in the direction of the driftwood piles. "Do you want to see it? I was afraid the tide would have carried it away."

"The tide doesn't reach that high, not usually." The waves drew foam-flecked lines on the beach.

Annie was about to suggest a voyage to Antarctica to see the penguins, when Ella's strident voice carried down from the bluff. "Annie, where are you?"

"Who's that?" Ronan asked.

"My sister. She's twelve. We could hide and pretend we're not here." She didn't like the thought of having to share Ronan with Ella.

"She'd come look for you. I'd better go," Ronan said, his eyes wary now.

"You don't have to—"

He put a finger to his lips. "Don't tell anyone about me. I'm not supposed to be here."

"Why?" He was the strangest boy. The strangest, most wonderful boy.

"My mother said. Promise." His look was piercing.

"I didn't show you the coracle—" She didn't want him to leave. There was so much more to show him, to say.

"Next time."

"But I don't know where you live," she protested.

"I'll find you. Remember. Promise."

"I promise."

He dashed down the tide's edge, his footprints erased by the waves, and disappeared into the rocks.

Ella appeared a few moments later. "What are you doing here by yourself?" she asked.

"Playing." Annie wanted to tell her about Ronie, but she'd made a vow, and truthfully, she liked having a special friend of her own. Ella had a tendency to take over. Was Ronie still watching from the rocks? She picked up a length of seaweed and wrapped it around her shoulders with a toss of her head, strutting along the beach like a supermodel. "Look, I'm wearing a mermaid's scarf."

"Ew. Take it off. It stinks." Ella wrinkled her nose.

Ronie wouldn't have said that. He would have laughed.

"It smells like the sea," Annie said. "There's nothing wrong with that. It's a brinny-briney, seaside-finey smell." She breathed deep as she let it slip from her hands. "Maybe I'll sew a gown and go to the sea sprites' ball!"

"Let me guess, hosted by the sea people."

"Exactly! You can come if you want."

"I'll pass."

"I bet you'd change your mind if one of those boys in town was going." She remembered the way Ella was looking at them.

"I don't know what you're talking about." Ella blushed.

She hardly ever looked unsure of herself like that, so Annie backed off. It was interesting: she'd noticed that Ella spent a lot of time talking about boys (to her friends, not Annie, who overheard their conversations back home), but rarely spoke directly to them. "Are you going to help me with the boat?" Annie asked instead, then groaned. "We forgot to buy paint for it at the store."

"We can use the leftovers from the cottage, if we ever paint the rooms." Their mother hadn't even taken the cans out of the bag. She stuck them in the closet, as if she wanted to forget the entire episode at the store, especially the woman, Maggie Scanlon.

"All it needs is a coat of varnish," said a voice behind them. "Boats like that aren't meant to be painted.

They need to be allowed to show what they're made of, the grain of their wood, their skin. They need to breathe."

An elderly man stood on the path above, leaning on a walking stick. He wore baggy twill pants, like their grandfather used to wear, a brown hacking jacket, and a faded tweed cap. He must have come from the bluffs around the bend. Annie suspected he might have seen Ronan pass by, but she didn't dare ask.

The man's border collie tore down the embankment, wagging his tail and barking. "Don't mind Patch. He's friendly. Happy for the company, no doubt. We don't get many visitors here," he said, his voice low, with a hint of a rasp. He was missing a tooth, like Annie. She wondered if the tooth fairy ever paid visits to elderly people. "Where did you two come from?"

"Boston," Annie said.

"Boston. That's a long way from here."

Patch leaped up and licked Annie's face. She supposed the dog must have been named for the spot of black over his left eye. "We're visiting for the summer," Annie said.

"Like the migrating swallows, eh? You've both come for the season. And where might you be staying?"

"At our great-aunt Maire's cottage, over there."

Ella tugged at her elbow. Annie shook her off. *What?* Aunt Maire probably knew him anyway, so what was the harm?

He paused for a moment. "The prodigal daughter returns. . . ."

"What do you mean?" Ella was clearly trying to make up her mind about him.

"That it's been a long time since your mother has been to the island. I remember her well."

"You were here then?" Ella asked.

"I've lived here my whole life. I'm one of the old-timers. Reilly Neale is my name. Fixing up the boat, are you? Used to be your grandmother's when she was young—and her father's before that. How that boat lasted so long, I'll never know," he went on. "Must have put a good finish on it. Wish I knew what they used."

"Maybe it's magic," Annie said.

"Maybe." His eyes crinkled. "I could get it seaworthy, if you promise to keep to the cove and not to get into too much mischief. Got materials at home for the job."

Annie looked at her older sister. They could certainly use expert advice.

"You know something about boats?" Ella asked.

"Know something about boats? Been sailing since I could walk. Would be still, if my sight weren't going."

"All right," Ella said. "You're hired."

"We can't pay much," Annie warned, not wanting to mislead him.

He laughed. "Consider it a donation to the cause. I'll be back shortly," he said. "I live on the other side of the point."

Reilly returned within a half hour, bearing not only caulking and varnish but potato and cheese pies, cookies, three cups, and a flask of lemonade, which he'd tucked into a carrier fastened to Patch's back. "Thought you might like to have a picnic after we're done working." He sat down on a piece of driftwood with a wince. He smelled strongly of cigarettes, but he didn't smoke in front of them. "It's the arthritis," he said. He walked with a hitch, he told them, due to a fishing accident and an accumulation of misfortunes. "Things start to wear out when you're old."

"How old are you?" Ella asked.

"Eighty-five, this July."

"That *is* old," Annie said.

"Spoken with the unflinching honesty of youth." He gave each of them a putty knife and held out a tin of thick brown goo. "Spread this on the seams. Not too thick. No need to frost it like a cake."

"Will there be a party and cake for your birthday?" Annie asked.

"Probably not."

"Sure, there will. Your family—"

"My family left years ago."

"Why?"

He paused. "It was right before your grandmother disappeared. There's no use dressing it up. The truth is, I used to drink too much in those days, and my wife eventually had had enough. Can't say I blame her, thinking back on it now, thanks to my dear friend, hindsight. She took my daughter and son and left the island for good. They've lived on the mainland ever since. She remarried, went on with her life, as she should have done, given the circumstances. Heard I have granddaughters your ages . . ." His voice trailed off.

"You haven't met them?" Ella asked.

He shook his head.

"You should write to them," Annie said.

"I did."

"When it's something important, you should never give up," Ella said, perhaps thinking of their parents.

Reilly took off his hat and wiped his forehead with the back of his hand, a pale strip above the weathered skin of his face, white hair ruffled by the wind. "When they talk about living the life of Reilly, they weren't talking about mine, that's for certain. I guess some of us are destined to navigate difficult seas."

"Maybe you should get a better boat to ride them out," Annie suggested. "The waves, I mean."

"You two have an answer for everything, don't you?" Reilly grunted. "Well then, maybe I'll give that a try."

Nora called to the girls, her voice borne away by the wind. To the east of the cottage stood the copse of spruce and fir. To the west, there were waves ragged as torn paper, as far as the eye could see, the mainland little more than a flat line beyond. Seals bobbed in the surf near the rocks, skin black, glistening, more of them now than when Nora and the girls first arrived, the silvery one too, ever present, barking orders, sunning herself on the ledges of the outer rocks. No sign of Annie or Ella anywhere. They'd taken off in such a hurry that morning, she didn't know which direction they'd gone.

The scene was deserted except for the cats, Flotsam and Jetsam, nearly identical gray tabbies (Flotsam was missing part of her tail; Jetsam had a nick in his left ear) that lolled on the deck.

"I don't suppose you know where they are." She squatted down and scratched Jetsam's ears, eliciting a motorcycle-engine purr. They weren't lap cats, but they tolerated demonstrations of affection on their own, decidedly feline terms. "I thought you two were supposed to be working. You eat your wages and laze about."

Jetsam winked and stretched with a contented sigh, aware, perhaps, that he'd already achieved tenure and didn't need to exert himself.

"They're down on the beach." Maire came up behind her.

"Oh, I didn't hear you—"

"I came through the trees. You don't need to worry about the girls here. It's not like the city. They can have some freedom to roam. Let out the lines a bit, so to speak." Maire was wearing white coveralls.

Nora couldn't think what she might be up to. "Has there been a toxic spill?" She smiled.

Maire laughed. "Oh, no. It's the bees. I left my hat and gloves at the house."

"Bees? Are you an exterminator too?"

"Heavens, no. I meant honeybees. I started keeping them after my husband and son died. At first, it was a way to pass the time, a hobby, but it's grown into something of a side business. I sell the jars at the farmers' market and by special order. I thought you might like to lend a hand today. It's time to check the hives. I'd ask Polly, but she's too much of a chatterbox. She sets the bees on edge."

"I'd love to help. But the girls—"

"Our houses are so close together, they'll figure it out. Or leave a note on the door, and they can find us when they're ready, though we'll probably be done before they are. You know children and their schemes. They could be busy for hours. Play is good for them. There's not enough play in children's lives these days, if you ask me. Too many schedules to keep."

It was hard for Nora to overcome her tendency to hover, her instinct to protect the girls heightened by what had happened in Boston. But perhaps Maire was right. The sooner the girls put some distance between themselves and the complications at home, by whatever means the island offered, the better.

Nora accompanied Maire to the garden shed at Cliff House and put on her aunt's spare beekeeper's outfit. She felt like an astronaut, the grassed meadow surrounding the hives at the edge of Maire's property a new frontier. At first her steps were ungainly, tentative, the suit cumbersome, the netted hat too, a pith helmet, really, with a mesh veil. Bees circled, seemingly curious about the visitors in their midst. They alighted on her gloved hands and shoulders and scaled her arms, antennae twitching, gossamer wings fluttering, exploring the peaks and valleys of the fabric.

Maire walked ahead of her, steps easy, measured, as if she were leading a procession. She opened and closed boxes, wafting smoke as she went to calm the bees. They didn't seem to mind the intrusion.

"Hail to the queen," Maire said. "She rules the hive well. See how the others follow her every move. They're Italian honeybees. I chose them because they're reputed to have the best dispositions. It rained the day I was supposed to put the bees in, so we had to wait. A keeper told me to put them in a cool, dry place until the weather cleared, so I sprayed them with sugar water and brought them into the house with me."

"In the house?" Nora asked. She couldn't imagine doing that.

"Polly just about had a fit when she saw them, until she realized they wouldn't do her any harm. In the end, they weren't bad tenants at all. I missed them after they moved out, though I think they're happier here, in their own place. Each hive has twelve thousand bees. Kingdoms unto themselves, I suppose you could say. Close your eyes. They beat their wings at two hundred and fifty cycles per second. That creates the humming sound. It's astonishing, isn't it, the complexity of life?"

Nora did as Maire instructed. The melodic hum filled her senses with a song of purpose and beauty. Moving among the colony, like swimming in the ocean, gave her a serenity, a oneness with nature, that seemed, however fleeting, a form of benediction.

"Like this." Maire showed her how to waft smoke over the boxes. Nora paused, the smoker dangling from her hands like a hypnotist's watch, swinging back and forth, the smoke rising upward in a twisting column.

"I know we haven't been acquainted very long," Maire said, "not in real time, but I want you to know you can depend on me."

Depend on her, as she hadn't been able to depend on her mother. Or Malcolm.

"I've been drifting these past few months," Nora admitted. "It's not like me. I don't like the way it feels."

Maire thought for a moment. "Perhaps not so much drifting as gathering yourself," she said. "We each have our own paths to walk. One isn't necessarily better than another. They jig and jag and turn back on themselves. They have dead ends and breathtaking vistas too, if we stop and look."

"Yes." There was, after all, Maire, standing before her, who she might never have seen again but for the letter. There were the girls, those challenging, precious bundles of humanity, the best things to have come out of her marriage. And her growing knowledge of herself, what she wanted, what inspired her. These things had come from that path, difficult as it had been. There was this island, this land, and the ways in which it offered sustenance. The ocean. The garden. The fields.

"After all, you have to understand where you've been before you can begin to move forward," Maire said. "You've already weathered some of the worst of storms."

Had she? "I'd rather have avoided them entirely."

"I've wished that myself. But life doesn't work that way, does it? We can't be in calm waters all our lives. I suppose our existence might be rather dull, in the end, if we were."

"Sometimes I feel like I'm fighting against a current—that I have been, my whole life. It's hard to explain."

"You had an unusual start, separated from the home, and some of the people, you loved. That would cause anyone to wonder about their place in the world, let alone the other things you've been through lately."

The bees hummed, a choir. "Thank you for finding me, for sending another letter," Nora said. "It must have been difficult, not getting anything in return for so long."

"I should thank you. For answering." Maire opened the box, exposing row upon row of labyrinthine honeycombs. "Whenever I have a problem, I bring it to the bees. Here, take this." She handed Nora the box lid. "See, that's the honey." She pointed to the glistening amber beads. "Even among life's stings, there can be sweetness. There will be for you too. Give it time."

Chapter Five

E very afternoon, Nora and the girls swam in the cove. They stepped carefully over the sun-baked stones. Their towels, draped over pieces of driftwood, snapped in the breeze like colorful flags. Sometimes they wore snorkels, so that they could observe the vibrant life beneath the surface—sea stars, minnows, anemones. They made the acquaintance of an eel that lived in the southern rocks. He peeked at them from his stone fortress, a sour expression on his face, thick lips moving soundlessly. He had an elder's visage, reminding Nora of a Confucian sage or an English magistrate.

"Will he bite?" Annie asked. They treaded water, a group of three, legs scissoring among the sea grass.

"Probably only if he feels threatened," Nora said. "Best to watch him from here, all the same."

What had he witnessed during his long life? Had he, or his ancestors, seen Nora and her mother the day they went out in the coracle for the last time? Had they overheard the conversations Nora had been too young to remember?

"Mom, you're drifting," Ella warned as Nora edged too near the rocks.

"Thanks, El." Nora kicked toward them. "Do you want to swim laps? How about if you go between these rocks?" She indicated a reasonable, safe distance in chest-high water.

"What about you?"

"I'll be right here." She gestured to the wider cove.

She dove down, surfaced, stroking through the water with ease. It was as if the ocean itself were breathing, its swell the rise and fall of its chest, as if she breathed with it, inextricably connected. A seal appeared, then another, swimming alongside, leading her into deeper waters. She felt as if she could go on for hours, as if she might never stop.

Maeve had taught her to swim in that very cove, a hand on her back. "Chin up. Eyes on the sky. It's all right. I've got you. There. You're floating. See. You're a natural, like me." They moved on to the breaststroke, which Nora liked because it made her feel like a tadpole or a water bug, skimming along the surface, then the freestyle. "Elbows up, reach and grab the water. Kick from your hips. That's where the power is. Head down, chin to your chest. That's it."

The seals had followed her and Maeve during the lessons.

"What do they want?" Nora asked.

"They're curious. They wonder what sort of creatures we are."

"What are we?"

"What do you want to be?"

"A sea creature."

"Then that's what you are."

"Mom!" Ella cried.

Nora turned, treading water. She was outside the cove now. Ella stood on an outcrop, waving her arms and yelling. "Didn't you hear me calling you? That's too far!" She looked so small, standing there.

The seals ringed Nora in a half circle, as if to see what she'd do next. She found their scrutiny odd, but she wasn't afraid. They fascinated her too. "What are you thinking?" she asked. "What do you want from me?"

They dove out of sight. She waited a few minutes, hoping they would reappear, but the water remained still. They had moved on. It was time for her to do the same. She stroked back to shore, limbs burning. She'd underestimated how far she'd gone, how much energy it would take to return.

"You need to stay closer. I could barely see you," Ella said as Nora emerged from the water.

"I was following the seals," Nora replied. Her body felt heavy, her muscles rubbery, now that she was on land, the waves no longer supporting her.

"It's fine for the seals. They live out there. We don't." Ella paused. "I swam the lengths faster than I ever have. You should have seen me."

"Me too," Annie said.

"Must be something in the water." Nora shook the droplets from her hair.

They spread the towels and collapsed on the beach, beads of water sliding off their bodies, absorbed by the sand, dried by the sun, a drop at a time, leaving a salty film on their skin. Nora recalled lying in the sun like this at the modest beach house of her friend Maria Cordova. From the ages of eleven to thirteen, when Maria and Nora were best friends, Nora would go to the Cape for a week each July. She loved the smell of paella and the boisterous conversation of Maria's extended family, in contrast to her own quiet home. She was the only student at her school, St. Agnes, without a mother.

"Will it stay warm like this?" Ella asked. "I want to work on my tan."

"It's hard to say. There might be a storm later," Nora replied. "Though they tend to blow through quickly at this time of year."

"How do you know?" Annie asked.

"The ocean is telling us." The waves had flattened to rolling swells that crashed against the shore, gaining momentum. Her father had told her what to watch for during their Saturday-morning sailings in Boston Harbor when she was a child.

"What else does it say?"

"That remains to be seen." Nora tickled her. "Let's go up to the cottage. It's almost time to make dinner."

While Nora washed dishes that evening (she and the girls each took a night—the dish democracy, they called it), the girls played Jenga and discussed the validity of fairy tales, a literary debate that was proving particularly contentious. Annie believed in them completely. Ella had her doubts.

"They aren't meant to be real," Ella said. "They're stories people make up to explain things they don't understand, that frightened them."

"I don't believe you."

"Your argument isn't sound. There's no evidence to support your point of view."

"You're sounding like a lawyer again."

Like their father. Nora turned a plate over in her hands. She glimpsed a shadow of her face, a mere suggestion of a person, half formed. Who was she now, apart from her role as politician's wife, a role she'd allowed to define her for so long? She had a law degree, she hosted visiting dignitaries for the municipal league, served on the board at the arts center, but who was she, really? What did she want? She was still figuring that out. Cleaning agents stood at attention on the counter, reporting for duty: Purpose, Aim. If only they could rout uncertainty as well as ketchup stains.

She stuck the plate in the rack and scrubbed, more furiously than necessary, at a pan coated with singed spaghetti sauce. She'd been having trouble keeping her mind on things lately. She felt at home at the cottage, but uneasy too. The place hadn't proven to be quite the refuge she expected. It raised questions, the little girl she once was falling into step alongside her, in double exposure.

"I'm right," Ella said. "You just don't want to admit it."

"You're like a dark cloud that rains on everything."

"Rain's good. It's cleansing. It makes things grow," Ella replied.

"Not the hard kind. The kind that makes mud and floods. The kind that beats things down and drowns people."

"What are you quarreling about?" Nora sensed it was time to intervene, before the conflict escalated any further.

"Rain, sort of," said Ella.

"Leave it to you two to find an argument concerning something as innocuous as rain. Sometimes I think we should rechristen the cottage the Bickerage, with the squabbling that's been going on around here lately."

The girls fell silent, thinking perhaps of their father, who when they argued in his presence at home might stage a mock mediation, wearing a funny hat or blowing a horn left over from a New Year's Eve party, assuming the persona of a comical judge, Hermunculus A. Budge ("That's Judge Budge to you"), dissolving their conflicts into laughter.

"Your move," Ella said.

"There's no move I can make."

"It's your turn. You have to—unless you want to forfeit."

"Cunninghams never give up."

Their father's words again. He was everywhere, in everything. Nora couldn't pretend he wasn't. She scrubbed and scrubbed until her shoulder ached, her fingertips pruned. He persisted in her thoughts, in her dreams, her feelings for him enduring, in fragments, along with the anger, the hurt, almost against her will.

After much deliberation, Annie removed a wooden piece from the game. The tower teetered one way, then the other. She flapped her hands in the air around the structure in a panic. "No!"

"Don't touch the other pieces. You can't touch them, only the one you're taking out."

"I know!"

The tower tumbled onto the table with a clatter. "I hate this game." Annie kicked a rectangular block across the room.

"That's because you always lose," Ella said. "You have to have a strategy."

"Your strategy is going first. You always go first."

"The privilege of the firstborn."

"It's not fair."

Ella leaned forward, her jaw thrust out. "Life isn't fair."

"El, that's enough. And Annie, don't kick the game pieces," Nora said.

The lights flickered.

"Is the power going out?" Annie asked.

"It might," Nora said.

"Brilliant," Ella grumbled. "Now I get to freeze to death and stub my toe in the dark."

"It's not that cold. You can't even see your breath."

"We have enough firewood for tonight," Nora said, though they'd need to restock. She'd have to bring more driftwood up to dry. "And candles if it does. Aunt Maire has a generator. We could always head over there."

"I don't want to go out in that storm, thank you very much," Ella said. "I'd be soaked in a second." Raindrops streaked the windowpanes, illustrating her point. It had been blustery all evening. "Why couldn't we have gone someplace warm, like the Caribbean?"

Where they'd been planning a family vacation that winter, until the trouble started, redirecting their itinerary, on and off the map.

"The storm should blow through soon," Nora said. "The moon is already putting in an appearance." Indeed it swept across the roaring surf at intervals, the beacon of a celestial lighthouse.

"It is?" Annie pulled up a chair and gazed out the window, elbows on the sill. "Aunt Maire said there were shipwrecks in the old days."

"Maybe the ghosts will come up here and haunt you," Ella said. "That's what happens when you watch for them out the window. Your eyes meet, and in that split second they make a connection to you. You let them in."

"They'd go for you first, because you're mean and you need to be taught a lesson."

"Oho! Listen to you!"

Nora sighed. She had suds up to her elbows and didn't want to rinse off and referee another spat. She often wondered what it would have been like to have another child. She and Malcolm had talked about having a third, before his affair came to light. (Though she spoke of it more often than he did, now that she thought about it.) There would have been another child, between the girls—a boy, perhaps—if she hadn't miscarried that winter nine years ago. Her mother or Maire might have cared for her after the procedure, if they had been a part of her life then. She hadn't told anyone she was pregnant, since it was so early, and in the end, she said she was down with the flu, because she didn't want to deal with others' pity or grief. Malcolm did what he could to support her, but despite his best efforts she'd felt alone in those weeks, hearing the latch click as he went off to work. She remained at home in the silent house, Ella off at preschool, a parade of black-and-white films showing on the television screen, *Bringing up Baby, Casablanca, The Third Man,* beloved classics that couldn't penetrate the fog of disbelief and sadness, until finally she couldn't stand it anymore and forced herself to get out of bed a few days later. She'd been afraid to try again, afraid during the first few weeks of her pregnancy with Annie, and yet the months went by easily in the end, the birth, too, more so than Ella's, who, being a firstborn, caused some pain and trouble.

Now she watched her growing daughters through the open kitchen door of the cottage at Glass Beach, considering how swiftly the years had passed, from infant to toddler to child to nearly teen. Annie, with her face close to the glass—or so Nora guessed from the halo of breath fogging the pane. Ella, her nose in her book.

Annie began waving. "I'm waving at the waves. They always wave back."

"One of life's deep truths." Ella snorted without looking up.

"I see something," Annie said.

"You're always seeing things," Ella replied.

"No, really. There's someone down on the rocks. They're not moving."

"It's probably a seal," Ella said.

"I know the difference between a person and a seal," Annie said, adding in a hushed voice, "What if they're dead?"

"Now *that* would be interesting," Ella said.

"Mama!" Annie appealed to a higher authority.

"Let me see." Nora joined Annie at the window.

Yes, something, someone, lay on the ledge. "Stay here." She tossed on a rain jacket. "I'll be right back."

Nora staggered against the gale, coat winging out behind her. The hood refused to stay in place. She let it go and was drenched in seconds, water trickling down her spine, hair plastered to her scalp in flat ringlets. The rain came down so hard, she could barely see. Clouds raced across the moon, casting shadows that swept over the beach, elusive, spectral. It was easy to imagine things that weren't there. The ocean reared back and threw itself against the rocks, sending up plumes of spray. Pebbles and shells tumbled over the shore with the sound of dragging chains and breaking crockery. Nora stumbled forward, the way slick and treacherous. She hadn't bothered to change into boots. Her only thoughts had been for the person below. She glanced in the direction of Maire's house, dark now. No time to wake her.

She slid down the embankment, a border of mud collecting on her shoes. She leaped across the rocks, nearly losing her footing. She could see more clearly now. It was a man. He lay on his side, as if sleeping. She called to him, but he didn't stir. She reminded herself to stay calm, to remember the CPR training she'd had years ago, after Ella was born. She checked for a pulse, for breath. Yes. He was alive. "Hello," she said into his ear. "Can you hear me?" Did his eyelids flicker? The rain was still coming down heavily; she wasn't sure. His skin was tan, scored, as if he spent a great deal of time outdoors. A fisherman, no doubt. A scar on his brow, others on his arms and chest too, his face strong-boned, his clothes—or what was left of them; they looked as if the waves had nearly torn them from his body—draped around his waist like a shroud. His feet were bare. He had a deep cut on his head, abrasions and scratches elsewhere; he'd probably need stitches for that nasty head wound. She tore the cuff from her work shirt, doubled the fabric, and pressed it to his temple. She felt the fluid warmth of his blood beneath her hand. Her biggest concern was hypothermia. She had to get him warm as soon as possible. She took off her coat and draped it around his shoulders. It wasn't big enough to cover him completely, but it would have to do.

How had he ended up there? It was as if the ocean had spat him out. He lay half broken on the rocks, too heavy for her to carry. She couldn't leave him. The waves were rising, driven by storm and tide. They might snatch him back.

"It is a man!" Annie exclaimed. "See—"

"I told you two to stay inside." Nora whirled around. There were her two daughters in their new slickers and boots, their eyes wide with astonishment. "You shouldn't be here. You could get hurt."

"We want to help too," they insisted, in agreement for once.

"He's not dead, is he?" Ella said, apparently regretting her earlier comment.

"No, he's just hurt."

"Badly?"

"I don't know. If you want to be useful, run and wake Aunt Maire. She'll know what to do," Nora said. "Hurry!"

They did as she said.

The man opened his eyes. "Where am I?" he asked, his voice deep.

"Glass Beach, on Burke's Island. We need to get help—"

"I'm fine." He was remarkably calm after what he'd been through. Perhaps he was in shock.

"Clearly, you're not," she said. "You have a bad cut on your head, for one thing. You're in danger of getting hypothermia, and—"

"I'm not cold." He stared at her, his gaze disconcerting, his eyes large and nearly black. He touched her hand. "See."

She drew back. There was something odd in that touch, a warmth, and another quality she couldn't name. "What happened to you? Was there an accident?"

"There must have been."

"Why were you out in this weather?"

"I can't remember."

"But your boat—" She scanned the waves and rocks. Nothing. It must have sunk fast, some distance from shore. She supposed he had insurance, still—

"At least I have my life," he said. "Speaking of hypothermia, it seems you're out here without a coat."

"I gave it to you," she said. "Please. Stay still. My aunt should be here in a moment. She has medical training."

"I told you. I don't need any help." His tone sharpened. He hoisted himself into a sitting position with a grunt, shrugged the coat from his shoulders, and handed it to her. "I think this fits you better than me. You should put it on. You're shivering."

Was she? Her hands were so numb she could barely move them. She didn't bother fastening the coat. "Who are you?" Nora asked. "What is your name?"

He frowned. "I don't know."

The bump on his head must be worse than it looked. She was about to question him further when Maire and the girls appeared.

"We're coming," Maire called, first-aid kit in hand. The rain drummed steadily on their hoods as they gathered around the man in a semicircle.

He was clearly bemused by the attention. "Maybe I should get shipwrecked more often."

"There are easier ways to gain a woman's notice," Maire said. "Now then, let's take a look at you." She was all business as she checked his eyes, asked questions, and applied pressure to the wound.

So, Nora thought, there was another side to Maire: calm as always, but steely too.

"And what do you see?" he asked Maire.

"A man who's lucky to be alive, after being in weather like this."

"I was catching the end of the run."

"And it caught you."

"I suppose you could say that."

"He can't remember his name," Nora said. "I think it might be serious—"

"A concussion, that's all," he insisted. "I told you not to trouble yourself—"

Maire turned to Nora. "I'll take it from here. Get the girls home. They shouldn't be out on a night like this—and neither should you."

Chapter Six

The next day dawned so clear, Nora wondered if she'd imagined the encounter. Yet there was her torn shirt, ruined now, the cuff missing, seams speckled with blood. Her coat and shoes were crusted with mud, hair stiff with salt, lips tasting of it too, the taste of her childhood. She needed to shower—they had shed their clothes and fallen into bed as soon as they got home last night—but the girls were already headed out the door.

"What are you up to?" she called through the open window as she pulled her hair into a high ponytail. The girls' movements were a mystery these days. She could barely keep up with them.

"We want to see the shipwrecked man." They paused among the buttercups.

"He's probably at the village clinic by now, or headed home," Nora said. Wherever that was. "And even if he isn't, we should leave him alone. He's not an animal in a zoo." There was no place to stay but Maire's, and surely her aunt wouldn't have suggested such an arrangement.

"We know," Annie replied. "He's a man. He must have visiting hours. Everyone knows there are visiting hours."

"That's for hospitals," Nora said. "And besides, I doubt he's there."

"We want to know what happened after we left," Ella said. "Don't you?"

She did, but she thought they could have waited until at least after breakfast.

The girls didn't wait for a reply. They made for the trees and Maire's house beyond before she could dissuade them.

Nora yanked on a pair of jeans, nearly tripping in her haste, and a sweater, then jammed her feet into a pair of sneakers. She jogged along the path in their wake, feeling like a child again, the child who'd raced over these very trails, laughing, playing, seeking, crying.

All was quiet at Cliff House. A line of crows perched along the roofline, commentating on the activity below, soot-feathered and gossipy, like some of the women at the last black-tie event she attended with Malcolm, whispering behind her back in the days before the rumors were confirmed. What made him stray. Whether she'd gained weight or aged. If the other woman was younger, smarter, more beautiful. The birds on the roof watched her speculatively, eyes hard and shiny as polished jet beads.

The sound of the girls' voices brought her focus back to the present. She came upon them talking with—or rather interrogating—Maire, who was planting tomato bushes, as if nothing out of the ordinary had occurred the night before, the trowel chinking against a buried stone as she spaded the earth.

"Where is he?" Annie asked.

"Who?" Maire shaded her eyes with a gloved hand, a smudge of dirt on her cheek.

"You know—the man on the beach," Annie said. "The guy Ella thought was a seal."

"I said he *might* have been a seal," Ella protested.

"He was a bit bruised and battered and needed a butterfly bandage or two—that wound wasn't as deep as we thought—but he'll be as good as new before you know it, once he gets over that bump on the head and regains his full memory. He's made of sturdy stuff, that one." Maire patted the dirt with a nod of satisfaction.

"His memory?" Nora asked. So the effects were lingering. "I hope he's being seen by a doctor."

"Didn't want one," she replied, turning to Ella. "Funny you thought he was a seal."

"It was dark."

"Is he here?" Annie stood on tiptoe.

"Yes, is he?" Ella echoed.

"He didn't want to impose. I offered him the fishing shack near the point as a compromise. To say it's rustic is an understatement, but it seems to suit him fine."

"For how long?" Ella asked. Things were apparently starting to get interesting.

To Nora, they were getting complicated. She shooed the girls off to pick flowers in the meadow. "I thought you were going to call for help and get him settled in the village," she began once they were out of earshot.

"The phones were down, and I don't have a cell—darn things can be more trouble than they're worth, if you ask me, but then I'm not much for technology—so I figured I shouldn't waste time driving into town until I knew his condition. And in the end, he didn't want to put anyone to the trouble. He's a considerate sort. A rare breed these days." She set down the trowel and she looked up at Nora. "My instincts tell me he's all right."

"Next you'll be reading tea leaves."

"Sometimes I do. But I don't take them too seriously. People have a tendency to see what they want to see. It skews the results," she said, half joking. "Polly says even the type of tea can influence the process. Earl Grey is better for cautious sorts; jasmine for the adventurous; white for the pure. Keep that in mind if she offers you tea. I suspect you didn't have much exposure to such things when you were young."

"No," Nora said. "My father didn't put much stock in the occult. And my mother?"

"She looked for signs. She liked the drama, the mystery."

"I wish I could remember."

"Perhaps you know more than you realize. The subconscious is key," Maire said. "It's most active in dreams. I had a dream he came to us. Our visitor. I have an active dream life, don't you?"

"Mostly nightmares, lately." And from childhood too, a recurring dream of being on the ocean, struggling to keep her head above water, the waves frothing, pulling her mother away; dreams in which she feels as if she's drowning, the last gulps of air squeezed out of her lungs, before she manages to save herself at the last minute. She always saved herself. Her mother's fate unknown. "And did your dream reveal exactly who he is?" Nora asked.

"No." She shrugged. "He told me himself. His name is Owen Kavanagh. He could remember that much at least, after I got him down to the fishing shack. We have a long tradition of aiding the shipwrecked on the island. It goes back to the time of the founding. When we were out there on the rocks last night, did you feel the pull of the past?"

More than she'd like to admit. More than she understood.

"I'm not about to break with tradition now." Maire tamped the soil down firmly. "Besides, if we don't like him"—she smiled as she flicked a weed into a bucket—"we can always pitch him back into the sea."

The girls stole over to the rocks near the fishing shack. The clapboards of the one-room structure had bleached gray, the shingles gap-toothed along the fringes, the door slightly off its hinges. It didn't look as if it could withstand the violent storms that battered the island many months of the year, and yet it had.

"I'm glad we're not staying here," Ella said. "It makes the cottage look like the Plaza." They'd gone to New York and stayed there for her tenth birthday. She'd loved the Eloise books then. She wasn't that girl anymore, too old for such stories. She gravitated to serious books now, with darker themes, reading far beyond grade level.

"It's not so bad . . ." Annie's voice trailed off. Even she had trouble finding something kind to say about the place. "Are those bones?" She indicated a pile of spined ribs, whitened by the sun, near the southeast corner, with a shaky finger.

"Fish bones, silly. It's a fishing shack, remember?"

"Are they from ancient times?"

"I doubt it. They'd have turned to dust by now if they were."

"I don't want to turn to dust."

"Everyone does, eventually."

"What about our grandmother? Do you think she turned to dust? It's weird no one knows what happened to her."

"Maybe she left. People do sometimes."

Like their father. They didn't say his name, but it hung in the air between them. How Annie kept setting a place for him at the table at home, thinking he'd show up. How Ella would find herself listening for the slam of his car door, the sinking disappointment every time she realized it was only Mr. Livingston, next door, arriving home from work, home, to his family. How she'd watched for her father from the stage of her final school play—she'd had the lead in *Alice in Wonderland*—another chair left unfilled, row D, number 3. Her mother sitting in seat number 2 at every performance, her face tight from smiling encouragingly, smiling enough for both of them, when really it only made it all the more apparent he wasn't there.

"Let's look inside," Annie said.

"We don't know where he is. This needs to be a covert operation."

There were no windows on the sides of the structure, only on the front, its back set into the surrounding rock, as if it sprang from the earth itself. The girls crept closer, their knees stained green, and ducked down behind a tangle of nets and floats, the plastic worn and cracked. The stoop was swept clean of sand. He must have intended to stay for a while.

The seals barked from the beach below. Ella put a finger to her lips. "Look. There he is."

He was swimming in the cove, the seals with him. He was an excellent swimmer, clearly at ease in the water, unafraid of the animals.

"Does he have any clothes on?" Annie asked.

"I can't tell," Ella said. "I'm not sure if I want to."

Annie stood taller, to get a better look.

"Get down!" Ella warned.

He turned, the water swirling at his waist, eyes seeming to meet theirs across the expanse, though he was too far away to say for certain.

Annie took another peek. "He's heading for shore. Do you think he's mad at us for spying on him?"

"Run!" Ella said, not wanting to find out.

They scrambled back to Glass Beach, crouching and darting through the grass. Their beach. Theirs. They would say they'd been there the whole time. They would say—

"Is he following us?" Annie gasped.

Ella looked over her shoulder, nearly tripping over a stone. "I don't see him. I think we're in the clear."

"That doesn't mean he isn't there. He might be hiding, like we were."

"He's a grown-up. He doesn't have to hide." She paused, thinking of her father, who seemed to be hiding quite a lot lately—from the reporters, even from them. Too many questions he didn't want to answer. *Why are you leaving? Where are you going? Is it true? What they're saying? Why can't you tell me? Why can't you stay? Do you love her more than us?* His eyes shiny with tears before he turned away abruptly, the car gliding into the night.

"We're not going to get in trouble, are we?"

"No," Ella said, though she didn't know for sure. "We didn't do anything. It's not as if there was a No Trespassing sign. The shack is Aunt Maire's. She's didn't tell us we couldn't go there."

"Just because someone doesn't say so specifically doesn't mean—"

"Stop worrying. Let's check on the boat, okay?" Ella said.

Annie brightened. The coracle was her favorite subject. She climbed in, ready to navigate imaginary seas. "Today we're traveling along the horn of Africa."

"Better set a new course. We don't want to risk being taken by pirates."

"I *am* a pirate."

"You weren't yesterday."

"Well, I am now. Look out. Cannons!" She held fast against the onslaught.

"It's not the same as being on the water," Ella said. "It would be better if we had paddles, if we could go out there." The ocean shimmered.

"We could ask Mama to get paddles at Scanlon's. Or maybe Aunt Maire has some."

"If we told them, it wouldn't be a secret anymore, would it? They wouldn't let us go on the water. At least Mama wouldn't. She'd want to come along."

They heard footsteps. "Hide!" Ella whispered.

They lay flat and held their breath.

Too late. The shipwrecked man peered down at them. "Permission to come aboard," he said. He wore a pair of baggy shorts and a T-shirt that didn't suit him, from the shack, perhaps. The material stuck to his back, his skin still wet. A piece of seaweed clung to his neck.

"Granted." Annie scooted over to make room.

"Denied." Ella frowned. "There isn't room." He was a stranger, and a strange one at that. "I'm the captain."

"You run a tight ship."

"I have to." Somebody had to keep an eye on things.

"You're well suited to the job."

Was he making fun of her? She couldn't tell.

"My name is Owen Kavanagh," he said. "We haven't been formally introduced."

"You remembered your name."

"I did, and little else."

"I'm Annie, and this is my sister, Ella."

"Thank you for helping me last night."

"Are you feeling better?" Annie asked.

"My head still hurts a bit."

"And yet you're up and about." Ella regarded him closely. Something wasn't adding up.

"I am. It's hard to stay down in such a beautiful place as this. I'm about to go fishing; it's one of the best spots." He indicated the rocks.

"You can tell already?" Annie asked.

"I have a sense for these things," he replied. "You heading out?"

"We don't have any paddles," Annie said.

"There are a couple at the fishing shack. I could get them for you, if you want," he offered.

Ella hesitated. She didn't want him to do her any favors, but the temptation was too great. "Okay," she said, grudgingly.

"You have experience?"

"Of course," Ella replied, as if there were any question. "We're McGanns, aren't we?" She thought of how she'd canoed at Camp Miniwaka last summer. Her team won first place in the race between the docks. She had a badge at home to prove it. She would have been there this summer too, if she were still friends with Sophie, and her mother hadn't decided to go to Burke's Island.

"Yes," he said. "You are."

They busied themselves, drawing maps of the oceans and continents in the sand, the routes they would travel, across the Atlantic, the Pacific, the Coral Sea. Owen returned a short time later with paddles and two faded orange life jackets Maire and their grandmother might have worn when they were girls. "You sure your mother won't mind?"

"We do this all the time." Ella pinched Annie's arm, so she wouldn't disagree. "She was going to get us paddles anyway. This will save her the trouble."

"You'd best stay in the cove," he said, dragging the boat to the tide line, holding the sides while they climbed in, the water pleasantly cool that afternoon. "The currents in the channel can be strong." He pushed them off.

The land fell away. They were weightless, free. "Hooray! We're part of the ocean!" Annie exclaimed.

Ella plunged her oar into the water, the paddle gliding backward, cutting through the waves like a knife.

Annie wasn't paddling. She gazed around her, awestruck.

"Who are you looking for?"

"No one," she said quickly. "We're floating. We're really floating!"

"Yeah, and we're going to end up beached if you don't do your job. I ought to fire you."

"You can't fire me. I'm your sister."

"Want to bet?" Ella said. "Paddle harder, will you? On my count."

"Why does it have to be your count?"

"Listen for once," she said. "It's about working together, having the same rhythm."

"Does that mean I get a promotion?"

"To what?"

"Second in command."

"Show me you're ready. Stroke. Stroke. Stroke."

They paddled back and forth across the cove, zigzagging at first, then straightening. Ella scooped up a palm-size jellyfish and threw it at Annie. "Got you!" She seemed disappointed when Annie didn't get upset.

Annie liked the jellyfish. She liked most of the sea creatures she'd met. She reached for another jelly. Ella ducked, but Annie bided her time. The back of Ella's head made a nice target. She knew Ella didn't like getting things in her hair, especially slightly slimy things. The jellies didn't bother Annie. This type had no stingers, nothing to cause harm.

Ella turned forward to see where they were going, casting glances over her shoulder. "I know what you're up to."

No, you don't. Not everything. Annie dropped a small stone she'd been carrying in her pocket over the side. Let Ella think it was the jellyfish, that she'd disarmed herself. Her sister relaxed then, and when she did, Annie lobbed the jelly at her head. It clung for a moment, then slid into the water with a plop.

"Ugh!" Ella swiped at her hair, frantic. "Is there anything there?"

Annie smothered a laugh. It was funny to see Ella so worked up.

"I'll get you back. I swear I will."

"Look," Annie said. A porpoise leaped at the mouth of the cove, its body making a perfect arc over the water. Another followed, then another. Annie counted four in all, the same number as their family, or their family, as it used to be.

Ella directed them to a sunken rock shelf, teeming with anemones, starfish, crabs, and fish. "It's an undersea garden."

Another eel lived there. Mr. Eel, Annie called him. She gave many of the creatures names. Anabelle, the largest anemone, waved her lovely pale green tentacles in the current. Carleton, the crab, liked to snap his claws like castanets; he was the size of a salad plate and had a bright red shell with a distinctive blotch on the top like a spin-art design. Stella, the sea star, had bristly skin the color of purple grape juice.

The girls paddled for the better part of an hour, until their arms were burning and their palms were scored with calluses. Owen watched over them from the rocks, casting lines and reeling in the catch. He moved with an easy rhythm, in time with the waves, as if he sensed the ocean's every move, the fish within it too. Ella acted like he wasn't there. Annie waved to him once, but really, she focused on the ocean itself, all of them working its surface, sounding its depths, in their own ways.

"I can't go any farther," Annie said at last. "My arms feel like noodles."

"Maybe the sea monster will make spaghetti of you."

Annie splashed at her with a paddle. "I wouldn't taste very good."

Ella splashed her back. "Let's race to the beach."

"Race what?"

"The sea serpent. Didn't you see it?"

Annie looked behind them in alarm, before she realized Ella was teasing again. But it was fun to paddle as hard as they could and feel the waves rise up beneath them, carrying them home. All too soon, the coracle plowed into the beach and they were on land again. They pulled the boat from the water and collapsed on the shore, spent and utterly content for the first time in weeks, making sand angels, tracing shapes in the clouds, gazing up into the depths of the blue, blue sky.

Chapter Seven

Every July for as long as Maire could remember, her family had picked wild blueberries that grew in the island's meadows. She gathered the buckets they'd need for the expedition—the fruit was early this year—and she had promised Nora and the girls she'd introduce them to the tradition. They'd have a picnic on the boulders once they were done. She couldn't have asked for better weather, not a cloud in the sky. Nothing tasted as good as the wild berries; the others tasted bland by comparison. She liked them best in pie, each slice a piece of heaven, made with her mother's crust.

Maeve had hated picking, finding it tedious work, and made excuses to be elsewhere as soon as she could, but Maire didn't mind. She loved being in the fields, feeling the warmth of the sun on her face, the smell of ripening fruit making her mouth water. She'd worn an apron to protect her clothes from stains, boots on her feet. She liked the sound of the berries pinging into the coffee cans her father had rigged with string handles, sneaking a handful of berries when her mother wasn't looking. *You're like me, Maire. You have a practical nature.*

She didn't necessarily want to be that way—competent, average. She was pretty, not beautiful. Intelligent, not brilliant. Quiet, not lively. She wasn't Maeve. She could never be.

"Aren't you coming with us?" she'd asked as Maeve dashed out the door. Maeve was thirteen that year, a year of change, when she suddenly began to care more about her appearance, styling her hair, applying makeup on the sly.

"I'm meeting Brenna in town." In other words, swanning up and down the street, hoping to catch the attention of the boys.

"What about Maggie?" Maire asked.

She and Maeve had been best friends for years.

"What about her? Save me a slice of pie, will you?"

"When will you be back?"

She didn't reply. She hopped on her bike and pedaled past the mailbox, onto the road that promised better things.

Maire remained behind at the point. Her mother said she was too young to go into Portakinney on her own. And so she stayed where she was.

Where she still was, all those years later.

She sighed. She'd spent far too much time dwelling on the past lately. She might not be able to remember where she put her keys, but she had remarkable recall when it came to the details of her childhood. Perhaps that's what happened as one got older, entering into a time of reflection and regret.

Nora and the girls came up the steps. They wore hats, jeans, and tees, Ella's from a Taylor Swift concert, Annie's with Mickey Mouse, Nora's the B-52's.

Maire distributed some of Joe's cotton work shirts. "You might want to toss these on to protect your arms. The bushes don't have thorns, but the twigs can scratch, and there are brambles about."

"How long is this going to take?" Ella asked, clearly lacking enthusiasm.

"It depends how fast you pick," Maire said.

"I'm a good picker," Annie said.

"Of your nose," Ella said.

"I am not!"

"Manners," Nora said.

"Oh, we don't stand on ceremony around here," Maire assured her, "in case you hadn't noticed." She put on one of Joe's caps.

They decided to walk. The fields were only half a mile away, and they could always go back and harvest more berries later. There was no need to resort to freezing yet.

There was no traffic on the road. There rarely was, no matter the time of day. The next house was a half mile in the other direction.

"It's so quiet here," Ella said. "Don't you ever get tired of it?"

That's what Maeve had said. "We're stuck on this little island, when there's so much out there."

"Then leave," Maire had said, though she didn't mean it.

"I can't."

"Why not?"

Maeve wouldn't say.

"I don't mind. I'm used to it," Maire said now.

"Have you ever been to the city? To Boston?"

"Once," she said. "A long time ago." She and Joe had visited for a weekend. They'd seen Faneuil Hall. So much traffic, lights, noise. She didn't have the best time. She'd had too much on her mind.

"It's not quiet here, not really," Annie said. "There are all sorts of sounds: the bees, the birds, the trees, the ocean, the grass, the animals—"

"You talking. Blah, blah, blah," Ella said.

Nora shook her head at her and whispered, "Stop."

"This way." Maire turned onto a wooded path, the shade cool.

The ground was carpeted with moss. Annie ran her hands over a patch, exclaiming in delight as she leaned down and rubbed her cheek over its softness.

"There might be bugs," Ella warned.

"I don't care. It's like velvet."

"It's just moss."

"Not any old moss. Island moss."

"As if that makes a difference."

"It does. I keep telling you, things are different here, but you don't listen."

"They're different here, all right."

They were, though not as Ella supposed. Even now, the island could surprise Maire. Life could surprise her, with its twists and turns.

The path wound through the pines. A squirrel scrambled up a trunk, chattering from a bough, another answering a short distance away. A warning or a territorial dispute. Annie stopped to watch, entranced, before falling into step behind her sister again, occasionally treading on her heels.

"Watch where you're going, will you?"

"Sorry, I didn't mean to."

Words Maire herself had said to Maeve, time and again, when she broke her lipstick or stained her favorite shirt or followed her without being invited. "Mae-Mae," she'd cry when she was little, stranded behind the gate in the yard. "Is that your little sister?" Maeve's friends would ask. "No," she'd say.

The path opened onto the field, the blueberry bushes scattered among the grass and boulders. The place had changed little since Maire was young. "Here we are." Some of the fruit hadn't ripened yet, the berries green and pink.

They fanned out, Nora and Maire working in the same area, Ella striding off on her own, Annie close behind. "Find your own bush," Ella said.

Annie stuck out her tongue and settled nearby.

Ella saw her reach for a pink berry. "Only the blue ones. Those won't taste good."

Annie ate it anyway, just to spite her, making a face at the sharp taste of the unripe fruit.

"Told you."

"I like them that way."

"Sure you do."

Soon the field rang with the patter of berries dropping into the buckets Maire had fashioned from cans, just like her father's. It was a sound like rain on a tin roof. In the distance, she heard the rumble of the sea—it was always there, the island not large enough to escape it. She was glad for that. The waves, whether near or far, made her feel as if she were part of something greater than herself.

"How many do you have?" Annie asked a short time later, clearly keen to outperform her sister.

"I don't know." Ella wiped her brow. "Thirty? They're small. It's hard to tell."

"I have fifty."

"Is that counting leaves?"

Annie wasn't the cleanest of berry pickers.

"No." She stood on tiptoe to reach the higher branches, upending her bucket. "Oh," she cried. "I spilled them."

"I told you to be careful."

"I know. I know." Her lower lip trembled.

"Oh, for heaven's sake, don't cry. You can have some of mine." Ella reluctantly poured half her berries into Annie's container.

They worked happily until noon, even Ella getting into a groove. "How much do we need for a pie?" she asked.

"We almost have enough," Maire said, inspecting the buckets.

"Can we make it this afternoon?"

"Of course." She could think of nothing better.

Nora had fallen silent. She was staring across the field, gripping the handle of her bucket tightly, her face pale.

Maire followed her gaze. Maggie Scanlon was standing there, a shadow beneath the pines. She felt a chill seeing her like that, so still, an unnerving intensity in her eyes.

The insects in the meadow whined louder, a shrill, almost piercing sound cutting through the quiet morning.

Maggie didn't move. She stood motionless, watching.

Maire waved, a neighborly gesture to break the spell.

Maggie didn't respond. She stepped back into the shadows and vanished from sight.

The girls hadn't noticed, crouched behind a tall clump of bushes. It was just as well.

"What did she want?" Nora asked softly.

"She was probably just out for her daily constitutional," Maire said, not very convincingly. "We're an island of walkers, you know, myself included." Though she too found Maggie's unexpected appearance strange, very strange indeed.

After lunch the girls and Nora cleaned the berries in the cottage kitchen, picking off stray stems and leaves, while Maire mixed the pastry according to her mother's recipe.

"Can we roll out the dough?" Annie asked.

"Yes," Maire said. "You can use leaf-shaped cookie cutters to make a design if you want to."

While Nora sweetened the fruit, the girls wielded the rolling pin. If the thickness of the crust wasn't quite as uniform as usual, it was of little consequence to Maire. It was their pie, after all—their first island pie.

"Careful," Ella warned her sister as they flopped the lower crust in the pan. "You don't want to put a hole in it."

"I won't." Annie turned back to the counter. "Look. I made a dough person." She held up paper-doll cutout she'd shaped from a scrap of crust. "Can we put her on the pie?"

"Absolutely," Maire said.

"I'll make three others. We can be a pie family."

"A fabulous idea. I've never had a pie family before," Maire said.

Nora poured in the filling. "This looks delicious." She licked the juice from her fingers. If she was still shaken from the encounter with Maggie, she didn't show it, but then, she was good at hiding her feelings.

"Now for the top," Maire said.

The girls flipped the other circle over the filling. They worked together to crimp the edge. Maire cut a slit in the top and Annie and Ella arranged the cutouts they'd made, so that the figures were holding hands. Maire smiled. "It's darling. Really, it is."

Annie clapped her hands, sending little clouds of flour into the air, Ella too. "Flour power!" Annie cried.

"Outside with that, you two." Nora shooed them onto the deck. "We'll call you when the pie's ready." She began wiping down the counters with a sponge. "Sorry about the mess."

"A happy mess. It comes with the territory." Maire caught her looking out the window, brow creased.

"Don't worry," she said. "Maggie's not there."

"I don't want to be paranoid, but that was odd, wasn't it, seeing her there? She isn't following me, is she?"

"She has a tendency to wander sometimes. It's nothing personal."

"It seems like it is."

A car horn blasted from the driveway, startling them. But it was only Polly, delivering the mail. She came in the side door, a circular and a copy of *Gardens Illustrated* in hand. "No bills today, you'll be happy to know. I smell something delicious," she said. "Blueberry pie? I don't suppose you could spare a piece." She turned to Nora. "Maire makes the best pies on the island. The best everything, for that matter. She's quite the chef. I can barely boil water."

"Have a seat," Maire said. "It will be coming out of the oven any minute. Your timing couldn't be better."

Both for the pie, and for the distraction.

Chapter Eight

Days passed. Annie had begun to wonder if she'd see Ronan again. She took to exploring the shoreline at dawn, when the mist rose from the sea, as if it were part of a dream. No one else was out at that hour, except for Owen Kavanagh, fishing or swimming in the distance. He'd nod or wave, but they were rarely close enough to speak. He tended to venture into more dangerous areas, farther out on the rocks and surf than she dared go.

This morning the tide was low enough to walk among the tide pools. "Hello, fish," she said. "Hello, anemones." They were her friends too. She slipped between the rocks at the end of the beach, the sand between exposed at low tide. She liked to hide. She'd hidden in the garden at home many times. The laurel hedge, filled with nesting birds, provided the best cover. She had a fort inside, perfect for her and perhaps a close friend. Not Ella—she was too big and bossy; the birds didn't like her tone of voice, so Annie stopped inviting her early on. She'd been in the hedge when she overheard her father talking to someone on his cell phone, under the guise of feeding carp in the pond, a can of fish food in hand. He stood near an azalea bush, a stray napkin and spent balloon (which had read "Cunningham for AG" before it popped) lying beneath it from the fund-raising party her parents had had a few days before, the weather being fine enough for the guests to spill outside. He spoke softly, with the same hushed tones she used when confiding in her best friend, Katie. "Do you have secrets too, Daddy?" she'd asked, startling him as she emerged from the hedge and followed him into the house. "Just business, Annie-pan," he said briskly. "I didn't realize you were there."

She felt a chill there on Glass Beach, in the shade of the rocks, and flitted out into the sun again. *I'm a butterfly.* She could transform herself. She could make anything new.

"Hi, Annie." Ronan stepped lightly along the lip of a pool. She'd never seen anyone with such perfect balance.

"Where have you been?" She'd been hoping to see him, and now there he was.

"Away, fishing. You haven't told anyone about me, have you?"

"No. I never break a promise."

"Good. I knew I could trust you. I have something for you." He handed her a shell—plain, white, flawless. It was threaded on a piece of braided sea grass. "Go ahead. Blow on it."

She did. "It doesn't make a sound."

His eyes sparkled. "Just because you can't hear it, doesn't mean someone else can't. Keep it. You might need it someday."

"When?"

"It's not someday yet. When it is, you'll know."

She slipped the necklace over her head. She liked how it smelled of the sea, that he'd made it for her.

"Do you want to swim?"

"I'm not supposed to swim alone."

"You aren't alone. You're with me. We won't go far. There's something I want to show you."

"We still haven't gone out in my boat. I have paddles now."

"This will be better. You'll see." He took her hand. The warmth from his skin spread through her body. "Still cold?"

She laughed and shook her head.

They ran through the shallows, water splashing behind them, spray iridescent in the sunlight, and dove in. The salt stung Annie's eyes, but she didn't close them. She wanted to see where Ronan was taking her. She'd never known anyone who swam as well as he did, not even her mother. She mirrored his movements as best she could. They surfaced at intervals, to draw breath, before submerging once again.

Ronan treaded water, cocking his head. "They're coming. Listen." He tugged her beneath the waves. She caught her breath, fast, before going under. Then she heard it: a basslike sound, like a muffled horn, deep, sonorous, followed by higher whistles—a symphony of the sea.

"What was that?" she asked after they surfaced again, gasping. She'd never held her breath so long. "It was beautiful."

"The whales, singing." He paused, noticing how breathless she was. "You're tired. We'd better go back."

"I don't want to."

"I know." He guided her to shore and sat by her side, drawing symbols in the sand.

"What do those mean?" She gestured to the marks, a series of curves and lines, as if in code.

"It's a special language," he said. "Maybe I'll teach you sometime."

"Would you write my name?"

He scratched loops and dashes that looked like sparrow's wings or fish scales.

"It's pretty. I want to write my name like that, always."

He shook his head. "It's between us—for the beach only."

"For the beach only," she agreed.

"So you're here with your family?" he asked.

"My sister and mom."

"And your dad?"

"He's coming, I think. Actually, I don't know. He hasn't been around much lately." She sighed.

He nodded, as if he knew exactly what she meant. "Things are always changing," he said, studying the waves. "Sometimes in ways we don't want them to."

They fell silent. Ronan was easy to be with. She could have spent hours with him, hours and hours.

He got up abruptly and crouched down behind a pile of driftwood. He seemed to sense things before she did.

"What's wrong?" she asked, wondering if she should hide too.

"Someone's there."

She looked in the direction he indicated. It was Owen Kavanagh, casting a net from one of the outcrops. "It's just Owen. He comes from the ocean, like you. Do you know him?"

Ronan didn't answer. He slipped away through a slit in the rocks without another word.

Maire met Annie on the path that meandered down the bluff. She was on her way to gather seaweed and shellfish, a basket on her arm. She'd glimpsed the boy before he'd dashed away. "I see you've made a new friend."

"Friend? There was nobody but me." Annie toed the sand. She wouldn't meet Maire's eyes. She was obviously hiding something.

There was a pile of beachcombed findings at her feet—periwinkles, clamshells, sea glass, a perfectly spherical granite stone. She'd already assembled quite a collection at the cottage. She'd shown it to Maire on many occasions. "You've found more treasures."

"There's something new every day. You never know what you'll find." Her gaze darted in the direction the boy had gone.

"A visitor too?" Maire gestured to the footprints the waves hadn't quite had a chance to erase.

Annie bit her lip. "No one is supposed to know, especially Ella. She gets so bossy. I don't think Ronan would like her very much." Annie covered her mouth. "Oh, no. I shouldn't have said his name. And I was doing so well, too."

"It's all right. Is he a summer visitor, like you?"

"I think so. I'm not sure. All I know is that he's my friend. He likes to play. Ella doesn't, not always. That's what happens when you get older, doesn't it? I won't let it happen to me."

Maire smiled. It was such a gift to have children at Cliff House again. She'd forgotten what it was like—their discoveries, their small joys, seeing possibility in everything. "Well, we'll keep it between the two of us for now, shall we?" She supposed there wasn't any harm. Perhaps Nora already knew. She kept such a close eye on the girls.

"Are you good at keeping secrets?" Annie asked.

Maire drew her fingers across her lips. Yes, she was. Too good.

"Some secrets are bad, aren't they?" Annie mused, perhaps thinking of her father.

"This one isn't. At least, I don't think it is. I'm glad you made a new friend."

"I am too. We're making lots of friends on Burke's Island—Polly, Alison, Owen, Reilly—"

"You've met Reilly?" She supposed she shouldn't have been surprised. He walked the bluffs frequently, though he didn't travel far beyond the point anymore, unless it was for Sunday mass. He sat in the same pew as Maire, third row, left, a small statue of Saint Rita, patron saint of impossible causes, in the niche nearby, candles burning at her feet.

"Yes. And Patch. I can't forget Patch."

Maire and Joe had had a dog too, a chocolate lab named Diggity, who went down with his master. She hadn't had the heart to get another, not knowing what the future would bring. "He's a sweetie, isn't he?"

"It's nice to get to know someone my own age," Annie said, speaking of Ronan again.

"Yes, I'm sure it is." Ella was the only one who hadn't formed a new friendship on the island, but then again, there weren't any other children near the point.

"Where are you going?" Annie asked.

"To harvest seaweed. Some types are good in salads, others for the garden. The vegetables are particularly fond of it. Would you like to help?"

"Yes." She took Maire's hand, looking up at her trustingly. "I'm glad we came here, Aunt Maire."

"I am too."

"Owen likes to fish, doesn't he?" Annie asked later after they returned to Cliff House. Maire had had her younger niece all to herself that morning. Nora had gone into town to run errands, and Ella remained at the cabin, engrossed in her book, *Mockingjay* being her latest selection. Maire and Annie were in the garden, laying the seaweed out to dry. Once it was ready, they'd spread it on the beds to nourish the roots of the plants. "He's always on the rocks, catching something."

"It's what he loves to do," Maire said. She shaded her eyes. There he was, coming up the path. He seemed to be getting along better now. At first, he'd been tentative in his movements, as if he didn't trust his feet to support him. "Hello, there. We were just talking about you."

"My ears are burning." He presented her with a batch of smelt.

"My favorite, ever since I was a little girl. I'd catch them with my dad. We were the only ones who liked them." Maire cherished those times with her father. He taught her about the ocean. The sailor's superstitions: Never sail on Friday. Never whistle aboard a boat unless it's to summon a fair breeze, when becalmed. The rules of navigation.

"Me too."

"We were just finishing up here." Maire rose to her feet, dusting off the knees of her jeans. "Why don't you come in for a cup of tea?"

"And cookies?" Annie asked hopefully.

"Before noon?" Maire smiled.

"It's never too early for cookies," Annie said. She'd hinted that snickerdoodles were her favorite.

"That's what I always say," Maire said as they went inside, leaving their boots at the door.

"Did you lose your clothes in the shipwreck?" Annie asked Owen as Maire set the kettle on to boil.

He shrugged good-naturedly. "I've never been much for fashion."

"I was going through the attic the other day, and I found some clothes that might fit you," Maire said. She'd been meaning to mention it to him. She'd noticed how he tended to wear the same pair of ragged shorts.

"That's not necessary—"

"You'd be doing me a favor. Keep an eye on the pot, and I'll bring them down." She'd already sorted the shirts and pants, running her hands over each piece of clothing, washing, folding, pressing, as she used to do when Jamie and Joe were alive. She wasn't sure the clothes would work, Jamie having been a rangy six-footer, while Owen was five-ten at most and strongly built. And yet Jamie had worn his clothes baggy, so perhaps some of them would fit Owen.

She lingered in Jamie's room—taking in the space in that had belonged to her son, in which he had grown from a small boy who feared the dark and loved basketball and astronomy to a young man who would barely speak to her, filling the room with his sheer size, with the force of his anger. Where did that rage come from? How did she lose the ability to communicate with him? The thoughts pained her. She wished she'd told him how much she loved him, but she'd gotten worn down by the arguments, the trouble.

There didn't seem to be anything they could agree on—and then he was gone.

She picked up the cardboard box with a sigh and carried it downstairs. "Here they are," she said, placing it on the table for Owen's perusal.

"What's your favorite color?" Annie asked him, taking a peek at the contents. "This shirt is nice." She fingered the collar of a gray flannel button-down.

He thought for a moment. "Blue."

"Mine too," Maire said. "A good thing, since there's so much of it around here."

"It's hard to choose," Annie said. "There's something pretty about every color."

"An excellent philosophy," Owen said, "seeing beauty in all things."

She smiled. He seemed to have her seal of approval too.

That night, Maire brought Owen dinner—crab cakes, beans, and honeyberries from the garden. She'd invited him to the house on several occasions, but he had yet to take her up on it, perhaps not wanting to intrude. He wasn't expecting her that evening. But she thought he could use a home-cooked meal; she had a feeling he hadn't had one in a while. She balanced the covered plate on her left hand as she wound her way down the point. She hadn't spent much time there, even in her youth, other than to summon her father for supper or to visit Patrick, when he first came to live with them. The memories of him still pained her, even after all these years.

Rabbits and voles had made homes just off the path. She glanced down at her feet, at intervals, to make sure not to put a foot wrong. It wouldn't do to twist her ankle. "Just sit for a moment," Joe would say. But she had to be doing. Maybe it kept her sane, or close to it.

She'd thought of bringing another plate for herself, to keep Owen company, but she didn't want to be presumptuous. He seemed to like his privacy. Smoke trailed up into the sky from the fishing shack. It had been decades since a fire had been lit in its small hearth. She hated to think of the condition the shack was in—the mice, the cobwebs. She'd warned him, but he hadn't been deterred. "I've seen far worse," he said. She didn't ask him what he meant.

A crow flew ahead of her, meowing like a cat. Such canny birds, they were. They used to frighten her when she was a child; her grandmother had said they were the harbingers of death, though as she got older, she realized that trouble could come unexpectedly, bird or no bird, and that perhaps the resident flock had been done a disservice. She suspected this one was poking fun at Flotsam and Jetsam, taunting them as it flew out of reach. "You're a clever fellow, aren't you?" she said to him. She often talked to the animals like this—to Joe too, especially in the months following the accident. She still felt him with her. She supposed she always would.

The path steepened and banked around a flat rock—the sunning rock, Maeve used to call it. She'd bask there in her bra and undies when their parents weren't around. Maire had her mother's skin, the pale Irish sort that never tanned. Maeve's turned a lovely honeyed shade, changing with the seasons, which only made her more exotic to the boys of Portakinney, who seemed to trail after her wherever she went. Maire soon learned that she couldn't keep up with her in the tanning department, after a couple of blistering burns that held the heat for days.

Owen had cleared the yard of debris and hung his nets up to dry. The place didn't look so desolate anymore. It was good to have someone in residence, a caretaker of sorts. She wished it had occurred to her before. She stepped onto the porch and tapped on the door. He'd fashioned a wind chime of shells to hang from the eaves. At first, there was no answer. Then she thought she heard a moan inside and became concerned. Maybe she should have watched him more closely. He'd been through a terrible ordeal. She pushed open the door and poked her head in. There he was, on his knees. What on earth could be the matter?

"Owen," she said. "Are you all right?"

He jerked his head up and his eyes met hers, a bewilderment in them she didn't understand, as if he didn't quite know where he was.

She set the plate down on the small table near the window and knelt down beside him. "Do you know who I am?"

His expression cleared, though a hint of confusion remained in his gaze. "I'm sorry. I didn't hear you."

She touched his arm. "What's going on? Is it the headaches?"

He stared at his hands as if they didn't belong to him. "This is harder than I thought."

"What is?"

"Everything."

She sat back on her heels. "You're safe now. You're on solid ground."

"I know," he said. "I'm not usually like this."

"You'll be your old self soon enough. Perhaps some dinner will set you to rights." She nodded to the plate. "Are you sure you don't want me to stay? It wouldn't be any trouble at all."

He got to his feet with some effort, as if he had an invisible yoke around his neck. She was curious about what was burdening him, but such symptoms weren't atypical of concussions. He might not be troubled by anything other than the pain in his head. "Seriously, Maire. I'm okay—and I very much appreciate your taking care of me like this."

"I think it's you who's taking care of me." She put a hand on his arm—she could feel him shaking, ever so slightly—and reluctantly went on her way.

Chapter Nine

As the days went by, Owen ingratiated himself with Maire further. He assisted with repairs, worked on the truck, the house. There didn't seem to be anything he couldn't fix. The Fixer, Nora called him, keeping him at arm's length with sarcastic humor, and yet whenever he was near, as he seemed to be all too often, her eye was drawn to him.

"I could fix that for you," he'd say. "I'm good with repairs."

"What about your memory?" she'd reply. "Is it coming back?"

"A little at a time," he said. "No earthshaking revelations."

He spent a morning fixing the railing on the deck at Maire's request, while Nora repaired the chair cushions with striped fabric from Scanlon's. (Alison had helped her pick it out. She had a good eye.) The girls were making mazes in the long grass of the meadow, their heads barely detectable above the tassels.

"You're the Minotaur," Ella called to Annie.

"Why do I always have to be the monster? Why can't I be the warrior princess?" Annie complained.

"Because your teeth are pointier than mine."

"I won't always have baby teeth. I might be bigger than you someday. I might tell you what to do. Ha!"

The sound of their voices faded as they moved into the shadows of the pines.

Nora stole glances at Owen. She'd been working outside when he arrived, and it seemed rude to abruptly move indoors. He labored steadily, bracing the railing and repairing the supports. He didn't seem to mind the silence.

She did. "I think Maire was afraid the girls might hurt themselves on a loose nail," she said.

"It needs to be completely redone."

"This part too?" She tapped her foot on the decking, worried about the possibility of it giving way.

He shook his head. "That's sound enough. It's been sealed."

She remembered her father installing the deck. Nora had begged to help—Patrick had given her a tool belt, complete with a plastic child-size hammer, with which she used to pound the boards; he'd never complained about her being in the way—but her mother wouldn't let her participate in the last step of the process. She closed the windows against the strong vapors of the sealant and insisted they vacate the premises for the day. Nora couldn't remember where they were going, only the trail, leading away, and her father growing smaller, until he disappeared from view.

"Is something wrong?" Owen asked.

"No, I was just thinking about my dad. He did most of the restoration work on the cottage." Patrick continued woodworking in his workshop at their home in Boston after they left the island. Nora would sit at the entrance, away from the whirring saws, the noise of the equipment making conversation difficult. She played with piles of sawdust, pretending they were the Gobi or the Sahara, her strong, quiet father wielding an adze nearby. He rebuilt their life too, as best he could, a roof over her head, a firm foundation on which she could stand. She understood that now.

"A fine job, too," Owen said.

"Except the railing."

"That wasn't his work. Maire said her son put it in."

That reassured Nora, somehow, to learn her father hadn't had a hand in creating anything faulty.

The conversation continued in fits and starts, but eventually she and Owen found a rhythm, after laboring in close proximity, that invited confidences. He seemed happy to let her talk. He didn't interrupt, didn't analyze. She hadn't realized how much she needed someone to listen. She told him stories about her childhood, when she climbed the tallest trees in the neighborhood or raced down the biggest hills on her bicycle, before she'd grown careful and cautious, raising her children, letting Malcolm take the lead. Perhaps she wanted Owen to think she was brave, that she could take chances. Perhaps she needed to be reminded that that person was still a part of her too.

"I didn't realize I was talking so much," she said, a lull in the conversation making her self-conscious. "I don't usually babble like this—"

"It's all right," he said. "I like having someone to talk to. I'm on my own most of the time."

"Me too."

Owen fell silent for a moment. "He was a fool to let you go."

"Maybe he hasn't," she said quickly. She wanted to be clear. "Nothing has been decided."

"No," he said. "I suppose it hasn't."

The hammer sounded sharper then, against the wood, as he rejoined the pieces that had separated and made them whole once more.

The next morning, as the sun began to cast its light over the meadow, streaming through the windows, Nora was surprised to find new driftwood furniture on the deck. Owen must have seen the poor condition of the old pieces early on and designed new ones, perhaps delivering them before sunrise, while she and the girls slept. She ran her hands over the wood, polished by the waves. The chairs were finely made, the work of a true artisan.

The girls appeared behind her, faces soft from sleep.

"Mermaids' chairs." Annie plopped down and placed her hands on the armrests. "Where did they come from?"

"Owen must have made them."

"They're the most beautiful chairs I've ever seen."

"You must not have seen that many chairs, then," Ella said.

"They're lovely," Nora said, thinking she must compensate him for the work. She didn't feel comfortable accepting such an extravagant gift—unless they were another project Maire had asked him to undertake. Somehow she doubted it. "Better than the others, that's for certain."

"I liked the old ones," Ella said, a note of challenge in her voice.

"They were falling apart," Nora replied.

"Someone's being a grumpy-pants this morning," Annie said. She moved out of arm's reach, to allow a buffer against sisterly retaliation.

Ella ignored her. "The cushions you made won't fit them," she told Nora.

"They'll be fine. Or I can make new ones."

"We could have fixed the chairs," Ella insisted, "if we'd tried."

Nora gestured to the side of the cottage, where Owen had rested the rejects. "There they are, if you want them. Don't get a splinter."

Ella wrestled with one of the chairs—its joints were jammed—as if locked in a clumsy waltz.

"You're going to break it," Annie warned.

"No, I'm not," she said through clenched teeth. The chair finally popped open with a snap. She set it in the corner and sat down gingerly. The legs weren't level, and she tottered, unable to fully relax.

"Comfortable?" Nora asked.

"Very. We'll need more chairs, anyway—for when Dad visits."

Polly was at Maire's that night, Owen too. Maire had apparently invited him to dinner. He had contributed the fish for bouillabaisse, she said, and it was only proper to include him. Besides, it seemed inhospitable not to. The fragrant broth filled the senses, scented with saffron and herbs from Maire's garden, tomatoes from her greenhouse.

"Not as good as sun-ripened," she said. "But they'll do until nature is ready to do its work." She passed bowls of bread, salad, and raspberries, making sure everyone's plates were full.

Maire had set the table for the occasion using the family silver, white napkins, candlesticks, and delft china with faded pastoral scenes. Ella seemed to study the pattern closely—she barely raised her eyes from her plate the entire evening and made a project of moving her salad—garden greens, nasturtiums, and pea shoots—around the rim as if she were redecorating a room.

Marie had placed a flag in the holder by the door, hung streamers from the light fixtures. It was the Fourth of July. Nora had forgotten.

"We're from Boston," Annie said to Owen, chatty as always. "Where are you from?"

"I live at sea," he replied.

"You're our first shipwreck in forty years," Maire said, "if the records my grandfather kept are correct."

"Glad to make it into the books," Owen said.

"In dramatic fashion," Polly added.

"It's like a story from our book of fairy tales," Annie said.

"Not that again," Ella muttered.

"The collection that belonged to you and Maeve?" Polly asked Maire.

"The very one."

"Which is your favorite?" Polly asked the girls.

Ella shrugged.

"I can't decide," Annie said. "I want to read the one about the selkie, but we're not there yet."

"Oh, that's a good one. The fisherman who snares a seal wife in his nets."

"How come it's always the men who get to catch interesting things?" Ella asked, ever the budding feminist. "It doesn't seem fair."

"Actually, selkies can be men too. There's another side to the myth, not as widely known, in which a selkie man comes to a woman who cries seven tears into the sea, to help her find happiness again. Would that we all were so lucky." She paused, winking at Owen. "That wouldn't be you, would it, washed ashore on stormy seas?"

He laughed. "The question is, which of you did I come for?"

Polly blushed. "Oh, what a flirt you are. Watch out for this one, Maire."

"Cliff House hasn't been so filled with life since—" Maire's eyes flitted toward the photos of her family on the mantel, then away. "It's good to have everyone here." She raised a glass of wine. "To homecomings."

"To homecomings."

Nora insisted on cleaning up while Maire showed the girls some things she'd saved in the attic. The kitchen reflected the warmth of its owner, the walls painted yellow, the countertops island granite, the floors well-trodden pine. Jars of herbs and dried flowers lined the shelves. "Headache," read one label. "Memory," read another, as if it could be stored in a bottle. The fridge door was covered with photos and Post-it notes, to-do lists and phone numbers, a testament to Maire's busy life. As Nora scraped the dishes, she noticed a burned pot in the garbage—Maire must have left it on too long, something that Nora had done herself more than once after the scandal broke, unable to concentrate.

She loaded the dishwasher and wiped the countertops, as she would have back home in their understated Georgian—the perfect residence for a budding statesman, not too ostentatious, respectable—on a shady avenue, the trees in full leaf, children at play on the sidewalks, the sound of a lawn mower whirring in the distance, a neighborhood of ordered gardens and ordered lives, hers too, until recently. She'd put a great deal of work into that house; it had been a fixer-upper when they bought it, fulfilling their dream of owning a house on Oak Street. They saw the possibilities, the good bones. A place where Nora could have a normal family, the family she'd never had. The door was locked now. The mail held. Dust gathering on their possessions. There was a time she had belonged to the city: its industry, its life, her soul. The sidewalks teeming with people—the successful, the bereft, the joyous, the mad, the estranged. She had separated herself from that. From Malcolm. Their Boston, gone.

Owen came up behind her. "Thought I'd lend a hand."

"No need." Being close to him made her fluttery. Polly was playing show tunes at the piano, singing slightly off-key. The voices of Maire and the girls grew distant as they explored the upper regions of the house. "You know the saying, too many cooks in the kitchen."

"But you're not cooking, and I'm an expert at cleanup." He brandished a tea towel like a matador's cape.

"So many hidden talents you have. Thank you for the chairs, by the way. You didn't have to do that. I'd like to pay you for them."

"They're a gift."

"You don't owe me anything. I thought I'd made that clear. All I did was find you on the rocks and give you a coat that didn't fit. You'd already saved yourself."

"Does it matter how we got here?"

"No. It's only—"

"What's bothering you?"

"Nothing. I want to be sure you understand."

He didn't say anything for a moment. "We're friends, aren't we, Nora? Why don't we leave it at that for now."

"If we're friends, why do I know so little about you?"

"You said I don't owe you anything," he said. "You mean, except an explanation?"

"Yes, I suppose I do. You have to forgive me, but I'm not used to men washing ashore and hanging around." She'd meant to keep her tone light, but it didn't come across that way. She could see that by the way his expression became guarded.

"You're used to them leaving?" he asked. Then, "We both have our reasons for being here. I took a hard knock on the head—"

"Is it that you can't remember, or that you don't want to?" she couldn't help asking. The question had been on her mind. It was the attorney in her, pressing for answers.

"The same could be asked of you, couldn't it?"

"What's that supposed to mean?" she demanded, on the defensive now.

"Look. I don't want to argue with you. I'm just trying to get my feet on the ground and repay Maire's kindness. Is that all right with you?" He'd leaned closer to make his point.

She stepped back, heart racing, as Ella appeared in the doorway.

"Mom," Ella said. "You have to see what we found in the attic."

"Coming." Nora caught the hint of suspicion in her eye and glanced away, the heat rising in her face.

She told herself Ella didn't have anything to worry about. There was nothing between her and Owen Kavanagh, nothing at all.

Owen went into the living room to join Polly, while Ella took charge of Nora. "This way, Mama." She took Nora's hand and pulled her upstairs, to the second floor. Maire was waiting for them on the landing. Nora guessed it was her room off to the left, with a view of the ocean, the walls and coverlet echoing the colors of the sky. An old copy of *Jane Eyre* was on the nightstand.

"One of my favorite books," Maire said, following Nora's gaze.

"Mine too," Nora replied.

"We all dream of finding a Rochester, don't we?" Maire mused.

"Mom doesn't need a Rochester," Ella said. "She has Daddy."

"Of course she does."

They passed Jamie's room down the hall, still carefully preserved, shelves displaying sports trophies, and a stuffed dog lying on the pillow. We were all children once, Nora thought. Filled with innocence and dreams. Higher they went, up a steep, narrow staircase, to the top of the house.

"Mind the ceiling. It dips low at the entrance, as if it were made for elves," Maire warned.

"It's like a tower room," Annie remarked.

"Off with your head," Ella said.

"I'll keep mine, thank you very much," Annie said primly.

A bare bulb burned in the center of the long, narrow room, its cord swinging. The attic shelves were filled with boxes and trunks, neatly stacked and labeled, shadows at the edges.

"Here it is." Ella gestured toward a chart spread out on the floor in the corner near a small, round window, overlooking the orchard and hives, bathed in evening light, below. There were additional charts stored in tubes in a bin nearby.

"Where did these come from?" Nora asked. The paper of the chart in question was tattered along the margins and stained the color of tea.

"They've been in the family since the old days," Maire explained. "This one dates to the first landing. There's Little Burke and the channel."

"Who made them?" Nora asked.

"There are no signatures. Some of our ancestors were navigators, I guess. I swear, each time I look at these— and I don't that often—they never look the same to me."

"What are these hatch marks?"

"My da said they were to indicate the seal colonies. Our ancestors tracked their movements, both the local seals, and those that came from the north, fishing for the summer. Apparently, there would be the greatest concentration of fish wherever the seals congregated. It was as if the family had worked out an arrangement with them, or so he said. Whatever the truth was, we did well with the fishing, until my generation. Then something happened. Bad luck or declining fish stocks or global warming—for whatever reason, the bounty lessened. Nothing lasts forever, I suppose."

No, Nora thought, it didn't.

After they lit sparklers and the few fountains Maire had purchased at a fireworks stand in town—Ella and Annie couldn't wait until dark to set them off, despite the lack of effect—Nora and the girls walked home in the afterglow of the day, the sun fading into golden haze and dusk shading the waves and hills plum and indigo. The larks chattered to themselves in that quiet time before sleep, and a heron stood motionless on the dock. Annie and Ella scampered ahead, figures in a shadow play, over the hummocked turf, the trees in the orchard bending low, branches laced with lichen and fall-ripening fruit, shiny and green. The evening smelled of wildflowers, grass, and the tang of the ocean, and something underneath, a deeper, unidentifiable note that passed on the breeze. There one minute, gone the next. Her mother's perfume? The oil Maire said she'd distilled from wild narcissus blooms? Intimations of the past snuck up on her at every turn.

"Almost time for a story," Annie said.

Ella pushed open the cottage door. The shadows seemed deeper than usual—perhaps Maeve's there too, disappearing around a corner, into the bedroom. Nora readied herself for bed, tracing the lines on her face, the gray strands that seemed to have multiplied at her temples, permanent souvenirs from the past few months, her features sharper. Was this how Malcolm saw her? His other woman a younger version of herself, skin smooth, life unencumbered, enthralling, mysterious. Was it possible to know each other too well in some ways, not well enough in others?

"Mama!" Annie called.

Nora roused herself to run a bath for Annie. She turned the tap and water poured from the faucet in a torrent. "Niagara Falls!" Annie exclaimed. "Iguazu!" Ella said from in front of the mirror, where she stood, untangling her hair. She was too old for mother-assisted bathing now, especially in the company of her little sister. She wanted her privacy, and yet she stayed with them, joining in the fun from her perch on the toilet lid, where she'd settled to paint her nails vermilion.

Annie hopped into the tub, its feet clawed as a beast; what better place to play sea monster, like the one in the fairy tale.

Nora ignored the discomfort of the hard tiles pressing against her knees and gave herself over to the warmth of the water, the iridescence of a single bubble floating up to the ceiling, the softness of her daughter's skin, the silkiness of her hair. They helped Annie sculpt the suds into shapes—mountains, wigs and beards and hats—*I'm a witch, I'm a shark, I'm a mermaid*—their laughter ringing through the house that had been silent for too long, their jubilance echoed by distant crackles and booms.

"It's a fireworks show!" Annie cried, running onto the deck in her bath towel.

Clusters of sparks and explosions lit up the sky at the docks in Portakinney, launched just high enough to be visible from the point. Ella and Annie broke into cheers.

"Happy Independence Day, Mama!" Annie said.

Independence Day. Nora liked the sound of that.

Chapter Ten

The wind spoke with a peculiar tone the next day, as if it were playing the calliope of a traveling circus, plaintive and slightly out of tune. The girls listened as they prepared to launch the coracle into the cove. They'd never heard anything quite like it before. Reilly Neale accompanied them, ordering Patch to stay ashore. (He consented with great reluctance, head on paws.) Reilly's boarding the boat caused some comical moments, his pants rolled up to knobbed knees, the coracle tilting dangerously, first one way, then the other, but in the end he managed to settle into the central position without capsizing them.

"I see you're properly outfitted now," he said.

"Wait. You don't have a life jacket," Annie said, as they floated in the shallows.

"Never've had one. Sink or swim and all that."

"We'll have to get you one before we sail. It's the rules."

"Let's not worry about that now. I'll bring one next time. The important thing is you girls have them. Time is of the essence. Listen." Reilly cocked his head as he and Ella paddled into the center of the cove.

"It's only the wind," Ella said. "And the seals."

"A special wind. Only comes once a season, if you're blessed enough to hear it: the sirens' song."

"It doesn't sound like a fire engine or an ambulance," Annie said.

Ella laughed. "Not that kind."

"Mermaids. They're rumored to visit, in a cave around the bend," Reilly explained. "Do you want to see it? The tide is right."

"Yes!" Annie cried.

Ella didn't believe in mermaids. She had her mind on other things. "Was this really our grandmother's boat?" She trailed her hand in the water. "Do you know what happened to her?"

Reilly shook his head. "I regret to say my mind was too clouded with drink in those days to make much sense of anything I might have seen or heard. Your grandfather was heartbroken, good man that he was. He bailed me out more than once when I'd gotten myself into a fix, on and off the sea."

Yes, their grandfather had hardly talked at all. They'd seen him for Sunday dinners when he was alive, solemn affairs with little sound track but the scrape and clatter of silverware. He kept a candy dish, a lidded tin filled with butterscotches and candy corn, treats their mother refused to buy, and could be persuaded to play marathons of gin rummy on those few occasions they went to stay with him. Ella remembered his sad eyes, his shoulders, hunched against an invisible weight, his patience as he taught her to tally scores, strategize the next move, the tick of the grandfather clock in the hallway marking the hours. There were crucifixes over every bed, a statue of the Virgin Mary, Saint Francis, and gnomes scattered about the garden, where she worked alongside him among the roses and played croquet with a set he'd bought at Mallory's, her hand in his, cradled gently as a tiny bird, as they left the store.

"Her disappearance is one of the island's great mysteries," Reilly said. "Bear left. Mind the rocks. See the arch? That's the entrance."

Puffins dove into the surf and gulls wheeled, the air filled with warning shrieks and the papery fluttering of wings.

"It looks like a castle," Annie said. The rock formations did indeed resemble turrets.

"So it does. Easy now." They negotiated a series of outcrops under Reilly's direction. "You must have done this before," he said. "You're naturals."

"If Ella's the captain and I'm the first mate, does that make you the admiral?" Annie asked.

"I'm whatever you want me to be," he said, apparently mindful of Ella's need to occupy the lead position. "Let's say I'm your personal maritime consultant."

They seemed satisfied with the title.

The dissonant melody intensified as they drew closer.

"It's not a pretty song," Annie said. "But it makes me want to listen. It's like you can't not listen. May we go inside?"

"We could get dashed against the rocks if a surge comes in," Reilly said. "Best stay here."

"In ancient Rome, sirens supposedly drew men to their deaths," Ella said.

"A fellow student of history and mythology, I should have known," Reilly replied. "My favorite subjects at school, especially the Greeks and Romans."

Each culture, even each family, had its myths, Ella thought, hers too.

"Did our grandmother visit the mermaids?" Annie asked. "Did she take the coracle out that last day?"

The sun glared on the lip of the waves, like a mirror tilted to catch the light. Reilly blinked, spots before his eyes, as there had been that day years before. The whiskey bottle rolling across the uneven floor, level with his one, half-seeing eye. The door open, with a soggy view of the beach, due not to the weather but to all he had imbibed. And through that opening, he'd seen, or thought he'd seen, Maeve and the girl, Nora, paddling beyond the cove, the water smooth as ice, their hair streaming in the wind, curled and shiny as black ribbons. A girl and her mother, on a fair afternoon.

It wasn't until later, when Patrick pounded on the door, that he came to the fuzzy realization that something was amiss. "Did you see them? Did you?" Patrick asked, but he couldn't respond. Patrick shoved him out of the way and sprinted down to the shore, hands and feet tearing at the bank. The beach giving its own account in the scored marks left behind, where Maeve had dragged the coracle into the shallows, and their bare footsteps pressed into the sand, two larger, two smaller, his women, his family, gone.

Days passed. The coracle eventually returned on its own, sitting on the beach as if awaiting the next passengers, leaving no clue as to where it had been or the fate of its occupants.

Maeve's granddaughters were the passengers now, Reilly too. He felt the weight of the past in the surrounding sea, in the curved boards that supported him and the girls. He ran his hand along the gunwales. *Coracle.* He remembered what his grand-da had told him when he was a boy: "Drop the *c*, and you have *oracle.*" This boat, holding secrets, still.

"Yes," Reilly told Annie and Ella quietly. "I think she did."

"Maybe I'll write a story about it," Annie said. "To add to the book of fairy tales."

"Go ahead," Ella said, "if it makes you feel better."

They turned back, into the cove. Nora was waiting for them on the beach, arms crossed over her chest, face set. Patch sat nearby with a guilty expression, as if he knew what was coming. He didn't even bark. The surf raced up the shore before backing away, as if it didn't dare so much as dampen their mother's feet, a margin of darker sand separating her from the waves that bore the coracle landward.

"Uh-oh," Annie said.

"That must be your mother," Reilly said. "She looks like Maeve."

"She's got her mad face on," Annie said.

"Didn't you tell her about the coracle?" Reilly asked. "I thought you had permission."

"Not exactly," Ella admitted.

"Well, you're arriving safely. Perhaps that's a point in our favor."

The bottom of the boat scraped against the pebbled shore. The girls jumped out and helped him drag the vessel up the beach. Nora met them halfway, her arms still crossed, fingers whitening at the tips from pressing into her skin. She wore a deep green tank top the same color as the pines near the cottage and a pair of jeans rolled to her calves.

"Hi, Mom," Annie said, as if a smile would set everything right.

"Hi," Nora said. Her voice was flat, her eyes narrowed. She was clearly attempting—not very successfully—to control her temper.

"I'm Reilly Neale, Mrs.—" He doffed his cap and made a little bow.

"Cunningham."

"Mama, Reilly is our friend," Annie said. She glanced at her older sister, who shrugged and rolled her eyes.

"I know your aunt," Reilly tried again.

"Funny. She hasn't mentioned you."

"You can ask her—"

"I will."

"I live down the shore a pace. I came upon the girls when I was out walking and gave them a hand with the coracle. I didn't mean to interfere."

"Coracle?" Nora looked more closely at the boat. She'd apparently been so focused on the returning crew that she hadn't examined it closely. Her face went pale.

"We spruced it up. I thought they should have a chaperone."

"A maritime consultant," Annie chimed in.

"We didn't go far," Reilly assured her, not that she appeared to be in the mood for assurances. "They wanted to see the mermaid cave."

"Next time, consult with me first. I live over there a pace, in the cottage," she said, her voice dripping with sarcasm.

He clapped his hands to Patch, who had been cowering at the sidelines, smart dog that he was, and headed for home, saddened that their excursion had ended on a bad note.

What were you thinking?" Nora herded the girls up the bank after Reilly had gone, a hand gripping each arm firmly.

"Ouch, that hurts. You made a red mark on my skin." Ella pulled away.

"There's no mark," Nora scoffed, though there was, a slight one that gave her pause, though it was already fading. She hadn't meant to handle her so roughly.

"You told us to experience the island," Ella went on. "That's what we were doing. It's a cove. We know how to swim. We had life jackets. And besides, Reilly was there."

"A man I don't know."

"He remembered you," Annie said.

"I don't remember him. He didn't have permission to take you anywhere. He gave you the paddles and life jackets too?" Her tone sharpened again. They didn't understand how worried she'd been, wouldn't understand, not until if and when they had children of their own.

"No," Ella said with a curl of her lips. "Owen did."

"Owen?" Her jaw tightened.

"We're sorry, Mama," Annie said. "Aren't we, El?"

Ella didn't reply. She pressed her mouth into a stubborn line.

"You're only seven and twelve years old," Nora continued. "I'm responsible for you. Don't you understand that? If anything were to happen—"

"But it didn't. It wouldn't have," Annie said.

"That boat is too old."

"It's lasted all this time. It was your mother's. Didn't you recognize it?" Ella asked.

"Yes, I did." The sight of it had stunned her, as if she'd been suddenly shoved into a dark room. Her pulse still hadn't slowed. She opened the door to the cottage and motioned them inside. It was dinnertime, after all. Maire had gone into town that night to play bridge. They were on their own. She checked the stove, the burners heating up, the liquid in the pots simmering. She poured in the pasta, checked the vegetables. She was serving penne with broccoli from Maire's garden that night, the girls' favorite. "Get changed," she said. "Your clothes are wet."

"They'll dry," Ella said.

Nora knew Ella didn't want to stay in her soaked garments; she was being recalcitrant. "Do as I say," Nora said sharply. She gripped the edge of the counter and took a deep breath.

The girls retreated to the bedroom, their voices a low murmur of conspiracy united against her, behind the closed door.

Nora stared at the waves. The waves her daughters had traveled, that she must have traveled, in that very boat. She remembered when Maeve first showed her the coracle. "This will be yours someday," she said. "A crafty little craft for sailing the sea. A crafty little craft," Nora had repeated with a child's love for alliteration, clapping her hands. It had seemed bigger then. Everything seemed bigger. Only the ocean had retained its size, larger than life, enigmatic as ever, holding the key to her mother's fate. The coracle was hers now, but she had no desire to take it out again. She didn't want the girls to, either, but they seemed to love it so much it would be difficult to prevent them. Best not to make the boat more intriguing than it already was. She would allow them to explore, but she would keep watch, as she always had.

Her cell phone buzzed on the countertop. She glanced at the display. Malcolm. "Hello?" she said quietly. She didn't want the girls to hear, to get their hopes up. There was no reply. "Hello?" Did he have a bad signal? Or was it *her*, calling to hear the sound of Nora's voice, curiosity getting the best of her? Nora had done the same thing weeks ago, thinking she might confront the woman, but she'd hung up quickly, her resolve faltering, the voice lingering in her ears. A prep-school voice, girlish, young, or so it seemed. A voice that couldn't have been more different from Nora's own.

The sun slanted in the kitchen window, catching on the diamond of Nora's engagement ring. A ring Nora continued to wear, because it was hers, because they were still married, she and Malcolm, weren't they, even if they didn't live in the same place any longer. The gem cast a spot of light that moved jerkily across the bare wall, as if searching for something lost, something that might still be found.

The path to the fishing shack was clear enough, though slightly more overgrown than the others that crisscrossed the fields and copses on their part of the island. The grass grew higher here, brushing against her legs, and the trees were more contorted, bearing the brunt of the weather that struck the point. As she drew closer, something tugged at her memory. She had been here before. It was a place her grandfather retreated to, to mend nets, to think. She remembered the bare patch in his beard, where the hair wouldn't grow because of a hook scar, the rich smell of pipe smoke, the rumbling lilt of his voice as he taught her sailor's knots—bowlines, angler's loops, clove hitches, figure eights, sheepshanks, reefs, eye splices, Windsor ties, rolling hitches—twisting simple lines and ropes into elaborate designs, his fingers moving with swift assurance.

The shack hadn't changed much, at least outwardly, set as it was into a knoll so that it seemed to emerge from the rock itself, moss and grass growing on the roof, no smoke in the chimney, no light in the windows.

Her grandfather wasn't there any longer, her father either, only Owen, the latest resident of that solitary place. Owen, with whom she needed to discuss the matter of the furniture, her daughters and what he had given them, innocuous as it may have seemed at the time.

She'd meant to knock, to confront him directly, but she became stealthy now that she was close.

"Looking for me?" He appeared behind her.

She started guiltily. "Yes, as a matter of fact. I came to give you this." She presented him with a check for the furniture, Malcolm's name still printed above hers on the upper left-hand corner. She'd left the amount blank. She would leave it to Owen to decide his worth.

He didn't extend his hand to take it. "I'll tear it up."

She supposed he didn't remember anything about his bank account either, if he even had one. She should have thought of that. "Were the paddles a gift too?"

"What?"

"The paddles you gave the girls—for the coracle. You did give them to them, didn't you?"

"Yes. I thought—"

"You thought wrong. You obviously don't have children. You don't understand the dangers—"

"You didn't know what they were up to?"

"No. I didn't." She blamed herself for having let her vigilance slip. "I want to make this perfectly clear," she went on. "I don't want you giving us anything. I don't want you—"

"Okay," he said, raising his hands. "Okay." He crumpled the check and tucked it into her palm, pressing her hand in his, then releasing her.

"Good." Not trusting herself to say more, she hurried back in the direction she'd come, to the cottage, to her daughters.

She paused in the meadow, composing herself. A flock of swallows swooped by, banking, darting, inches from her face. One alighted on a reed and trilled at her, an admonishment, perhaps, for shattering the calm of the evening with harsh words. She regretted losing her temper. She regretted many things.

The door to the cottage opened, and a small figure ran toward her: Annie, her ever-cheerful emissary. "We want to read the next story in the book of fairy tales."

"Which one will it be this time?"

"The story of the shell people," Annie said as they reached the door. "I peeked."

"Sneaky girl."

"Hurry! It's time to turn the page and find out what happens next."

Behind them, the light left the sky, a curtain closing on the day, another opening, the coming of night, and the dreams it would bring.

Chapter Eleven

Nora woke with a start. She could have sworn someone had spoken to her—a faint echo of her mother's voice in the air—but the room was still. A shadow slid from the edge of the mirror and across the floor, causing her to sit upright, hands clenching the sheets, but it was only the sun rising higher, the start of another day. The compass needle trembled on the nightstand, as if it too had been moving in the minutes before dawn, charting a course through the waters of memory and dreams. She cupped it in her palm, but it revealed no answers. It could not guide her unless she knew where she wanted to go. She had the sense of the room having been animated before she woke, of things shifting, and yet they appeared to be as they were the night before, years before, for that matter.

A mausoleum to her parents' past lives, a marriage that fell apart. Hers too.

An eye peered at her through the crack in the door. Nora stifled a shriek.

"Scared you!" Annie laughed.

"It's too early for scaring." Nora swung her legs over the side of the bed and stretched. "You nearly gave me heart failure."

"Your heart can't fail, Mama. It's too strong."

Sometimes she wondered if it truly were. She pulled on a sweatshirt.

"What were you thinking about? You looked like you were remembering something."

"Waking up."

Annie smiled. "Aunt Maire told us to come over early today, remember? She's going to move more plants out of the greenhouse and said El and I could help." She picked up the compass. "Has it told you which way to go?"

Nora rubbed her eyes. "It's only a tool, honey. You need to have a destination."

"Whatever you say." She darted out of the room and jumped on Ella's bed, or so Nora deduced from the squeaking of mattress springs. "Get out of bed, sleepy-head!" she cried.

Then a thump as Ella most likely threw a pillow at her, with sufficient force to knock her sideways.

"Ow!"

"Go away! God, you're such a pest."

Yet within minutes, both girls were dressed and eating cereal at the table. Ella eyed Nora over a spoonful of Cheerios (the same cereal she'd fed them as toddlers; she remembered how they'd pick up each piece with stubby-fingered precision, one at a time; how Malcolm would leave a trail of them along the newly washed floor, to illustrate a reading of Hansel and Gretel, doing all the voices, including the witch's).

"When are we going home, Mom?" Ella asked. The girls used various words for her: *Mom* when they were serious/put upon; *Mama* when they were wheedling, or doting, or in need of consolation; *Mother* when they were disdainful or angry, Ella being most likely to employ the last.

"I told you, El, at the end of the summer."

"It's fun here. I don't care if we ever go back," Annie said.

"What about your friends?" Nora asked.

"They can come visit. And I'll make new ones." She paused. "Besides, Aunt Maire needs us."

"She's done fine without us," Ella said.

"How do you know?" Annie asked. "You weren't here. She must have been lonely."

"What about Dad?"

"He can move here too."

Nora didn't like to hear his name mentioned, but she knew she couldn't, shouldn't stop them talking about him. She'd have to make a decision soon, to give Malcolm another chance or strike out on her own. Thinking about it set her on edge. She accidentally tipped a cup of coffee down her front. "Damn it!"

"Language," Ella said with an evil smile.

Nora blotted the stain. She recalled the morning some weeks ago when she'd thrown a cup of coffee at Malcolm, the color bleeding into his pristine white shirt, not dissimilar from this one. She'd drunk too many cups, brewing pot after pot, waiting for his return; she'd been up all night, her nerves screaming with caffeine and fury, because she knew exactly where he'd been. The girls had gone off to school, unaware. She'd covered for him, saying he'd gone to work early.

"Jesus, Nora!" Malcolm whipped off the shirt and left it wadded up on the kitchen floor. The skin on his chest was red, where the liquid had scalded him. "You burned me."

"Now you know how it feels," she said. It was minor enough, not even third degree. He'd heal. And the shirt? She let it sit. She was damned if she was going to treat it for him.

"Must have been some strong coffee," the dry cleaner said, unable to get the stain out, and yet she'd thanked him for the news, because it seemed appropriate somehow. She hung the garment at the front of Malcolm's other dry cleaning, bagged in smothering plastic, the last batch she picked up before he moved out. That brown blotch a statement of his betrayal, of the stain he'd made on their lives, deepening and spreading.

This morning's stain would come out. She slipped off the shirt, to get a better angle, and stood at the sink in her bra.

"Couldn't you at least put on a T-shirt or something?" Ella wrinkled her nose.

"We're all girls here," Nora said. "And besides, a bra isn't that different from a bathing suit top."

"Let's go, Annie-pan. This view of Mom's love handles is disturbing."

"Not nice, El."

"Is that what made him leave? Is she prettier than you?" Ella asked, her eyes widening with the shock of what she'd said, giving voice, at last, to something that must have been on her mind for weeks.

Nora turned, conscious of where her skin had slackened, from childbirth, from the effects of time and gravity. She refused to do Botox or surgery. Let time do its work. She'd earned every wrinkle. She looked good, not perfect. She didn't have to be. Not for Malcolm. Not for anyone.

But those words, her daughter's words . . . She pulled the damp shirt to her chest, droplets of cold water rolling down her stomach.

"Who?" Annie asked.

"That woman Dad is with."

"Of course she isn't. Mom is beautiful," Annie insisted. "She's ours. Dad's too. He just has to find his way back."

"And whose fault is that?" Ella said, as Nora left the room to find a clean top.

Whose indeed.

The girls walked a certain distance ahead, Annie moving between Nora and Ella, negotiating a peace. Nora wanted to shake her eldest daughter. *Don't you realize how much I've shielded you, without lying to you? Don't you realize how hard that is? How I don't want you to hurt anymore? Don't you realize that if you went back to Boston, if you lived with him, as you've sometimes said you want to do—not that he'd permit it—he'd disappoint you? Because he can be that amazing person we all know him to be, yes, he can, but not for us. Not anymore.* But she didn't. Because then it would be about her, Nora, her pain, her losing control. She couldn't do that to them. She would take whatever Ella chose to inflict. Deflecting, disciplining when the need arose, absorbing; they just had to ride this out, this long, crashing wave.

"Mama, look!" Annie cried. Painted lady butterflies clung to her arms. "I'm a fairy queen, like Grandma Maeve."

"They probably smell the milk and cereal you didn't wipe off your face," Ella said.

"You're jealous because they like me best. They don't like angry people."

"I'm not angry."

"Then hold out your hands. Mama, you too."

Ella sighed and extended her arms, Nora as well.

"Don't move," Annie whispered.

"Yes, Your Highness," Ella replied.

"Shh. You'll scare them away."

They stood motionless, holding their breath, the wind stirring their hair and clothes, the limbs of the trees, the grasses. A butterfly tiptoed over their fingers, then another, and another, wings fluttering, antennae probing.

Annie twirled in a circle, Nora and Ella with her. "Fly!" she cried. "Up to the sky!"

And the butterflies rose in a cloud of orange and black, like sparks, like cinders, into the gray pearl clouds.

Onward they went, into the woods. The pines gave off a sharp green scent, thick, pungent. The shadows were deep for the short length of the copse, before Nora and the girls stepped into the light of the meadow closest to Cliff House, the grass a riot of daisies and lupine.

"Mom, why is Aunt Maire lying on the ground like that?" called Ella, who'd gone ahead a length or two, as always. "Mom!"

Nora ran to Maire's side. Annie began to cry. Ella was shaking. "Get Owen," Nora said. "Now!"

They didn't have to be told twice. They raced down the path.

"Maire." Nora listened to Maire's heart, her breath, checked her pulse. "Maire—"

Why hadn't she sent one of the girls to the phone? She couldn't think straight. She had nearly shouted for them again when Maire opened her eyes, her gaze faraway. "Oh, it's you," she said. "You've come back."

"Yes." Nora held her hand.

Maire's grip tightened. "I didn't mean what I said—"

What on earth was she talking about? "I'm here now."

"I wish I'd—" Maire stared into Nora's face, and yet it was as if she didn't see her.

The way she looked at Nora, the vacancy in her expression, gave her a chill. "It's all right," Nora said.

Maire blinked rapidly. "Nora?"

Who had Maire thought she was? Maeve?

"What happened? I—"

"You must have fainted."

"I lost track of time, of where I was for a moment."

"Where did you think you were?"

"A place where the fog never lifts." Her voice trailed off.

"What do you mean? Are you sure you're okay?"

Maire breathed deeply, collecting herself. "It's only dizziness. A momentary lapse." She brushed at the dirt on her arms. "Ah, well, no harm done. Not even a scrape."

"But you fainted. Don't you think—"

"It happens sometimes." She scoffed. "Darn diabetes."

"We should call your doctor anyway."

"There's no need. Really. One of my spells. I'm sorry I gave you a fright. What you must have thought, finding me this way."

"You've had them before?"

"It's no cause for alarm."

Nora wasn't convinced. "At least go in and rest for a while."

"I suppose a cup of tea wouldn't hurt." She took Nora's hand.

Nora felt her sway slightly as she got to her feet, hands shaking. Something had clearly unsettled her, something she wouldn't talk about. "Yes, I suppose it wouldn't."

The girls and Owen rushed in the door as Nora got Maire settled on the couch and put the kettle on to boil. A smear of dirt on Maire's arm and a sprig of chickweed in her hair were the only signs left of the incident.

"I should at least put out some treats. What a poor hostess I am." Maire started to get up.

Nora put a hand on her shoulder. "I'll take care of it."

"I'm not an invalid," her aunt protested. "I wish you'd stop making such a fuss."

Owen took a seat next to Maire and attempted to distract her. "The girls and I were wondering if you could tell us more about the shipwrecks offshore."

"Intrigued, are you?" She turned to him, her face softening. His presence had an immediate calming effect. "You may have passed some of the wreckage on your way in, the night you first arrived. There aren't many sailors who manage to make it to shore in conditions like that." Her eyes clouded again, perhaps thinking of Jamie, of her husband, and their own fateful meeting with the rocks.

"I'm counting my blessings, that's for sure."

"How many were lost?" Annie asked.

"Too many to count. Their ghosts are rumored to hover over the water on winter nights when the mist is thick and swirling."

"I told you," Ella said to her sister.

"I'm glad it's not winter." Annie shivered.

"Oh, they mean no harm, most of them, lost souls that they are," Maire assured her. "There's nothing to be afraid of."

"Don't worry," Ella told Annie. "We won't be here that long anyway. We're only staying for the summer."

"For the summer." Maire gave them a searching look before continuing. "Whalers, shrimpers, passenger ships veering off course, so many types of men and vessels, have gone down out there—a woman, Molly Gerrin, too. She captained her husband's ship when he was swept overboard. Sailed for ten years in the late 1800s, until she was taken herself, the mast of her ship, like the others, at the bottom of Solomon's Rift."

"Solomon's Rift?" Annie repeated the words, scooting closer.

"That's what they call the undersea canyon where the first recorded ship went down. Named for the fact that only King Solomon can decide who will survive, separating the living from the dead."

The kettle whistled, a long hard blast. Nora rose to take it off the burner, Owen following along behind.

"Thank you for coming. I didn't know what to do." Nora took a plate down from the shelf. She arranged shortbread on one side, tea cakes on the other. "She seems fine now, but—"

"She fainted?"

"I guess so. We found her in the garden. She said she was only out for a moment. That she sometimes gets lightheaded, because of her diabetes. She has type two, apparently. I wish she'd see her doctor. I'm not sure how much to say."

"Your being here is enough."

"Is it?"

"Think if she'd been on her own. Better keep an eye on her, in case."

"Yes." Nora paused. "About the other day—"

"It's fine. I understand."

"I shouldn't have spoken to you that way."

"You don't have to explain. You're their mother. A good mother. Anyone can see that."

She bit her lip. "I'm trying to be."

He studied her hands, the gold rings encircling her finger, skin pale beneath the bands: the diamond solitaire, the plain wedding band.

She curled her fingers inward.

"Is he coming?" he asked.

She stared out the window at the orchard, with its fruiting trees, their gnarled, grasping branches. "I came here to get away from him."

"And have you?"

"I'm beginning to think we can never fully escape the past."

"Still looking for answers?"

"How can I stop? I was left behind. First by my mother, now by my husband. It's not a good feeling. . . . And you?"

"It might be easier if I don't remember everything. I'm content here. Maire needs me. Maybe you do too."

She didn't reply. She rested her hands on the counter, near his.

"Mom?" Ella said behind her, not so much inquiring as commanding. To come out of that room, away from him.

Nora picked up the tray, its pot of tea and floral, gold-rimmed cups rattling in an effort to remain upright as she returned to her aunt and children and the safer realm of fireside conversation, where there was no danger of lines being crossed.

Chapter Twelve

Maire opened the churchyard gate of St. Mary's by the Sea. She'd walked there, a pleasant stroll through the woods and meadows by one of the island's many footpaths. She liked walking. It helped her think.

The white church with its simple spire was small, more of a chapel really, with room for a mere two hundred and fifty congregants, if they squeezed close together, though fewer attended now, given the decline in the local population. The church door was cracked open. Votive candles flickered within. She might light one and make a petition. Every little bit helped.

There was a single stained-glass window above the altar. The others were plain, long and narrow, to let in the light. The benches were worn, the kneelers too, from the countless parishioners who had worshipped there. No tower, only a bell in the yard that Father Ray or one of the children rang before mass Sunday morning. A plaque was embedded in the wall to the left of the main door. "Est. 1855," it read. The building had withstood many a gale and harsh winter, a testament to the strength of their faith, the more devout among them might have said.

Father Ray's motorcycle was parked out front. A vintage Harley, no less. It made Maire happy to see him riding around the island, a leather jacket over his blacks, white collar around his neck, a smile on his face, a pair of old-fashioned German goggles shielding his eyes. Not today. Today, she found him planting cucumbers in the church garden. (He gave the overflow to parishioners in need, bags of produce and flowers at a roadside stand at the entrance for Friday pickups, no questions asked.) Maire often helped with the harvesting and packaging. She and Father Ray shared a love of gardening and swapped tips about the best means to repel pests ("Even some of God's creatures need a blast from the hose now and then," he said, referring to the rather persistent aphids that had taken too much of an interest in the zucchini) and methods to encourage heat-loving plants to grow in cool climates. He wore a pair of jeans with a hole in the knee and a Notre Dame sweatshirt (his nephew played football there) that afternoon, which only accentuated his powerful build (he had more of a belly now that he had entered his sixties), along with a pair of rubber boots and a canvas fisherman's hat, both of which worked equally well for jigging for squid from the pier or mucking about in the yard.

"How are you today, Maire?" he asked, getting to his feet. He took off his work gloves, tucking them under his arm, so that he could shake her hand. She was one of his favorite parishioners.

"I'm well, Father Ray."

"How are your guests settling in? A welcome change from the city, I imagine, especially this time of year."

"Yes, the heat has been particularly bad," she agreed. "I suppose you might have heard about my niece's troubles."

He nodded. "I'm afraid it was hard not to."

"The coverage has been relentless."

"No reporters on Burke's Island though, unless you count Jonathan Dee." Dee was the writer and editor of the local newsletter, the *Burke's Island Record*, and was, thankfully, visiting his daughter in California that summer, or he almost certainly would have been on the prowl.

"Not so far. I wish there was something more I could do for her."

"I'm sure you're doing everything you can," he said. "Is she finding some peace here?"

"She keeps a tight rein on things. The only time she seems truly relaxed is when she's in the sea."

"The sea reinvents itself with every wave, doesn't it? Maybe she will too, eventually. We need time to find our way, on our own terms," he said, adding, "I hear you have another visitor, too."

"Yes, Owen. Owen Kavanagh." She gazed out in the direction of the ocean, biting her lip.

"Is something wrong?" He sat down on the garden bench and patted the space beside him.

She sighed and settled next to him. "The wreck has brought back the day I lost Joe and Jamie, just when I was starting to feel as if I were ready to move forward." So many questions remained: Had the depleted fish stocks caused Joe to take more chances than usual? Had the accident been preventable? Had Joe or Jamie made one small miscalculation, one misstep, that set off a catastrophic sequence of events? She'd never know. They'd lost radio contact early on—he'd been meaning to get the antennae fixed—the last conversation they'd had filled with lingering tension and static.

Father Ray nodded, waiting for her to say more.

"He wasn't mine, you know. Jamie. We adopted him."

"I didn't." Father Ray had taken over the parish when the elderly priest, Father Noonan, passed away ten years before. "He was yours, all the same."

"I couldn't have children," Maire went on. "The doctors couldn't pinpoint why. The women in my family had never had fertility problems. There was no history to suggest. . . . We went to Boston, looking for answers"—she'd driven by Patrick and Nora's house, hoping to catch a glimpse of them, though she didn't dare ring the bell—"but they didn't have the technology they do now, not that it would have helped."

"Why do you say that?"

"Because it was a judgment, a curse, for my having failed Maeve."

"Your sister."

"She lost a child, before Nora. And I always felt it was my fault. I was there. I should have—"

"I'm sure it wasn't. You need to forgive yourself."

"I felt Jamie was taken away from me as some sort of karmic retribution."

"And now?"

"And now, with Nora and the girls here, with Owen coming to us, it's like a second chance."

"Life is full of second chances, Maire, you know that."

"Yes, but not for me. I'm afraid there won't be time—"

"For what? You're only sixty. You're still relatively young. There's plenty of time for new beginnings."

She hoped he was right.

Maire dropped by the cottage on her way home. Alison's black Capri was parked out front. (The letters had fallen off; Alison's brother had reattached them to read "Crapi," a jibe at the car's unreliable nature.) She was helping test the paint colors they'd purchased at Scanlon's. At the girls' urging, Nora had finally opened the cans.

"Let's paint the rooms now," Ella said, pushing a chair away from the wall.

Nora shook her head. "We need to live with the swatches first. See how they look at different times of day, as the light and weather change."

Annie sighed in disappointment. "How long?"

"A day or two, perhaps more. Don't worry, we'll break out the paintbrushes again soon enough."

Alison fingered a necklace Nora had been working on. "This is beautiful, Nora. Do you have more?"

"A few. I'm dabbling."

"She made me this too," Maire said, showing off the eyeglass chain Nora had crafted for her.

"I'm sure there would be a market for these. I have a friend in New York who works as a stylist. Local girl made good and all that. I could send her some samples, if you'd like."

"Mom, your stuff might be in a magazine!" Annie clapped her hands.

"Let's not get ahead of ourselves."

"Seriously. Keep it in mind," Alison said, and Nora agreed. She certainly wouldn't mind having that kind of publicity, something to truly call her own.

"Are you an artist too?" Annie asked Alison. "You look like an artist."

"Yes, what's in the bag?" Ella gestured toward Alison's open pack, which overflowed with curious-looking tools.

"I'm headed to Nell Grady's after this. She's an old school friend of mine. She wants a tattoo."

"You're a tattoo artist?" Ella asked. "That's so cool!"

"Studied with the best, Paul 'The Needle' Foley, in Portakinney. I'll be taking over his shop in town, once he retires."

"Is there enough of a clientele?" Nora asked.

"Are you kidding? With an island full of fisher-men?" Alison looked at Nora, speculatively. "You should get one too. I don't know why I didn't think of it before."

"No, thank you," Nora demurred. "I'm not really the type."

"You don't have to look like you belong in a carnival. I meant something small and tasteful."

"Your mother used to have a wave, right here," Maire said, touching the inside of her left wrist, "so that wherever she went, the sea would always be with her."

"What sort of wave?" Nora asked.

Maire drew a picture on a piece of scratch paper. "Something like this."

"Can we get one?" the girls asked.

"Maybe when you're older."

They groaned.

"You're old enough," Ella said to Nora. "What's stopping you?"

"That's not the issue—"

"We could put it on the inside of your wrist, or the base of your spine, where no one would see," Alison said.

"You're not going to give up, are you?"

"You need to do this, Nora," Alison insisted. "I've been tattooing long enough that I have a sense of these things. C'mon. What do you say? You trust me, don't you?"

"It's not a question of trust."

"Does it hurt?" Annie asked, voicing a question Nora probably had herself.

"For one this simple, not too much."

"How about you, Aunt Maire?" Nora asked.

"I already have one." She showed them the tiny Celtic cross on the inner arch of her foot. "Alison is very persuasive. I got mine for my sixtieth birthday. Polly put me up to it. She has a grace note behind her ear. Says it's the only way she can carry a tune. You'll see it if you look closely. We're a bunch of subversives here."

"Rebels with a cause." Alison grinned. "You'd better watch out, Nora. Soon, I'll have a stud in your nose too."

"I draw the line there." Nora laughed.

In the end, Nora went with the placement on her inner wrist, like her mother, so that she might look at the mark and take courage from it, a reminder that she could do the unexpected, that she could surprise herself.

Owen was waiting for Maire on the porch of Cliff House, bearing a basket of crabs. "I see you've brought dinner again," she said. "You spoil me. Why don't you come in and help me cook them up?" She was grateful for the company.

"Will Nora be here?"

"Not tonight. They're dining in."

Owen followed Maire into the kitchen. If he was disappointed at Nora's absence, he didn't show it. They put the shellfish in a pot of water to boil. Some melted butter mixed with white wine was all they needed for a dipping sauce. A salad of garden greens and slices of the crusty bread she'd baked earlier that week would complete the simple meal.

"Nora and the girls have taken to the water well," Owen remarked as he set the smaller table in the kitchen, two places across from each other, as if they'd been dining together for years. "They've been swimming nearly every day."

"Noticed, have you?" She'd seen the way he looked at Nora.

"Well, they do live right next door." He smiled.

"You're a strong swimmer. Perhaps you'll enter the race in August as well. The inhabitants of the point might sweep the categories."

"Only if you enter too."

"My sister, Maeve, was the swimmer in the family. I could never keep up with her. No one could. There had been talk of Maeve leaving to train on the mainland when she was fourteen, but she didn't like the thought of being in a pool, of leaving the island. 'I need the sea,' she said. My mother wanted her to go. But those were my mother's dreams, not Maeve's." Maire wondered how different their lives would have been if her sister had left.

She scooped the crabs out of the pot, placed them in a serving bowl, and set them on the table, along with crackers and forks for extracting the meat. She took the seat across from Owen.

"So swimming runs in the family," he said.

"Yes, I suppose it does." That, and other things. "Yours too?"

He shrugged. "I guess you could say that." He didn't need the utensils. He broke the claws open easily with his hands. She was glad to see he'd recovered his appetite.

"Should I make more salad?" she asked. She could rarely interest him in fruit or dessert. He didn't seem to have much of a sweet tooth.

"No, thank you. You've made a feast as it is."

"You have to regain your strength. Are you feeling stronger? You weren't in the best shape when we found you."

"I'm getting better, thanks to you. Is there anything more I can do to be of help? I want to be sure I'm doing my share, to compensate for the rent."

"I told you. That's of little consequence. The fishing shack is barely habitable. You're doing me a favor, keeping the mice away."

"It suits my needs."

"Which are, apparently, few."

"I'm a simple man."

"So you are. And for that very reason, your being here is compensation enough."

"Really—"

She thought for a moment. "Well, I suppose you could fix up Joe's boat. I'd been meaning to have it seen to."

"The wooden boat at the dock? It must have been a beauty in its day."

"It's been in his family for years. An antique now. Doesn't have any of the modern conveniences. Joe hadn't taken it on the water in quite some time—he'd bought a new one for fishing—but he couldn't let it go. He knew it would be of some value once it was restored. It was to have been his retirement project. Our getaway fund. We thought of cruising to Bermuda, doing some fishing along the way."

He reached across the table and touched her hand.

Tears came to her eyes at the gesture. She dabbed her cheeks with a napkin. "Sorry about the water-works," she said with a sad smile.

"No need."

"I miss my boys. I wish I'd hadn't been upset that morning. I wish they knew how much I loved them."

"They knew. I'm sure they did. You're a kind woman, Maire. The kindest I've ever known."

"I'm not, really. But I try."

"That's all a person can ever do."

She buttered a piece of bread. "So you don't mind seeing to it? To the boat?"

"I'd be happy to. Is there more I can do at the cottage?"

Maire sensed he was asking about more than standard repairs. "I'm sure things will come up. It's a work in progress. I know Nora appreciates your help."

"Does she? It doesn't always seem like it."

"She's suffered disappointments. They've made her cautious." She held his gaze to make sure he understood. He didn't look away, as Joe and Jamie might have done. His eyes remained steady. They were beautiful eyes, dark, long-lashed, shining with intelligence. "Are you going to tell her who you are?" Maire asked, curious about how he would respond. She knew there was more to him than met the eye, from the minute she saw him, exactly what, she couldn't say, though she guessed. She hadn't pressed him. She didn't want to drive him away.

"I'm not sure I know myself—and would she believe me if I did? She doesn't trust easily."

"She needs time. She doesn't fully understand the island yet. What's possible. I'm not sure I do myself, and I've lived here my whole life."

It was enough that he was there, sitting across from her, this man who had come into their lives so suddenly, who filled a void she hadn't known existed.

Chapter Thirteen

Nora heard the sound of tires negotiating the drive, their steady progress crushing the shell fragments before halting in front of the cottage. The engine went silent. The radiator ticked and hissed, as if, in the process of cooling, it might detonate. A door slammed. Footsteps crunched. She didn't pay them much mind. She was in the middle of gluing fasteners onto the sea glass, drilling holes, linking links, tasks that required focus and a steady hand. One or two more, then she'd rise and see who it was. After all, no one would be visiting except Polly, with the mail, or Alison, delivering an order from the store or dropping by to say hello.

Ella, however, seemed particularly attuned to the arrival. Out the door she went, and into the blinding light, a single word leaving her lips like the cry of a gull, shattering the tenuous quiet: "Daddy!"

Nora dropped the piece of glass she'd been working on. It skittered across the floor and spun before going still.

Annie looked up from her puzzle. She held the fin of an angel fish, feathery, brilliant, in her right hand, a question in her eyes.

Nora nodded, fighting the instinct to grab her and hold her close. Annie raced out of the cottage and into her father's arms. Through the curtained window, Nora saw her daughters and husband. Malcolm, tall, slender as ever, more tan than when she'd seen him last, the girls wrapped around him like vines, all arms and legs.

What was he doing there?

She opened the door. The light, coming from the east at that midmorning hour—a long day ahead—cut into the room, forcing her to squint against the glare, he at the locus of its brilliance, as always, a second sun around which others orbited, with his smile, his very presence. She looked past him to the road, expecting others to appear in his wake—advisers, journalists, photographers—for he was rarely alone. The road was deserted.

Their eyes met over the girls' shoulders, their disheveled hair, their expressions wild with hope and abandon.

He was here, at last.

"Malcolm." Nora spoke as if moving a chess piece across a board. No matter what she was feeling right now, no matter how much her heart thrummed at the sight of him—not so much with anticipation as with anxiety and confusion—everything would have to be handled with utmost care.

"Nora."

They used full names now, the time of endearments in the past.

The girls slid away from him, watched her, watched him, watched them watching each other.

"Why don't you play on the beach for a while?" she suggested. As much as she wanted the girls there as a buffer, that would only prolong the encounter and expose them to unnecessary tension. She hoped it would be short, this meeting or whatever it was—a few minutes, an hour, a day at most. She could entertain the thought of sitting down together for a meal, lunch or, if need be, dinner. That, she could manage. Then he would get in the car and drive away. He was good at that. She wouldn't allow herself to be drawn in—into a fight, or into revisiting the piercing sense of loss that had once driven her to break a full set of dishes and scream obscenities while the girls were at school. And yet the wound was there, refusing to heal. She felt a tug now at the edges. She hadn't realized how easily it might break open. She didn't know what she'd do if it did.

Ella's eyes darted from one parent to another, her expression pleading.

"Your mother and I need to talk." Malcolm backed Nora up for once. How odd to be united in this one small thing.

Ella motioned to Annie. "Let's go," she said. Nora clenched her teeth at how easily she obeyed him.

Ella paused after a few steps, looking over her shoulder. "You're not going to leave, are you?" she asked her father.

The wind ruffled his hair, still wavy and brown as ever, the hair she once ran her fingers through. "I'll be right there," he said.

He made promises easily, Nora thought.

The girls disappeared over the bluff in the direction of the coracle.

"So this is the place," Malcolm said, taking in the view. "Burke's Island." The words sounded foreign on his tongue, wrong.

They stood there, suspended, he in the drive, she on the threshold. She held on to that moment, weighing whether to admit him or turn him away. He was on her turf now. "I guess you'd better come in," she said finally, the flush of power already ebbing. She couldn't disappoint her daughters, and so she motioned him inside, offered coffee, as if he were a friend or acquaintance dropping by for a chat. "I confess I'm surprised to see you."

"Ella called. I wanted to see the girls."

She'd forbidden the girls cell phones, at least until they were fourteen, clearly in the minority among the other parents, but holding firm, for now. The separation was forcing her to rethink the rule, but she hadn't planned on revisiting the matter until they returned to Boston. Her gaze fell on her own phone, resting on the desk. Ella must have used it to text him.

"And to see you." The transition was nearly seamless. Maybe he meant it, maybe he didn't. Sometimes it was hard to tell.

"Really? What for?"

"Nor—" His eyes softened as he resurrected the nickname, deep-set blue eyes holding the same expression that had attracted her all those years ago, making her feel as if she were the only person in the room. A look she'd thought was meant specially for her. Maybe it had been, for a time, though over the course of their marriage she'd seen it at work as he wooed everyone from colleagues to constituents to waitresses with a nearly indiscriminate charm.

"How long do you plan on staying?" she asked.

"I have a few days off."

Remarkable.

"And you have a place in town?"

"I thought—" He gazed around the interior of the cottage, taking in the dimensions, the number of rooms.

"You'd stay here?" She laughed, incredulous. "That's presumptuous, even for you."

"Burke's Island isn't exactly tourist central."

No, it wasn't—which was precisely the point.

"I'm thinking about what would be best," he continued.

"For whom, exactly?"

He reached across the table.

She kept her hands in her lap.

"I've missed you," he said. "I've missed the girls."

"Have you?"

"Do you think the life we had means nothing to me?"

"It does seem that way."

He shook his head. "I can't separate myself from you. I don't want to."

"You have a funny way of showing it."

"I'd like to try."

"I wasn't the one who called you," she said. There had been times, many times, when she had, leaving countless unanswered voice-mail messages, until finally one night that spring, she'd thrown the phone against the wall in frustration. "What happened?"

Ella had asked. "It broke," Nora said, sweeping up the pieces with a broom and throwing them away, the metal waste-bin lid clanging with a finality she wasn't quite willing to accept.

"I understand." How penitent he was, how attentive, now that she'd made a break from him—or attempted to.

She pursed her lips. It was up to her, for once. She glimpsed the girls watching through the window. They hadn't gone to the beach after all. They'd lingered to see what would happen when their parents were alone in the same room. "You can sleep on the couch," she said at last. "I'm doing this for their sake, not yours."

"I'll take what I can get," he said.

"You always do."

The girls led him to the coracle, each daughter holding a hand, their father suspended between them, their prize. Across the wildflower meadow they went, making new paths through the grass, down the bluff, their footsteps sinking in the sand. Nora walked some distance behind, a bystander, as the girls skipped across the shore, the beach a darker gray where the waves had rushed in. A flock of shearwaters made for the point in a hectic dash, startled from their shoreline scavenging, their wings and voices slashing the quiet afternoon with a screeching white fury. The girls too flailed their arms, chirped and shrieked, hungry for their father's affection.

"Look at our boat! Daddy, look!"

"Yours? It was waiting here for you, was it?" he asked.

"It was!"

Each sentence marked with an exclamation point, stabs of joy flying at her, across the sand, where she stood, apart.

"Come with us," Ella said to him. She looked at Nora then, daring contradiction. There wasn't room for all of them. Ever since Malcolm had arrived, there had been new tension between Ella and Nora, intensifying after Nora reminded her to ask first before using the cell phone.

Malcolm raised an eyebrow.

Nora inclined her head slightly. *Oh, go ahead.* The three of them could have their fun.

Annie hesitated before getting in. Nora made no move to stop her. Safety had been the primary concern, and Malcolm was with them, after all, an honored passenger. He sat up tall in the boat, like a mast, at the center of everything yet again. Ella had never asked her to join them, and Nora hadn't wanted to, the very sight of the boat filling her with an inexplicable dread. She sat on a piece of driftwood as they cut across the cove, the boat riding low in the water, their voices ringing happily, cheering when Malcolm launched into a song. "*The Sailor McNee went to sea on a trim little boat called the Fiddle Dee Dee.*" "*Fiddle Dee Dee,*" they joined in the chorus. "*Fiddle Dee Dee.*" It was as if he'd been there for days, as if the family had never come to the island without him. How easily he slipped into their lives, like a hand into a glove.

The fortifications of a sand castle lay at her feet, shaped by father and daughters with buckets and funnels. Between the encroaching tide and inherent design flaws, it had become a ruined kingdom, the ocean flooding the battlements, crumbling the walls.

Back they came, Annie waving to her, Nora waving in return—a convivial scene, if one didn't know better.

Malcolm crossed the beach and stopped before her, droplets of water rolling down his calves, handsome as always. "It's your turn," he said to her, as the girls bobbed in the half-grounded boat.

She shook her head. "I'm good."

"Mom never comes out in the coracle," Ella called. "She doesn't like boats."

"I never said that," Nora replied.

"It's a fabulous little boat." Malcolm's mood wouldn't be dampened. "I've never seen such a fine design for something so simple. It's an antique, isn't it? Whose was it? Do you know?"

The sun brought out the gold in his hair, no hint of gray—even after all they'd been through—gilding the highlights in their girls' hair too, the same shade as his.

"It was my mother's." She'd rarely mentioned Maeve, even to Malcolm. Their history had been so brief, she had little to work with. It wasn't until Maire's letter arrived and Nora came to the island that she'd been compelled to question the past more fully, to attempt to confront what had happened, that early loss amplifying the more recent one, her life turned upside down once more, everything jarring loose.

"And the cottage?"

"We lived there when I was small. The details aren't important. Sometimes it's easier to move on." She gave him a pointed stare.

He looked away. "I don't have the talent for that."

"Don't you?"

"And what about you?" An edge crept into his voice.

"What do you mean?"

"Haven't you met someone?"

"Who would I have met?" She didn't like being interrogated, least of all by him.

He jerked his head toward the rocks at the point, where Owen was fishing. She hadn't seen him there earlier. He must have been around the other side of the rocks, only recently shifting his position so that he was in full view. The girls must have pointed him out. Ella must have.

"He was shipwrecked."

"How dramatic for you."

"It had nothing to do with me. I don't control the weather or the shipping lanes."

"No, you like to control everything else."

She bit back a reply. He had her there. She'd been careful, watchful, ever since she was a child. It had served her well in law school—drawn, as she was, to the precision, to the enforcement of rules—and in raising the girls. During the separation, as things seemed to be slipping from her grasp, she had felt the need to tighten her hold; especially now, with Malcolm here, with his forcefulness, his recklessness.

"Ella said you were first on the scene," he continued.

"What were we supposed to do? Leave him there?"

He shrugged.

"Maire asked him to stay," Nora said. "It wasn't my doing. Don't assume everyone shares your wandering eye."

"I'm not assuming anything."

"Aren't you?" She paused. "What is this really about?"

"You tell me."

"Oh, I see, you don't want me—but you don't want anyone else to have me either, is that it?"

"I never said I didn't want you." His gaze fell on the tattoo. "When did you get that? Part of a midlife crisis or something?"

"That would be your department. No, it's an island tradition, I guess you could say."

"I didn't think you had it in you."

"You don't know everything about me, Malcolm. You might think you do, but you don't."

Annie came toward them. "Are you fighting?"

"No," they said, in unison.

"Because it sounded like you were."

Nora sighed. She felt Owen's eyes upon her, but she didn't look in his direction. Were they making a spectacle of themselves? It wouldn't have been the first time.

"I don't want you to fight in front of Aunt Maire," Annie said. "I don't want you to fight at all."

"Aunt Maire?" Nora asked.

"Don't you remember?" Ella fell into line next to Malcolm. "We're supposed to go to her house for dinner tonight."

Nora had forgotten. "I'll let her know we can't make it."

"Don't cancel your plans on my account," Malcolm said, "though I'd like to meet her."

"We can't leave Daddy by himself," Ella insisted. She wouldn't let him out of her sight. "Aunt Maire always says the more the merrier. She won't mind."

No, Nora thought, but I do. Having Malcolm in such close proximity, seeing him with the girls, made her, by turns, nostalgic and furious.

"She'd want to meet him. Everyone loves Daddy," Annie said.

Yes, everyone loved Malcolm. Which was precisely the problem.

That evening, true to form, he charmed them all— the girls, Maire, even Nora. After a glass or wine or two, Nora wondered if he was truly regretting what had happened, what he too had lost. No, it wasn't a question of if. She knew he did. But how much? Enough to change? He caught her gaze across the table and smiled, as if sharing an inside joke.

Owen wasn't at dinner that night. Maire had invited him, but he told her he would be up the coast, night fishing. Nora had to admit she was relieved.

Maire presided over the meal, magnanimous as ever, not taking sides. She hadn't missed a beat when Nora told her there would be a fifth for dinner.

"I'm surprised more people haven't discovered the island," Malcolm said as he sampled Maire's rhubarb pie, proclaiming it the best he'd ever had.

"Too far afield and rough around the edges for most," Maire said.

"That must be what I like about it."

"We all feel that way, Burke's Islanders and off-islanders, few as they are, alike. It's an in-between place, my grandmother used to say. A thin place."

"People aren't that thin here," Annie said.

Maire laughed. "Not in terms of physical appearance," she explained. "It means a place where the past and present meet, and in the case of Burke's Island, the new and old countries too."

"And, most importantly, it's the place my wife is from," Malcolm added.

My wife, as if she still belonged to him.

"And it's got magic and secrets," Annie said, "like the coracle."

"The coracle? I'd forgotten about that thing," Maire said. "Didn't realize it was still seaworthy."

"Reilly Neale helped us fix it. We took Daddy out today," Ella said.

"Our grandmother disappeared from the boat, that's what Reilly told us," Annie volunteered.

"You never said—" Malcolm turned to Nora.

"That's because there wasn't anything to say," she replied curtly.

The seals barked down on the beach, first one, then a chorus. Maire closed the sash. "Heavens, I wonder what they're going on about. They usually don't cause such a commotion."

"Maybe they've seen a sea monster," Annie said.

"Sea monster?" Malcolm asked. "Now that sounds exciting."

"It's from a fairy tale in a book of Mom's," Ella said.

"Something else for you to show me later," he said, though it was Nora at whom he gazed over the top of the girls' heads.

There was barely room on the couch for everyone, and yet they piled on, Malcolm in the center, Nora balancing awkwardly on the armrest, the only spot available. "You can squish in, Mama," Annie said.

"I'm fine, honey." She didn't want to squish in. She preferred to maintain her distance.

"Daddy can read tonight," Ella said, her gaze flicking to Nora with whiplike speed, then away.

"I don't have to," Malcolm said. "It's your mother's book. See, there's her name."

Below Maeve's and Maire's. Ella's and Annie's would be next.

"It's okay," Nora said. "My voice could use a rest."

Malcolm was a gifted orator. He could read anything and make it interesting. He used to read Nora poetry in law school as they lay in bed together. Frost. Blake. Keats. Long afternoons when the sun streamed through the windows, and hours could pass by.

He read the story of the selkie, caught in a net. The fisherman hid her coat so that she couldn't swim away, and she bore him children and lived with him for years, all the while yearning for the sea.

"What do you think, girls?" Malcolm said. "Is your mother a selkie?"

"She doesn't have a fur," Annie said. "She doesn't like it."

"Not that kind of fur," Ella said. "The story's referring to the type that's actually a part of you, like an animal pelt."

Annie studied her arms, as if examining them for evidence, apparently disappointed that only a light down covered her skin.

"What do you say, Nora?" Malcolm asked.

She forced a smile. She refused to play his games. " 'Fraid not."

She wasn't the one who'd left one night and not come back.

A single ember glowed in the fireplace, persisting in the dark. There he was on the couch, his arm thrown back in repose, as if he'd only been exiled for snoring. The nobility of his profile—the strong, straight nose, the chiseled chin—not quite matched by his character. The sigh of his breath, steady as ever. He could sleep through anything, anywhere, putting troubled thoughts aside. She'd never had the talent. She lay in her bedroom, in the dusky light—for on moonlit nights such as this, it was never truly dark, but rather half illuminated—and in that grayed world, with its blurred margins, her awareness of him, of his nearness, intensified. He had not been this close in weeks, and the proximity filled her with expectation and anxiety.

Sleep didn't take her until one a.m. Dream after dream washed over her, before the one she would remember, hazily, upon waking. She was in the coracle, her mother sitting in front—at least, she thought it was Maeve. She couldn't see her face, her back to Nora, a child once more. *Mama*, Nora said, *Mama*, her voice rising when her mother didn't respond, the ashen terns flapping overhead, wings tattered and sullied as crumpled newspaper, the pages turning, turning, headlines of disasters, disappearances. Her mother's arms moved in time with the wings above, the waves beneath them deepening, bottomless—the sky too, everything the color of steel, polished, cold, the wind blowing, lightly at first, then wildly. *We have to go back*, Nora cried. Maeve didn't answer, didn't turn. The wind lifted her mother's hair from the nape of her neck, revealing a single green strand, a piece of sea grass, among the ringlets. Nora reached forward to remove it, the boat shifting beneath her, listing precariously. When she glanced up again, she saw that her mother's hair was made entirely of sea grass, that one lock no different from the rest. She stared at the piece that had broken off in her hand, taking in the slickness of it, the green. *Your hair—* And then Maeve was gone. A wave crashed over her. She was going down, her mother a shadow, receding into the depths. *I can't breathe.* No words escaping her lips, only a stream of bubbles racing to the surface, lost to spray.

She woke, gasping, Malcolm's arms around her. The familiar scent of him, close, warm. She held fast for a moment.

"It's all right. I'm here," he said, his cheek pressed into her hair.

She recovered herself enough to pull away and clutch a pillow to her chest.

He sat on the side of the bed, the same side on which he used to sleep next to her. He wore a plain gray T-shirt and checked pajama pants. They'd never worn bedclothes at home. "The same dream?" he asked.

A version of the recurring nightmare she'd been having for years, from which she'd wake, thinking she was drowning, him soothing her, when he was there. "Yes," she said.

"Is it worse since you've been here?" The edges of everything softened in the dark, their voices hushed too.

The dream had intensified the week before she received Maire's letter, as if her psyche were attuned to what was coming. He hadn't been home then. "I'm all right."

He got up, awkward now. His hair stood on end, giving him a comical appearance about which she would have teased him, under different circumstances.

"You should go," she said.

He nodded, a slow movement, as if this were part of a dream from which they might wake, shaking their heads over their estrangement.

They knew it wouldn't be good for the girls to find him there, to think—

He turned in the doorway. "I'm here if you need me."

The ache, the regret, didn't hit her until after he'd closed the door, a quiet click of the latch articulating their separation, he on one side of the wall, she on the other.

One day passed into the next, flowing together. Nora swam for hours, training for the race. She felt stronger, venturing farther each time, Malcolm small in the distance, the girls swimming near shore, showing him their strokes.

He showed no sign of leaving. He stuck to them like a burr.

"Don't you need to go?" she asked one afternoon, a couple of days later, toweling her skin and hair.

"Where?"

"Boston."

To his work. His life. *Her.* Though they hadn't spoken of her. Here, she was only an idea. She had no shape, no form.

He shook his head. "Not yet."

"When?"

He sighed. "It's good here, isn't it? We're good here, away from everything."

Everyone. Was that what he meant?

"I didn't know you were such a strong swimmer," he said.

"I didn't either. I like the open water." She hadn't realized how hemmed in, how limited, she felt by the pool at the health club. It was freeing to be in the ocean, with no walls and lanes, whistles and lifeguards, to hold her back.

"You look good."

She'd done something else he hadn't expected. It made her more interesting.

"I'm not doing this for you," she said. "I'm doing it for me."

He'd brought a kite. An ornate paper bird with hinged wings that caught the wind, diving and soaring. The patterns of its flight were intricate, thrilling. He and the girls ran through the grass, creating a labyrinth of passageways in the green, crisscrossing, intersecting, breaking away. The girls swooped through the blue-bells, while Malcolm worked the lines, the cables humming. "Higher, Daddy, higher!" they begged, and he complied. If they'd asked for the sky, the clouds, he would have pulled them down. Or tried to—a blanket of blue, a pillow of cumulus. "Mama, come on!" Annie called. Nora cut the safety cord that had held her at a distance from Malcolm and joined them, arms outspread, opening herself up to the wind. "Are you flying, Mama?" Annie asked. Nora felt the warmth of the sun on her face, the breeze on her skin, a sense of lightness, uplifting, exhilarating. "What are we?" Nora asked. "Sparrows," said Ella, banking right. The most aerodynamic birds of all. "Sparrows!" Annie cried, taking up the call. "Sparrows!" Nora threw back her head and laughed, the meadow spinning. Malcolm, the kite in one hand, took flight as well, not to leave, but follow. "This way!" Ella led, bending low, the grass, tasseled, braided, tickling arms and legs. Annie jumped off a log, airborne, then landed, light-footed, barely touching ground. "This way!" Nora right behind, breathless, Malcolm in pursuit. A perfect summer scene. A scene that almost made Nora think they could spend many days like this, countless days.

A sudden gust blasted the meadow, testing their balance. It snatched the kite from Malcolm's hands. The bird flailed and then plummeted into the top of the spruce tree.

"No!" Annie cried.

They stopped below, the joy of the afternoon draining away.

"Sorry," Malcolm said. "I should have held on."

Nora's eyes met his. The words didn't have to be spoken to pass between them.

"It's roosting," Ella said hopefully.

"So it is," he agreed. "Still, I might see if I can persuade it to come down."

"The tree is like a mountain," Annie said. A mountain of needles, of green.

"I can buy another," he said, as if the time in the meadow, already receding into the past, could be recreated. He tugged on the line, tentatively at first, then harder. The bird hopped down a branch, then held fast, taunting him.

"Let's go inside and make lemonade," Nora suggested, sensing his mounting frustration. "You must be thirsty."

"Do you want some, Daddy?" Ella asked.

"I'd love a glass. It's hard work, being a bird, and negotiating with one. You know where to find me," he said.

For once, Nora did.

The girls darted ahead, still birdlike in their movements, into the cottage. Nora skirted Malcolm's sedan, a sporty, sleek model. The buzz of his cell phone cut the quiet of the afternoon through a half-open window. She'd heard him at the car earlier that morning, the click of the latch, the ding of the warning light, as he retrieved the kite and, in all likelihood, checked for messages in privacy.

She glanced up. He was out of her line of sight—and she from his. The phone buzzed violently as a trapped insect against the hard plastic receptacle. The call might be important—to his career, or, more to the point, to her, to ascertain his intentions, to find out if she'd been, careful as she was, fooled yet again.

The screen flashed. It might as well have been a billboard, given how large the letters seemed. It was a text message from *her*. Nora hesitated before pressing the button. Did she want to know? To violate his trust? Too many choices, the thirst for knowledge, as benign or terrible as it might be, winning in the end.

Have you given her the papers yet?

He rounded the corner, saw her standing there with the door ajar, the warning bell still doing its *ding-ding-ding*.

"You have a missed call," she said.

"You didn't have to answer it."

"A message." She thrust the device at him. She was aware of the girls inside the house, making the drinks, juicing the lemons, adding water, pouring in sugar, making everything sweet. The day, and all that lay between them, fragile as glass.

"I can explain."

She stared at him. She felt tightly coiled as a spring.

"Nora—"

"Remember, I'm your wife, not one of your constituents."

"That's not fair. This isn't what I want."

"What isn't?" Her words rat-tatted in the quiet afternoon.

"A divorce."

"But she thinks you do."

"I didn't say—"

"Didn't you?"

"She has her own situation to work out."

So that's what marriages were. Situations—the Situation Room taking on a whole new meaning. "Sounds like a fine start to a relationship, one built on mutual destruction and deceit. I'm glad you two have so much in common." She paused, the words leaving a bitter aftertaste.

"I'm hurting too."

"My heart bleeds for you."

"Don't raise your voice."

"I'm not raising my voice." How dare he tell her what to do? How to feel? She wanted to scream at him.

"You are. They might hear you."

The girls, their mutual trump card. The one they tried not to use.

Maybe she was talking too loudly. Though it was more her tone than anything else that probably got to him. He wasn't used to her speaking to him that way— sharp, biting, judging, no hint of affection, not even a glimmer. She'd been indulgent of him, loved him, for so many years.

"Why did you come here?" She dropped her voice lower. "Why did you, really?"

"I just wanted to see—" He faltered. He never faltered, but he did now.

"What you're missing?"

He looked at the ground, unable to meet her gaze.

"And is it enough, Malcolm?" Enough to make him stay? And if it was, did she care enough, trust enough, to let him?

He stroked the keys of his phone, absently, his fingers perhaps itching to dial the number he knew by heart. He caught her staring at his hand and froze, too late. He'd given himself away. She knew it wasn't calculated. For all his faults—and hers, she wasn't perfect either, she knew that—he wasn't manipulative. Defensive, exasperating, deflective, deceptive, yes; manipulative, no. He was, simply and finally, himself, perhaps ultimately unable to change for her, or she for him. "And what about what I want? Have you thought about that?"

"I thought you wanted to try."

"I did. But you haven't. You haven't done a damn thing."

"You don't know that."

"Don't insult my intelligence," she said. "Right now, I want you gone. Do you hear me? G-O-N-E." She shoved him. "You shouldn't have come here in the first place."

He stood his ground, striking the same pose he did in court, the one that won him case after case. "I don't like being jerked around like this."

"That's right, Malcolm. You're the victim."

"What's going to be enough for you?"

They weren't hearing each other, their words ricocheting. "You already know the answer to that."

He took a different tack. "And what about the girls? You're supposed to protect them."

"Seriously? Screw you."

"There's no call for that kind of language."

"Oh, yes, there certainly is. Protect them? That's exactly what I've been doing. I doubt you can say the same." She turned her back on him and walked away. She would not let him get the best of her.

The rest of the day passed. They spoke to the girls too brightly, their words so vehemently upbeat they shone. To each other, they said as little as possible, their movements as carefully choreographed as steps in a dance, their lines so well spoken they might have had weeks of rehearsal.

The next morning, she woke to find he'd gone. And while she had expected it, it surprised her too. She felt his absence more keenly than she might have thought. He was still a part of her, whether she liked it or not. She put the spare blankets in the closet, the sheets in the bag, to be transported to Maire's for washing.

Ella's eyes brimmed with tears. "Where is he?"

As if Nora had misplaced him. "He went back to Boston."

"What?"

"I'm sorry, honey. He was visiting. He couldn't stay."

"Why?"

"His work—" And the other things she couldn't speak of.

Ella sputtered. "You drove him away, didn't you? What did you say to him? What did you say?"

"El, I'm doing the best I can, for all of us."

"Your best isn't good enough."

Annie put her hands over her ears. "Stop shouting! Stop!"

They turned and looked at her.

"He didn't even say good-bye." Annie cried softly. "He always says good-bye."

Nora pulled her close. Annie's tears dampened the front of her shirt. Ella ran out the door with a slam.

"El—" Nora called after her.

Malcolm hadn't told the girls he was leaving, to spare them—and more likely, himself—a scene. Nora supposed it was better that way, in the end.

Ella sat below the spruce, gaze fixed on the kite, still high in the tree. She stayed there for some time, as if by the force of her will she could bring the kite down, bring her father back. When she returned to the house at last, exhausted, Nora ran her a warm bath, to wash away the tears.

Over the passing days, the kite faded and tore, a ribboned piece of its tail catching on the roof, where it fluttered, a hapless banner of the days they'd spent as a family, before the wind ripped it free at last, carrying it past the cove, twisting in midair, out to sea.

Chapter Fourteen

The girls sat in the beached coracle, the surrounding sand, rocks, and driftwood their sea. The pebbles shone. The tide retreated, leaving behind petticoats of white-laced foam. The shore smelled strongly of seaweed, and their lips had an invisible crust of salt. Their hair broke free of its braided restraints, falling into their faces in tangled strands they kept pushing behind their ears, so that they might contemplate the forbidden ocean, its currents summoning them, its waves promising adventure.

"It's not the same." Ella threw down the plastic tube she'd been using as a telescope in disgust.

"We can't take the boat out. We promised." Annie hopped out of the vessel and waded in the shallows—oh, that breath-catching, skin-prickling, delicious cold, like no other—as if that would suffice.

If their father had been there, he would have gone with them. But he was gone.

Ella tromped along the tidal margins, leaving footprints in the wet, slate-colored sand, the heels filling with water, legs splattered with the ocean's damp breath, its gritty muck. "No, we didn't. We didn't promise anything." She set her lips in a sullen line.

"But she thought we did." Annie cupped the water, marveling how it went clear when she held it in her hands, divided from the larger body.

"She thought we did—in her mind. It was never spoken of, and therefore, it doesn't count."

"We'd still be breaking the rules. We'd still be lying, indirectly. She's been sad enough already lately."

"Sad and mad are two different things."

"She's both, isn't she? I don't want her to be mad at me."

"Suit yourself. I don't care if she is, when it comes to me."

The seals appeared in the cove, observing them from the rocks. "They want us to play," Annie said. She missed Ronan. She hadn't seen him in days. Did the seals know where he was? They weren't saying. "They like hide-and-seek."

"I wonder if they'd come closer, if we went out in the coracle," Ella said.

"Maybe if we sit here, they'll come ashore," Annie said. "They like the rocks on sunny days. They leave their babies there, while they fish." It was pupping season. Reilly had warned them to keep their distance.

Ella flopped down on the sand. The clouds moved across the sky in a steady line, a processional, heading south, to Boston—to their father. She pointed her finger at the tip, as if she could catch hold of the plume and ride it all the way home.

Patch barked from the point. Reilly was nearby, casting a line, a slope-shouldered silhouette, eyes fixed on the waves that would not give up their catch easily that day, neither side willing to admit defeat. He must have been staying away, thanks to their mother.

"Let's go." Ella grabbed Annie's hand and set out to join him.

"But Mama said—"

"She didn't say we couldn't talk to him. There's no harm in talking, is there?"

"No," she admitted. She'd missed Reilly, Patch too.

As they drew closer, Patch dashed down the path and perched on a slab of granite, woofing a greeting. Reilly patted the space next to him, large enough to accommodate two slender girls under the age of thirteen.

"Where have you been?" Annie asked.

"I might have asked the same of you."

"Under house arrest," Ella said.

"And now you're on parole, eh?" Seabirds spiraled above the pinnacles, up into the clouds. "When I was a boy, I used to want to fly like that, above everything. Be able to dive in, catch all the fish in the world, their silver scales turning into coins. Such an imagination I had."

"Have you caught anything today?" Annie asked. The earth fell away beneath their feet—Reilly's booted, the girls' laced in red and black Converses—dangling above the thrashing surf.

"Not much of consequence. The big fish like deep water. Here, I only hook the little ones. They aren't as tasty. Not enough fat stored in the tissues, you see. I miss being at sea."

"So do we."

"Give it time. You'll earn your stripes—and your mother's support."

The line went taut. So did he. Then it slackened, his body too, before he set his shoulders again. "Patience," he told himself.

"My mother's always telling me what to do—and not do," Ella said.

"She's keeping you safe."

"From what?"

"All that might harm you."

Ella contemplated the ocean. "Since we're confined to shore," she said, "would you teach us to navigate?"

"We're already on probation," Reilly said. "Don't want your mother to have my head. A formidable woman, she is."

"She just doesn't want us on the water. It doesn't matter if we learn skills on land. You have a compass, don't you?"

"I do. I keep it in my pocket. It was handed down through the family. Something of an island tradition, you could say."

"Please, show us," Annie said.

"The points of the compass rose," he began with a verse his great grandfather had taught him, "hold more wisdom than you suppose. . . ."

Polly Clennon came by that afternoon, announcing her arrival with a beep of the mail van. Her hair was now deep purple. "Do not, under any circumstances, go to Merry Manes to get your hair colored. I should have known better. Merry is my friend, but she's never been the best with dye, and what with her sight getting worse—she needs to up her eyeglass prescription, if you ask me, but she'd have to go to the mainland for that, and, well, that's a hassle—she can't make out the labels. At least I didn't end up puce, like Maura O'Donnell."

"You wear it well." Nora smiled.

"My husband's taken to calling me Violet. Or Aubergine. He's quite the cutup, believe me. Ah, well, it will grow out; it will fade, as things do, given time." She paused. "Here's your mail."

Two letters; no legal documents, as Nora supposed. One had no return address. The other was a note from her friend Miriam, probably in the vein of her last. "Please know I'm thinking of you," she'd written, her effort to find the right words apparent in the brevity of the message, one that sounded like a sympathy card, for that's what it was. Nora was far from the world of 16 Oak Street and the neighbors like Miriam who'd appeared with dinners of lasagna or enchilada casserole in the days after the scandal broke, as if she'd lost the ability to cook, as if someone had died (not someone, though something, yes). Like those who'd peered from behind their Venetian blinds, noting the media trucks with avid curiosity, those who'd hovered by their mailboxes, hoping to be interviewed, taking their turn in the spotlight, to talk about her, Malcolm, the girls, suggesting a deeper acquaintance, a knowledge, than they actually possessed.

On this part of the island, there was only the shell road, with little or no traffic. A road that glowed on clear nights, when the shadows fell between the broken cockles, and the moon lit the nacred edges to brilliance. A road that disappeared into the mist on foggy evenings. A road few others had taken. Nora hadn't been followed, except by the past.

"News from home?" Polly asked as the van idled, the engine rumbling as if clearing its throat. She had the window rolled down, her freckled arm resting on the door. A single mailbag sat on the seat beside her. Aretha Franklin's "Respect" played on an antiquated stereo system, the cassette tape tinny, hissing.

Nora gave a dismissive wave of her hand. The wind snatched at the envelope. "A note from a friend," she said.

"Will they visit?"

"I hadn't really thought about it."

"Not much room for guests, is there?"

"No, there isn't." Nora knew she was fishing for details about Malcolm and what had transpired during his stay.

"Houseguests can be wearing. Not that I mind, myself. I like company," she paused. "And where might the girls be?"

"Down on the beach. They found a coracle."

"Maeve's coracle? We could put it in the museum, if you ever get tired of it," she said, clearly turning over the possibilities in her mind. "Some said your ancestors made a deal with the sea," she added, "so that they might always travel its waters safely. Didn't work for Maire's husband, poor man. But then, he wasn't a McGann."

"Or my mother." Though she was.

"So many stories." She gave Nora a considering look. "We all have our histories, our mythologies, don't we? The historians think they're being impartial, relying on facts, but even the facts can be mighty unreliable, depending upon who's doing the telling."

"What do you mean?"

"Oh, you know how I go on. They called me Babs, short for Babbling Brook, when I was a girl. My family started it. Nicknames. The perfect thing to call them, eh? A little cut, a little jab, in the saying of them? Not that I minded. Rise above has always been my modus operandi. It's gotten me far enough in life, if not off this island. Anyway, it's the old-timers who might be able to tell you more about Maeve. They—along with a host of others—gather at Cis McClure's on Wednesday nights."

"My mother seems to stir up strong feelings in people."

"She was memorable, that's for certain."

"I've lived most of my life not knowing whether she left or disappeared. I told myself it didn't matter—" The words tumbled out before Nora could stop them.

"But it does. It cuts to the very heart of you, of course it would," Polly said. "Go into town later. Most everyone should be there, or at least the usual suspects. I'll introduce you."

"I'd like that."

"I'm sure Maire will watch the girls. She doesn't go in for that sort of thing, not since Joe died. He was a fiddler, you see. Performed regularly at McClure's. Brings back too many memories for her to even consider setting foot in the place. She still feels the loss keenly. I think there's a part of her that expects he'll come sailing home one evening, from wherever he's been. Some things are too hard to get over, no matter how much time passes."

They fell quiet and turned toward the ocean, that magician, whose greatest trick, it seemed, was making people disappear.

After Polly left, Nora opened Miriam's letter:

How are you doing? You've been on my mind. Will you really be staying on the island for the summer? It's strange not having you here. The house is so quiet. I have to stop myself from going over and knocking on the door. I keep forgetting you're not there. I miss you—

She should write back. She knew she should, but she didn't know what to say. She'd sat down before, pen poised over paper. The words wouldn't come. She'd try again soon. She'd ask Miriam about her life, rather than speaking of her own. Maybe that would make it easier.

She went inside and turned to the other letter. "McGann," read the name in labored print. It must have been a mistake—Maire's married name was Flanagan, Nora's Cunningham. The address matched the number for the cottage, not Cliff House. Odd.

She tore open the envelope, nicking her index finger in the process. There was only a scrap of lined yellow paper inside. She pulled it out. "Why are you here?" it read. No signature. The writer appeared to have pressed the pencil so hard into the paper that it punctured it in places.

The girls came into the house, faces flushed, hungry for a snack.

"What's that?" Ella asked. "A letter from Dad?"

"No." She crumpled it up and threw it in the garbage. "Just junk mail."

Night had fallen by the time Nora drove into town, the stars and occasional streetlamp dotting the velvet darkness with pinpricks of light. Moths fluttered before the headlights, cream-colored, fragile. Hers the only vehicle on the road, making its way to the center of things, Cis McClure's, where people drank and sang and danced their troubles away. The spots outside the bar were taken. She had to park up the street and around the corner, down a deserted alley. Her boots clattered on the cobblestones, conspicuously loud in the quiet. Even at that distance, she felt the throb of the music, as if it came from the earth itself. She passed Scanlon's, closed now after hours, the bakery, the shoe repair, no sign of life within, the windows dark.

The entire population of the island, or close to it, seemed to have crammed into the pub that night. Every seat taken, every space to stand occupied. Girls in short skirts and low-cut tops, chests pale, freckled, young men in knit hats and flannel shirts, hair black or blazing red, the old men in tweeds and patch-elbowed jackets, either hanging off shoulders or straining across bellies. Nora stood on tiptoe, hoping to spot Polly Clennon, but the loquacious postmistress was nowhere in sight. The drone of voices filled the space, a hive of gossip, conviviality, and intrigue. Patrons sat, head-to-head, in tense or jocular debate; others clustered around tables, chiming in. Some danced. Some sang, to themselves or in small groups. A band tuned up in the corner, preparing to play.

A seat opened at the bar, and she took it. The stool was wooden, offering little comfort. She caught the bartender's eye. Cis himself poured the drinks—Cisco being his full name, she gathered. Broad-shouldered and spade-faced, he was an imposing presence amid the greater chaos around him, the only suggestion of gentleness in his hands as they swiftly, neatly poured the drinks, not spilling a single drop. "New, are you?" he asked.

"As a penny," she replied.

"Worth a sight more than that, aren't you?" he said. "Though that's what I'll charge you."

"The going rate?"

"Newcomer's special."

She ordered the house ale, the foam poised perfectly on the lip of the glass. She would have preferred a glass of white wine, but had the feeling such a request would have been verboten. Cis set the drink in front of her with a nod.

The local priest, Father Ray, tapped her shoulder. Nora had seen—or rather heard—him tearing around the island on his motorcycle, though she'd never actually met him. She felt some embarrassment over having not been to mass (Maire asked if she'd like to join her those first weeks, but then let her be), but clearly he wasn't the sort who went in for guilt trips. "Joining the congregation tonight, are we?" he asked.

"They don't look very holy," she said with a smile.

"This is their second church. Some worship here more regularly than others." He wore a collar and blacks, which made him stand out in the crowd. His stocky build hinted at a youth spent on the football field.

"They do seem devoted."

"It is a sort of religion."

"Maybe you should talk to the Vatican about introducing a communion ale."

"There's a thought." He laughed. "Might like that better myself. They send the most awful wine." He paused. "You're Maire's niece, aren't you? I can see the family resemblance. How are you getting on?"

She took a sip of ale, considering. She decided to go with the simple answer. "Well enough."

"I hear you're quite the swimmer."

She wondered what else he'd heard. "I like the ocean."

"It's special here, isn't it? A unique convergence of currents, they say."

"Yes. And you?"

"I'm better on land. I tend to get seasick. Don't tell anyone. I don't want to ruin my credibility."

"Your secret's safe with me."

He paused for a moment, as if she might be compelled to share a confidence.

One of the men called to him from across the room.

"Someone needing to confess?" Nora asked.

"Or, hopefully, wanting to buy me a drink." Father Ray winked. "Well, I'm off to minister to the flock. Drop by St. Mary's for a visit anytime. The door is always open."

Alison breezed past with an empty tray. Nora had forgotten she waitressed there.

"Busy girl," Nora said. She considered mentioning the disturbing letter, but then thought the better of it.

"Keeps me out of trouble." Alison balanced the order with ease. "And pads the bank account. My travel fund."

"Any thoughts about where you'll go?"

"A vacation someplace hot and sunny—Thailand, Brazil."

"I might have to join you," Nora said. "Have you seen Polly? She was supposed to meet me."

Alison shook her head. "Not yet. Maybe the van broke down again. She doesn't have much luck with cars. Or she stopped to chat too long. The woman's a talker, if you haven't noticed."

She was indeed.

"But here's her father, Gerry." Alison nodded to the red-faced man who'd taken the seat beside Nora. He appeared to have had a good start on the evening, judging by the shine in his eyes. "The next best thing."

"Next best thing, am I?" He grinned. "I'll do better than that." He must have been in his eighties. He was spry, a touch of arthritis, perhaps, giving him the jerky movements of a marionette. Before Nora knew what was happening, he'd hopped off his stool and taken her by the elbow, jigging her through the crowd near the door. The pubgoers parted to let them through, some laughing and clapping indulgently, others scarcely registering them. Nora sensed Gerry made a regular habit of such displays. "Good for the heart," he said, as he deposited her in her seat, with a gentlemanly tip of his cap. "Thank you for the dance."

"You're welcome." He was quite the character.

He leaned closer. "I'm looking to get laid tonight." He wasn't necessarily propositioning her, merely announcing his general intentions, in an almost wistful fashion.

"Happy fishing." She took a demure sip of her ale, suppressing a laugh. She imagined he'd never say such things when sober. She wouldn't drink much that night herself. She needed to have a clear head, the roads and the people of Burke's Island being challenging, at times, to navigate.

Gerry skipped off for a solo and returned a short time later, leaning on the bar for support. "Out of breath, I am." He panted. "Gone are the days when I could close the place down."

"It's the dancing."

"And the age. More's the pity." He paused.

"You don't look a day over—"

"A hundred?" He cackled. "Soon to be. Ninety-five, this last January."

"That can't be."

"Oh, but it is. How the time does pass. I was in the world war. The first one. Saw a lot of action, especially in France." He gave her a playful jab in the ribs.

"You're quite the flirt, aren't you?"

"Don't tell my wife."

"Is she here too?"

"Lord, no. She's up at St. Mary's."

"Praying?"

"In the cemetery, God rest her soul."

"I'm sorry. I didn't realize—"

"Years ago, it was. Still miss her." His gaze clouded, before he fixed on her face again. "You remind me of someone."

"I have one of those faces."

He snapped his fingers, after a couple of unsuccessful goes. "That McGann girl. A fine one, she was. Maeve."

"My mother."

"That explains it. Sure. You're the child, all grown up. The spitting image."

"So I hear. Did you know her?"

"We all knew her. Or wanted to. The Queen of the Fleet. Won the sea race too, time and again. Never been a girl that pretty who could swim that fast. Like a fish, she was. Got to lead the parade. Can't recall the year. She would have been eighteen or thereabouts. Not long before she met that fella. A string of broken hearts, to be sure. And jealous women."

"She didn't have many friends?"

"More men than gals. And I don't mean she was too free. She got on better with the lads. Never went in for the gossip, maybe because she was the focus of it herself. Didn't endear herself to the female population, except my daughter, Brenna. Thick as thieves, they were." His gaze drifted. "It's a sad thing to have your children go before you."

"I'm sorry. Polly mentioned she'd passed away."

"You know my Polly?"

"Doesn't everyone?"

"She's everywhere, isn't she? Always has been, ever since she was little. Didn't want to miss out on the fun." He nudged her. "Gets that from me, I suppose. . . . Maeve McGann. What a girl. And the sailor got her in the end, didn't he? The sea delivering a man to her, when she couldn't find the right one here."

Nora waited another hour, but Polly never showed, Alison had to work, and Gerry, who seemed to know the most about Maeve, or was at least the most inclined to talk, had passed out at the bar. The band started up in earnest, making conversation impossible. She listened to the first set before stealing a glance at her watch and deciding she should probably head back to Cliff House and pick up the girls. She reluctantly waved to Alison, shouldered her bag, and went out the door.

The clatter of her footsteps was a lonely sound, moving away from the festivities to the car that would carry her along the deserted road, to the cottage by the sea. The car used for ferrying the girls from one place to another in her previous life, the one she'd shared with Malcolm, as wife and mother. Here, mother only, and she wasn't sure what else. She was still gaining a sense of herself apart from those roles.

She turned down the alley where she'd parked the car—on a dead end. She heard a shuffling behind her. She tightened her hand on her bag, ready to stand her ground, if necessary. It would be just her luck to have Maggie Scanlon show up and assail her again.

But it wasn't Maggie Scanlon. It was a group of men from the bar.

There were three of them, one short and wiry, the others larger, six feet at least and heavily built. They blocked the only way out. The alley smelled of damp, and now of them too—beery, musty. She had her keys out. If she could get inside the car, she could lock the door, press her foot on the accelerator, and go.

The wiry one darted closer. "Going somewhere?" He was fox-faced and glassy-eyed, a wispy stubble on his chin, patchy, as if he'd missed a spot or two shaving. She guessed he'd started drinking early that day.

"Home." She hoped they didn't hear the shakiness in her voice.

"Boston. That's where you belong."

So there had been gossip. "Get out of my way."

"We're on to you. Biding your time, aren't you? Waiting to get your hands on Maire's land. Tear it down, build a new house or a resort for the big-city assholes. We don't want that here."

"I don't know what you're talking about." It was no use trying to reason with him in his present condition, with his minions looming in the background. They were clearly bent on ascribing the worst possible motives to her.

He stepped in front of her. "Still, we might have a little fun with you, before you go."

Nora felt a chill of apprehension. She had to get out of there, fast. "You're drunk. You're not making any sense. Now get lost." She dodged him and fumbled with the key in the lock, her hands trembling. It slid into the mechanism, turned with a soft click. Broken glass crunched underfoot. She was halfway in the car when a hand grabbed the door. No words now, only breathing. Hers. His. The others behind him. She felt a rush of adrenaline. She shouted for help, but the noise in the bar was too loud for anyone inside to hear. She wrestled for possession of the door, nearly smashing his fingers in the jamb. She kicked at him, hard. "Fuck off!" she cried. They backed away, reconsidering. She was clearly more than they'd bargained for.

"That's enough," someone shouted from the entrance of the alley. A familiar figure approached. Owen.

Nora stared at him in disbelief, her breathing shallow. Where had he come from? He hadn't been in the pub; she would have noticed.

The fishermen laughed, though they'd retreated a few paces at his voice. She didn't know he could sound like that. He'd always been so soft-spoken.

"Only one of you, isn't there?" the tallest one said, peering behind him for confirmation. "Who are you to tell us what to do?"

Owen didn't reply but continued to advance toward the group, undeterred. Nora moved her keys to her right hand and made a fist around them.

"He wants a fight," said the ringleader. He grabbed an empty bottle from an overflowing garbage can and waved it in the air, hopping with excitement, clearly expecting the others to take the first swing. He'd taken the lead with Nora, but he appeared more cautious when it came to dealing with an adversary like Owen.

"Steady, Dec," the biggest said, putting a hand on his shoulder.

Owen stopped directly in front of them. She couldn't see his face. "You need to leave. Now." His voice was guttural, almost a growl. She couldn't be sure what he said next, because as he spoke, the seals barked from the harbor, obscuring his words.

The men retreated. "No harm done, eh?" As if it had been a joke. They shoved each other and traded insults as they repaired to the bar, evidently in search of less complicated company and another round of drinks.

Nora rested her chin on the steering wheel, spent. She raised her head when Owen came up to the car. "I had things under control," she said, feigning calm.

"Of course you did." If he noticed her shaking, he didn't say so. "Doesn't hurt to have some backup, though, does it?"

"I suppose not." Her pulse was still racing. "Do you need a ride?" she managed to ask.

"Why not." He got in beside her. "It's a long walk home. Good thing I happened by. Not the friendliest guys, are they?"

"No, they're not." She wondered if she and the girls were safe at the cottage, how much she had to fear the men stalking her. "I hope they don't come looking for me."

"If they do, they'll find trouble. I'll see to that."

"So now you're our bodyguard too? You're developing quite a résumé."

"I wouldn't worry about them too much. They're all talk."

"And drink."

"Exactly. They probably won't remember anything in the morning."

"I hope they have one hell of a hangover." It wouldn't be so easy for Nora to put the encounter out of her mind. She turned the key in the ignition and pulled onto the road. The indicator lights glowed on the dash. Oil. Gas. Speed. She told herself she was in control now, foot on the accelerator, hands on the wheel. She glanced at her passenger. "You're all wet," she observed.

His hair was slicked down. "That's what happens when you've been out in the rain."

"But it's not raining."

A drop, then another, hit the windshield.

"Your powers of intuition are truly remarkable," she said.

"Not really. There's a squall, making landfall, moving in from the docks. It should blow through in a moment or two."

"What were you doing here, anyway?"

"Just out for an evening stroll."

"Quite a distance to go."

"Only a couple of miles or so. I like being outdoors."

They passed the outskirts of town. "Well, I'm glad you were here tonight," she said. "I know I haven't been completely welcoming since you arrived."

"Makes your regard all the more worth attaining," he replied. "The point has become like a second home to me."

"Where is home?" she asked. "Surely you must have family, a life elsewhere. Someone who misses you—"

He didn't say anything for a moment. "I remembered something today, when I was swimming past the cove. That my parents were killed in a boating accident when I was young," he said. "It's coming back to me, one piece at a time. I think I've been on my own, for the most part, ever since. Funny how things like that can occur to you out there."

It was. "I'm sorry. I didn't realize—" At least she'd had her father, at least she hadn't lost everything. She'd held his hand while he lay in a hospital bed those last hours, felled by a stroke, unable to communicate, his eyes half closed, fixed. She hoped he'd heard her when she'd thanked him for everything he'd done for her. She'd never told him before. She hadn't anticipated him going so quickly.

"There's no reason you should have."

They lapsed into silence, the only sound the wiper blades moving across the windshield in half circles, the rain coming down harder. She put on the high beams, casting the road before them in shades of gray.

"So he's gone?" he asked.

"Who?"

"Your husband."

It was odd to hear him say the word. She hurried to explain. "Yes. I wasn't expecting him. To visit, that is."

"You weren't?"

"No. He didn't come for me. He came for the girls."

"Are you sure of that?"

Yes. No. She didn't want to get into it, not then, not with Owen. It was as if Malcolm was riding along with her, the backseat husband, still calling the shots. "I thought we said we didn't owe each other explanations."

"So we did." He gazed out the window at the streaming dark, the headlights trained on the road before them, its margins appearing narrower in the nighttime hours. "Though that doesn't mean we can't get to know each other better. I thought we were."

"We're friends, remember?" Goose bumps prickled her skin. She supposed she should have worn a heavier coat. "Aren't you cold?" She should have thought to have had the car serviced before they left Boston. The heater still wouldn't work, not an issue on the mainland during the summer, but here, on the island, it could be.

"Not really. I'm used to it."

"Well, I am." She tried the heater anyway, to no avail, the radio too, fingers pressing busily, to break the silence, to give her something to do. All she could get was static. "What did you say to those guys, anyway?"

"Something they'd understand."

Nora and Owen alighted in front of Cliff House. The moon appeared, the squall having passed, as he predicted. His skin was luminous in that light, his eyes searching. She looked away, feeling the warmth in her cheeks. "Well," she said, suddenly awkward as a teenager. "Thank you." Maire's house stood behind her. The girls were there, upstairs. She should bring them home, get them to bed.

"For what? You would have done the same for me."

"To less effect."

"Oh, I'm not so sure. You can be rather intimidating when you want to be."

"Hardly. You scared the hell out of them. What's your secret?"

"Ah, but it wouldn't be a secret if I told you, would it?"

They went their separate ways, he to the fishing shack, she to Cliff House. A single light burned in the front room, the curtains half open, Maire, still awake, knitting. Nora tapped on the door.

"You don't have to knock. The door isn't locked. It's your home too. I keep telling you that." Maire motioned her inside, a basket of knitting at the foot of her chair, a half-finished multicolored sweater—perhaps for one of the girls, judging by the size of it—draped over the side, awaiting the next purl. "You look pale. Did something happen?"

Nora paused at the foot of the staircase.

"Maggie wasn't at Cis McClure's, was she?" Maire asked.

"No." Nora told her about the incident in the alley.

"Must have been the Connelly boys. That Declan has been a problem for years. We should report them. I could ask John O'Connor to give them a talking-to. Wouldn't be the first time he's had to do it, believe me."

"I don't think they'll try it again," Nora said. Reporting them would only stir things up, if they did indeed forget the encounter. "They were drunk."

"I'm sure you're right, but it bears watching. It's good Owen was there."

Nora nodded. All she wanted to do was return to the cottage, take a long, hot bath, and pretend none of it ever happened. "I'll grab the girls and—"

"Don't worry about them. We had a lovely evening. They taught me how to play Snap and Golf—such fun card games—and we made sugar cookies." She nodded at the kitchen counter, where the frosted treats in shapes of flowers, butterflies, and trees rested on cooling racks. "I love getting to play the grandmother. They're fast asleep. Let's leave them for the night. Why don't you stay too? There's plenty of room. We could have breakfast together in the morning."

"That's all right," Nora said. "My things are at the cottage."

"You could probably use a little time to yourself."

"I didn't mean—"

"Of course you didn't. You're a mother. You put them before yourself, always. Go have a nice long bath," Maire said, as if she'd read her mind. "A glass of wine. Whatever would make you feel better. You've had quite a night, haven't you? I should have thought of that before."

"No, you shouldn't have. You've already done so much for us," Nora said. "Thank you, for everything."

Owen was waiting for her when she returned to the cottage. She wasn't completely surprised to see him. It was as if they'd reached an unspoken agreement earlier, as they'd driven home together in the dark, a sense, perhaps, that they'd been moving toward this point for days. She hadn't realized how much she'd wanted this—to lose herself in the moment, to stop thinking. It seemed as if all she'd been doing lately was worry, keeping her emotions in check. The effort was consuming her, suffocating her. And there he was. A means to forget, offering escape, sensation, desire . . . If she'd stopped to consider the implications, she might have gone inside alone. But for once, she didn't stop, didn't consider. She wanted to know what it was like—to see if she could still feel.

The moon bathed the cottage, the landscape, in shades of blue and gray, as if they were underwater. Owen pulled her toward him. She did nothing to stop him; if he hadn't reached for her, she would have reached for him. He pushed open the door, led her backward to the bed. And then everything fell away a layer at a time—her clothes, her responsibilities, her past.

She looked into his face; his eyes held hers, never breaking contact. Malcolm had always kept his eyes closed. He tended to take her quickly, holding her apart from him, as if to get better leverage. When she tried to tell him what she wanted, he became defensive, fearing he'd failed, and so she let it go. Sometimes he pleased her, others she'd lie and say he'd made her happy, because she couldn't bear to see the shame and disappointment on his face, because it was fine, really. Sex didn't always have to be earthshaking. They'd been married fifteen years, after all.

Owen was different, and she was different with him. He turned over her hand, traced the tattoo on the underside of her wrist. They whispered to each other, guiding, exploring. *This. This.* Everything was new with him. Everything. She cried. She felt as if she were breaking apart. "What's wrong?" He stroked her cheek. "It's so beautiful," she said through her tears. The room seemed to glisten, just the two of them, together, while through the open window the waves kept cadence, rushing up the beach, covering the rocks, the sand, the hour changing over, the tide coming in.

Chapter Fifteen

Voices warbled, swooping closer. Nora squinted in confusion. Who was outside? Where was she?

Her vision cleared, her mind too: in the cottage at Glass Beach.

"We're home! We're home!" The girls, running along the path.

She sat up in panic. Owen. They mustn't see him. She glanced around the room. He wasn't there. Where had he gone?

No time to think about that now. Things were looking different in the light of day—messy, in every sense of the word. She pulled on a T-shirt and shorts as Annie threw open the door and pounced on her. "Wake up, sleepyhead!"

"Is it late?"

"No, it's early. We missed you, so we came home."

Ella stood in the doorway, examining the scene with forensic intensity.

"Were you lonely here by yourself?" Annie asked. "You have sparkles on you." She flicked at Nora's skin.

"Must be sand," Nora said. "I didn't bother to shower."

"How European of you. Aunt Maire said you were going home to take a bath. I heard the car last night. I saw you from the window," Ella said.

"I didn't get around to it." Nora yawned and rubbed her eyes, partly for effect. She could smell him on her, hoped to God they wouldn't notice.

"Were you up late?" Annie asked.

"A little."

"I thought you said you were tired," Ella said. "What were you doing?"

They couldn't imagine her having a life separate from theirs. "Reading." It didn't feel right to lie to them.

"You didn't get far." Ella considered the paperback copy of *The Woman in White* on the nightstand, the bookmark indicating meager progress, the needle of the compass quivering nearby, as if it were a polygraph.

"I wanted to take my time. It's too early for conversation. I'm not a morning person. You know that."

She had to be careful what she told them. They had a certain idea of her. She was not so much a person as their mother; she couldn't disappoint or confuse them by revealing herself to be anything more or less. She had to be the one they could rely on—especially Ella, the intensity of her feelings almost too much for her to handle, a spark that might fan into flame.

Now her older daughter considered the rumpled sheets, the dent in the second pillow. "You moved around in your sleep a lot."

"I always do," Nora replied. "You know that. Dreams."

"Bad ones?" Annie asked.

"I don't remember," Nora said, changing the subject. "You must be hungry. I'll get you breakfast." What better way to divert them than catering to their most basic needs? She herded them out of the room and busied herself pouring cereal into bowls and making toast.

Ella regarded her closely, her chin dipped down over the bowl of Cheerios, little O's of cereal expressing collective surprise below her disapproving face. "So"— she crunched—"have you heard from Dad?"

"No." Nora hadn't expected to.

"You didn't turn off your phone, did you?"

"You'd know better than I would." Nora raised an eyebrow at her.

Ella slurped the milk.

The noise served its purpose, setting Nora's teeth on edge. "I know you miss him."

Annie's gaze moved between them.

"You haven't forgiven him, have you?" Ella asked. "You tell us to forgive and forget."

Yes, the inconsequential things siblings tended to argue about. This was different. "Just because your father and I have separated doesn't mean we don't love you," Nora said, a sentence she'd repeated over the course of the last few weeks. "We both love you, very much."

"Do you? Then why did you bring us here?"

"I thought it was best. Aunt Maire's letter arrived at the right time. You know what it was like at home."

"El—," Annie interceded.

"Coming here hasn't really fixed anything, has it?" Ella set her spoon down on the table with a clatter.

"I came here for you."

"No, you didn't. You wanted to know what happened to your mother. You wanted to escape—from the stuff with Dad." She flung her chair back and stormed outside.

"El, wait." Annie went after her.

The door slipped its latch and creaked open. It hadn't closed completely, revealing a slice of empty sky, heavy with clouds. It was raining over the ocean, raining hard. Nora picked up the chair Ella had thrown and put it back where it belonged. There was a gouge now in the wood. "Maybe I did."

A few moments later, there was a footstep on the deck, another. Nora's heart beat faster. She would turn Owen away. She would say last night was a mistake. Because she wasn't that type of person—

"Good morning," Maire called.

Nora sighed in relief, in disappointment; she wasn't sure which was stronger.

"How was your evening?" Her aunt's face was bright as ever as she pushed open the door. "You didn't sit and brood, did you?"

"Not too much." Nora gave her a wry smile.

"He'll be back."

Who did she mean? "Perhaps," she said, to be safe.

"Anyone can see he still loves you."

Malcolm. Of course she meant Malcolm. "Sometimes I think he loves the idea of me, more than the reality."

"It's good you're here, to give yourself time and space. He'll come to his senses. You'll see." Maire went on. "I thought you might like these." She proffered a basket of produce—baby carrots, lettuce, radishes, and beets. "I was going to give some to Owen, but he wasn't home."

"Do you know where he's gone?" She made the question casual. She'd thought she'd built a fortress around her heart that nothing, no one, could breach. No one except her daughters.

"Out fishing again, most likely. I suppose he must leave us someday. He has his life, though I hate the thought of him going. I've gotten used to having him here. He knows this coast as well as I do by now, probably better. I've been thinking about giving him Joe's old boat. It's hard for him, not having his own. I've gotten him started, fixing it up. He's made remarkable progress. Must work on it day and night when he's not on the cliffs or wherever he goes. I wonder if he ever sleeps."

Did Maire know more? If so, she wasn't saying. Her aunt sat down quickly, steadying herself.

Nora rushed to her side. "You're not feeling dizzy again, are you?"

"A little. Happens sometimes, in the mornings, mainly. Silly diabetes. A most inconvenient condition. Remember, I told you?"

She did. "Have you been to the doctor? You said you'd go."

"Yes, yes. Told me what I already knew. Now, don't you go worrying about me. You have enough on your mind." She took a deep breath and stood again.

"There." She demonstrated a little twirl. "All better. Besides, I didn't come over here to bother you. It's time to check on the bees again."

As they strolled next door, Maire chatted away about the state of the garden ("The lemon cucumbers are really coming on; wait until you taste them—you can eat them, skin and all") and her desire to keep chickens ("I hear the Araucanas have particularly lovely eggs"). Nora stepped into the bee suit, the fabric crinkling, settling. She put on the veil, the gloves. There were smaller suits now too, for the girls. Maire had made them herself, since they didn't come in children's sizes. The women walked to the edge of the orchard where the hives were sited to catch the rising sun, the light waking the bees each morning, calling them forth to greet the day. But there would only be the two keepers today. It was better that way. The bees might sense Ella's mood.

"The bees command our full attention, don't they?" Maire said. "Giving us a break from our troubles, whatever they may be."

Yes, if only Nora could focus on the task at hand. Her thoughts kept drifting to Owen and Malcolm. "When will the honey be ready?" she asked.

"Not for a while yet. The bees are only getting started. They need the warmth, the sun, the flowers.

We have all those things now. There's nothing like high summer on the island."

"It's beautiful," Nora agreed. Perhaps one of the most beautiful places she'd ever been. Nowhere else had she experienced the connectedness of things, the sustenance and solace nature could offer. Beyond the boundary of the orchard, the property went wild, grass and trees and brambles running free, the bees curled into nodding bluebells nearby, humming with contentment and industry.

"Do you like him?" Maire asked.

"Who?" She was grateful the veil obscured her expression.

"Owen. I know you weren't sure about him staying on."

"You've been so welcoming—to both of us." A successful dodge.

"I'm happy you're here. This place has had just me rattling around for too long." She looked small and vulnerable then, against the wide open landscape. "Do you feel at home? I want you to feel at home—because it is your home. It always has been," Maire said, a plea in her eyes. "I've been thinking. There's so much you could do here, if you decided to stay. The island doesn't have an attorney, or you could focus on your cooking or the jewelry you've been making. The pieces are lovely. Maeve would be proud."

Nora could imagine staying beyond the summer, more so every day, but it was too soon to be making such decisions. "We'll see," she said. "I love it here, but I need to think things through."

"I know. Life is complicated."

"And I need to understand the island and my history better. For some reason, I can't let the past lie."

The bees buzzed louder, a dirge. "No, I don't suppose you can." Maire kept her eyes on the hives.

"What is it you haven't told me?"

Maire hesitated. "I've been waiting for you to get a sense of the strangeness here, the otherness that isn't widely understood. And I was afraid that once you knew, you'd leave, that there would be nothing for you here, that you would think us all mad. I don't want to lose anyone else." Her eyes brimmed with tears.

Nora touched her arm. "You're not going to lose me. Please. I can't begin to understand until you share what you know."

"I'll tell you, but you might not believe me. I'm not sure if I believe it myself. Remember the charts in the attic and how I mentioned that our ancestors had supposedly reached an agreement with the sea and the seals that lived within it? There was a balance in all things in the beginning. That's what people thought. But as I told you before, with my parents' generation, something changed. I can't help but think it had something to do with your mother's disappearance and an argument I overheard my parents having one night. I was fourteen that summer, Maeve sixteen; she'd won the swimming race again. My mother was convinced that Maeve wasn't hers, that she was a changeling, a creature of the sea. That her ability to hold her breath so long and swim so fast proved it. That my father had found her on the beach and substituted her for their biological baby, who had died in childbirth before my mother regained consciousness. Maeve and my mother had never gotten along, you see. The conflicts between them intensified, as they often do with firstborns in the teenage years, Maeve more so than others, her will being particularly strong. Perhaps my mother was looking for reasons for their estrangement, though I too had always felt there was something different about Maeve. Anyway, Da found me outside my parents' bedroom door, eavesdropping. He told me to never tell a soul. That some things were best left alone."

"Did my mother know?"

"Oh, yes. I told her. I was angry one day, and I said she wasn't really my sister, and why. We got into a terrible fight, drawing blood, making scars, physical and otherwise." She pulled back her collar to reveal a pale crescent on her neck. "She withdrew after that, from all of us, until your father arrived."

The humming of the bees grew louder, ringing in Nora's ears. "Is it true?"

"I don't know. No one does."

"But if it were," she said slowly, "then I'm not a McGann—"

"Yes, you are, through my father, at least, if not more. We are bound together, aren't we, though perhaps not in the way we supposed."

"Were there any medical records?"

She shook her head. "There was no doctor on the island until after you were born. Before that, only midwives, from our family. My mother gave birth at home, no one but my father in attendance. That was the way it was done then."

"But the death your mother spoke of—"

"Swept under the carpet, never recorded, or not true in the first place. The birth had been hard. She had a fever. She could have been hallucinating about the stillbirth and the substitution. It took her weeks to recover, and she had severe postpartum depression afterward."

"And my grandfather?"

"He never spoke of it again."

Nora nodded. That sounded like her own father, a man of few words, especially when it came to difficult subjects.

"Are you all right?" Maire asked. "I know it's a lot to take in."

"Yes." Though, truly, she didn't know what to think.

Maire put a finger to her lips. "We're disturbing the bees. I guess it's too much for them too. They're still getting used to the new queen. If we don't give them enough time, they might reject her."

"And what happens then?"

"They could kill her."

"Oh, dear."

"Yes." She administered liberal puffs of smoke to calm the insects, and within seconds, the air was so thick Nora could barely see. She and Maire were mere outlines then, not forms so much as suggestions, lacking definition, moving through a space in which landmarks were no longer visible, and great care must be taken.

Chapter Sixteen

Ella didn't remain on the beach for long. She waited for Nora to leave the cottage, then went inside, shutting herself in the bedroom, retreating behind the pages of *Little Women*, "literature as armor," as their mother called it. Annie stayed where she was. She built a fort of driftwood, made castles of sand, cairns of stone, an architect of the shore. The sun was breaking through the clouds. Clear skies were still a possibility. The ocean too seemed calmer, the underside of its waves a lovely shade of turquoise. Annie studied the herky-jerky progress of a hermit crab over the sand. He could make his home anywhere, soldiering on. She would do the same. She would choose to be happy.

A shadow fell over her: Ronan, a bracelet of seaweed around his wrist. He wore the same shorts.

She wondered if he had another pair, or if they were all identical. "You're back," she said, picking up the thread of their conversation, as if they'd stopped speaking moments, rather than days, before. "I was wondering where you'd gone."

"Visiting relatives," he said.

"A family reunion?"

"Something like that."

"We don't have much family left for those kinds of gatherings." Her father's side had many relatives, but they mainly saw each other at weddings and funerals, his sisters, except Aunt Ro, having moved far away. "Though we've found some here. Maire."

"The woman in the big house? I've seen her working in the garden."

"I could introduce you."

"You're the only one I can talk to."

"Does your mother know about me?"

He shook his head.

"I'd like to meet her sometime."

"Maybe, someday. How long will you be here?"

"Probably for the summer."

"Same here. We travel from place to place."

"Sea gypsies."

"And what about you? Where did your father go? I saw him with you on the beach."

"I wondered if you had. I looked for you."

"I was hiding."

"You're good at that," she said, adding, "We took him out in the coracle. It was fun, mostly."

"Mostly?"

"When my parents weren't arguing. They don't know how to be together, but they don't know how to be apart."

"It's like that sometimes."

"What about your father?"

"He's gone."

"Gone? Did your parents get divorced?"

"They were never married."

"Oh. What was he like?"

"You already know."

"What do you mean?"

"You've met him. He's the man you know as Owen."

"Annie?" At the sound of Ella's voice, Ronan dove into the surf with barely a splash.

"Who were you talking to?" Ella clambered down the bank. "I heard voices."

"I thought you wanted to be alone." Annie was still processing the startling piece of information Ronan had given her, which she couldn't mention, not even to Owen himself. The secret was getting bigger, almost too big for her to contain. But she had to. She'd promised.

She'd already slipped that one time with Aunt Maire. She couldn't slip again.

"What can I say? I got bored." Ella sat down beside her. "So? What's going on?"

"Nothing. Playing with one of my imaginary friends. I have lots of them, remember?" Her heart pounded. It was hard to deceive Ella. Her eyes were sharp. Sometimes it seemed as if she could read Annie's mind.

"Didn't sound so imaginary to me. I could have sworn there was someone else talking. And I thought I saw something in the water."

"I guess you're seeing things too." She smiled. "Because there's no one here but me." And there wasn't, not any longer.

Ella grunted.

"Are you still mad?"

"I wish we could go home." Ella sighed. "That things could be the way they used to be."

"But they aren't. They've changed. Things are always changing."

Ella took Annie's hand, interlacing her fingers, the way she used to do when they were small. "Promise me you won't change, not in the ways that matter."

Another promise she would do her best to keep. "I promise."

Polly was late with the mail that day. Her hair color was less vivid. "At least my hair doesn't look like grape Kool-Aid anymore. My husband has been singing the song from the old commercial every time I walk into the room."

"What's he calling you now?" Nora asked. She sat on the porch with a cup of coffee, mulling over what Maire had told her in the orchard. She still couldn't get her mind around it. Perhaps it was another family myth, a smokescreen for that which no one wanted to confront. She was happy to be distracted by Polly. She always lightened the mood.

"Lavender. Soon I'll be back to Poll, which would be fine with me."

"I'll miss it. The hair."

"Maybe I'll do it again sometime—on Halloween."

"You're later than usual." Polly generally came by late morning. "Did something happen?"

"The radiator overheated," Polly explained. "What a to-do. Had to stay put until Dozer McGettigan lent a hand. Have you met him? We called him that in school, because he always fell asleep during math class. Never did have a head for numbers, that one. But he's good with anything mechanical, including dealing with my recalcitrant vehicles. He put in some Stop Leak, which should do until I can get it into the shop." She turned to address the van directly. "I might have to sell you, if you keep this up, though I doubt anyone would have you."

The van hiccuped dolefully.

"Ah, that's right. All penitent now, aren't we?" She turned to Nora. "Got an important letter for you. Looks official—you have to sign for it. Never happens around here."

The papers, at last? Nora scribbled her signature at the X, an all-too-apt designation, she thought ruefully, wishing she'd set things in motion herself.

"I'll file this"—Polly waved the receipt—"when I get back."

As Malcolm must be filing for divorce. What conditions would he set? She didn't want to be in the same room with him again, facing off across a table, attorneys by their sides. What stories would he spin to cloud the issue, to get the advantage?

Polly's eyes darted from the letter to Nora's face, inquisitive as ever.

Nora didn't open it, not then. She didn't know when she would—that letter, a Pandora's box of legal motions.

"I'm sorry I missed you the other night," Polly said.

"The other night?"

"At Cis McClure's. Alison said you'd been in. Da too. You made quite an impression on him. He's talked of little else since."

"He jigged me around the room."

"He didn't! Lord, that man."

"It was endearing."

"Thank you for putting up with him. Did you have a chance to learn anything?"

"Not as much as I would have liked. I left early."

"I heard the Connellys were making a nuisance of themselves. You didn't let them intimidate you?"

"Dark alleys aren't the best setting for testing one's courage, but no. And Owen showed up, though I had the situation in hand."

"I'm sure you did, though it's nice to have a knight in shining armor about; not many of them in evidence these days. Is there something else on your mind? You seem distracted."

Nora sighed. She shared what Maire had told her about Maeve. "Did you know anything about this?" she asked.

"There are always rumors of one sort or another on the island, though there was certainly an otherworldly quality to Maeve no one could quite explain."

"I'm trying to figure out where that leaves me."

"Right here, on the front step of your cottage. Solid ground—and don't you forget it. We all have our genetics, our myths, don't we? They shape us, inform us, but they aren't the essence of our identity, unless we want them to be. You are your own person. You always have been."

"Thanks, Polly."

"No need to thank me. I'm on your side, Nora. We all are—Alison, Maire, and me. No matter what." She glanced down at her watch. "Jesus, Mary, and Joseph, I'm running late. I'd best push on. Remember what I said, eh?" She hopped in the driver's seat and roared away, the van belching exhaust, leaving Nora to contemplate the letter in her hand.

"What's that?" Ella had apparently been spying from around the side of the house. Her feet were caked with dirt.

"El, I told you to wash off your feet with the hose before coming inside," Nora said. She hadn't been able to bring herself to open the letter, which she'd set before her on the kitchen table.

Ella swiped it before Nora could stop her. "Solomon & Gates," she read. A Boston address, the perfect name for a firm handling divorce cases. One of Malcolm's law school classmates was a partner there.

Nora snatched it back. A corner of the envelope ripped. The triangle of paper fluttered to the floor. "I don't want to get into this right now. The letter is addressed to me, and I'll deal with it when I'm ready."

"It affects me too."

"Yes, but I'm in charge."

"Are you in charge of Dad not being here?"

"That was his choice."

"You've made choices too."

Because there were no viable alternatives. Nora would not be the side-wife. She would not share him. The other woman apparently wouldn't either, Malcolm stringing them both along. The humiliation had been the hardest thing to deal with. Nora didn't know if she could forgive him that—what he'd put her through, continued to put her through. Perhaps he thought it worth the cost; he came out of it with a new love, a second life, or the prospect of one. And she, what did she get?

Ella balled her hands into fists. "All this stuff is happening, and there's nothing I can do about it."

"I know this is hard."

"No, you don't." Her voice cracked with anguish. "You're not me. You don't know how it feels."

"How does it feel?"

"Like everything is falling apart." Her voice dropped a note lower.

Nora reached for her, but she spun away and shut herself in the bedroom. Maybe it was better that way, before they said things they regretted. Her head throbbed from the effort of keeping her temper in check.

Annie tiptoed inside. She'd been playing with the cats on the deck. "When is she going to stop being angry?" She glanced at the bedroom door—she must have heard the slam, the raised voices—with caution.

"She has a right to her feelings." Nora pulled her close, the one daughter who would let herself be embraced. The other, who needed consoling as much if not more, closing herself off.

Annie slipped away, a movement smooth as water. She would not be held this way for long, would not take sides.

She sat across from Nora and toyed with a piece of sea glass. "Can we make something?" She held a piece of glass up to the light. "You can't see through it, not like other glass. It's misty." She turned it over.

But once she found the right angle, it glowed.

Chapter Seventeen

Nora threw the pages across the room. It was night outside, the sky black, cobwebbed with clouds, like a large, unoccupied room. She'd held off until now, while the girls were playing quietly in their room, to slit open the envelope and peruse its contents. All day she'd avoided it as it lay on her bedside table, the compass alongside, needle twitching. *North. North.* The papers fluttered at her, making reasonable arguments, stating the case. The document pertained to a formal separation. Malcolm wanted it his way, to have them in his life according to his terms, no question as to what Nora desired. A personal note inside, written on a piece of memo paper in his scrawling script. "This is a compromise that should suit all of us." No closing, just "Malcolm." For what would he have said:

284 • HEATHER BARBIERI

sincerely, yours truly, best regards? Certainly not *love,* not anymore.

The pages skittered, animate. She sat on the edge of the bed and dug her fingers into the lace spread, into the intricacies of threads that joined, that bound, unraveling now, here and there. She wished she'd filed for the separation herself, rather than going the informal route, that she'd kept control. She thought she had, by coming to the island, giving herself time and space. She wondered how what's-her-name felt about the arrangement. Had he told her the truth, or was he letting her think he'd filed for divorce? It was untenable, this in-between, this matrimonial limbo, these steps he took without consulting her.

The bedroom door opened with a hinged whine. Ella stood on the threshold. "Does he want a divorce?" she asked, looking at the fallen sheets of paper with their cold typed legalese. *The first party, the second*—as if they described a gala Nora and Malcolm might once have attended.

"No."

Ella's eyes shone with tears. Nora's heart broke at the sight of her dear, troubled face.

"Then what are you upset about?" Ella asked.

"Nothing." Nora couldn't tell her that a petition for divorce would almost have been a relief, an absolute. "The wind blew them off the dressing table."

The sea breeze obligingly stirred the curtains.

Nora wouldn't sign the agreement, not right away. She'd decide what she wanted, what was best for the girls, then she would act. Not on cue. Not according to his rules. But her own.

Annie plopped the book of fairy tales on Nora's lap when she came into the room to get the girls settled for the night. "It's time to read."

"Is it?" Nora was beginning to feel they had been written into the pages of the collection, their lives increasingly entwined with the stories depicted within.

"It's dark out. Didn't you see? The darkest dark."

It was. How long had Nora sat there in the bedroom before being summoned by her children? Minutes. Hours. Probably the former, and yet it seemed interminable—time, her very self, suspended.

"Have you been playing statue in your room? Like in freeze tag?" Annie asked.

Nora shook her head, though in a way she supposed she had been.

Annie tapped her arm. "There. I freed you."

If only it were that easy.

"Now we can read, right, El?" Annie turned toward her sister.

"I'm busy." Ella picked up her own book.

"Anti-gone." Annie sounded out the cover.

Nora suppressed a smile. Greek tragedy as laundry detergent. "It's *Antigone*, honey."

"What a weird way to spell it. Why are you reading that, anyway?" Annie asked.

"It can't be a summer reading assignment," Nora said. The title seemed far too demanding, even for the honors program.

"I came up with my own list," Ella informed them. "I'm improving my mind. I have to be ready for fall term."

"That's pretty heavy subject matter," Nora said.

"It has more relevance than you might think." Ella held Nora's gaze for a moment before looking away.

"Come on, El," Nora wheedled. "Tragedy can wait, can't it?"

"I suppose." She made a show of relenting.

And so both girls crawled into Annie's bed, as they had on other nights in Boston, when everything was changing and they didn't want to be alone. They huddled against Nora, snuggling into the blankets like kits in a burrow. She basked in their warmth. There could be moments like these. There could—

Annie turned the pages.

"Which one?" Nora asked.

"El can pick," Annie said.

"All right. This one." Ella chose a story that recalled the *Odyssey*, about a man who'd become lost and struggled to find his way back to his family. " 'Nial woke one morning in the middle of the sea, far from land and everything he knew. He had only one thought: Home. . . .' "

Nora heard the chatter of the girls in the meadow the next morning. She glanced at the clock: 9:30 a.m. She hadn't meant to sleep so late. Still groggy, she pulled on a pair of jeans and a T-shirt and brewed a cup of coffee. The world outside the cottage was a blur of sky and land, all greens and grays, mottled blues and dashes of yellow, the daisies blooming, cheerleaders of the floral world. *Rah-rah-rah.* A bouquet on the table too, which Annie and Ella had picked the previous day, filling the place with a clean, grassy perfume.

She slipped on a pair of flip-flops and filled a watering can at the sink. The window boxes needed watering. The plants were looking peaked, given the recent run of nice weather. She considered the front yard, such as it was, scrub mostly, the meadow grasses encroaching. The beds had been neglected for too long, Maire's influence not having extended to this section of the property. A new scheme took shape in Nora's mind, to be undertaken if they stayed—a mix of perennial grasses and lavender, easy to care for, dancing in the sea breeze. She'd discuss it with Maire. There were so many improvements that could be made, given the proper time and incentive.

Her gaze swept toward the drive, and the SUV parked there. The Cunningham family car. She stopped, mid-stride. There was a word scrawled on the windshield. It must have happened during the night. She drew closer, eyes darting to the tree line, to the road. Sometimes she thought she saw Maggie Scanlon watching the house, but she knew she was only imagining things. Maggie was ill, after all, the cottage too far from the village for her to reach in her present condition—though she'd gotten as far as the berry field. . . . Nora drew closer. She couldn't make out the word at first. She had to shade her hand against the sun's glare for the meaning to become clear: *Bitch*.

She felt as if the word had flown through the air and punched her in the stomach. Heart pounding, she fumbled for the chamois cloth in the glove box and set to work wiping the letters away. The girls mustn't see.

Sensing movement in the copse, she froze. She was reminded, yet again, of how isolated they were on that part of the island. A golf umbrella lying on the back seat was the only weapon handy.

The figure advanced with purpose, against the wind, along the path, exiting the woods. She felt an overwhelming sense of relief when she realized it was Owen. His hair had grown shaggier over the past few weeks, grazing his collar (one of her cousin's shirts, a dark green plaid), hanging in his eyes, yet his gaze was still piercing. He was carrying a creel.

"Washing the car, eh?" he said, setting the basket down.

"Sort of." She couldn't stop her hands from shaking.

"What's wrong?" He touched her cheek, then glanced at the cottage windows and took his hand away.

"Some island vandalism." She gestured at the windshield.

A faint outline of the word was still visible on the glass. "When did this happen?" he asked.

"It must have been last night or early this morning."

"You didn't hear anything?" He took the cloth from her and scrubbed the remaining residue away.

"Not a sound."

He thought for a moment. "When I was talking to Maire this morning, she mentioned that Maggie Scanlon drove her son's truck into the ditch about a mile north of here last night. It's within the realm of possibility that she might have been returning from paying you a visit."

That woman. Was there no end to her obsession? "Is she all right?"

"Bumps and bruises, apparently."

"I didn't know she was still driving."

"Her son reported the truck stolen. He didn't realize she was the one who took it until they found her. Are you going to call the authorities?"

She shook her head. "We erased the evidence, and besides, I'm not sure that's the right thing to do. There's something that's driving her, that hasn't been resolved. Something that she's fixated on. If I can find out what that is, maybe that will put an end to it."

"Whatever you think," he said, clearly unconvinced. "I almost forgot. I brought you this." He flipped open the lid of the basket revealing a catch of rockfish. "I was in the north end this week."

"I was wondering what to make for dinner," she replied, then, "You've been away a lot lately. I was beginning to think you might have left the island."

"I'm not like him," he said. "I wouldn't leave without saying good-bye."

Nora heard the voices of the girls behind them, louder now, as they attempted to extricate the kite from the tree. Ella wouldn't give up. She didn't want another kite, though Nora had offered to buy one at Scanlon's. Only this one would do. Her father's kite, an emblem of all that was broken, all that might be mended.

"What are you talking about?" Annie cantered up to them.

"That's a fine gallop," Owen said, evading the question.

"I'm an Arabian horse. I thought if I stood on my hind legs, I could get the kite, but it's not working."

"Of course it's not working," Ella called. "The kite's too high, and you're not a horse. Though if you were, I'd hitch you to a carriage and make you drive me into town."

"I'd kick you and run away," Annie said. She turned to Owen. "Can you get it down?"

"You don't have to," Nora interjected.

"Let's have a look." He set the basket down at Nora's feet, the fish staring up at her mutely. She felt a current run through her as he touched the small of her back and set off toward the tree.

"We don't want your help," Ella told him.

"Do you want it down or not?" he asked.

She fell silent, her gaze alternating between him and the kite that continued to dangle out of reach. "Maybe," she admitted.

The tree stood before them, its splintered branches reaching toward the ocean, bark rough as hide. The kite remained lodged in the crown, an effigy. Its wings rattled in the breeze, bits of red paper scattered on the ground, confettied by marauding crows and heavy winds.

Owen circled the base, studying the network of needled boughs, gauging distances.

"We don't have a ladder," Nora said, thinking that would put an end to it.

"Wouldn't reach high enough anyway," he replied.

To her surprise, he began to climb, moving higher, until he was lost in the upper boughs, a shaking among the branches the only indication of his presence.

"He's going to fall," Ella said, anticipation in her voice.

"No, he's not," Nora said, with more vehemence than she intended. "He's doing this for you, you know."

"Is he?" She gave her mother a probing look.

The kite nosedived into a hedge of broom, yellow petals exploding, then luffed in the wind, as if drawing its last breaths.

"Oh, no!" Annie cried.

One of the wings had split in two—recent or old damage, it was hard to say. Ella, however, had reached her own conclusions. "You broke it," she said, when he came down, hands sticky with pitch.

A cloud moved across the sun, and a shadow fell over the meadow and those who faced each other there.

"It was already like that," Annie pointed out.

"No, it wasn't," Ella said.

"We can get another," Owen offered.

"I want the old one," Ella said. "I want the old everything."

"At least Owen got it down. That was what you wanted," Nora said, which Ella clearly took as a criticism of her father, her face darkening. "Stop being rude and say thank you."

"That's your department," Ella said.

"What is?"

"Expressing gratitude."

Nora felt her face grow hot. "If you mean being polite, that would be true. I expect the same of you."

"Oh, sure. Be polite. Look where that's gotten us. Everyone else seems to say whatever they want," she said. "Even stupid people on the Internet who don't know us." She grabbed the kite and retreated to a rock a short distance away, where she sat and glared at them.

"Sorry about that," Nora said to Owen.

"Don't take it personally. She's mean to everybody," Annie added. "We're waiting for her to outgrow it."

"No worries. I'd be mad too, if it were mine." His kite, his young life.

"Where have you been, anyway?" Annie asked. "You haven't been around in a few days."

"I had business at sea."

Annie opened her mouth to ask him something else, then changed her mind. "It's so magical deep, the sea," she said instead.

Ella cradled the kite in her arms. She cast a baleful eye on the basket. "We're not having fish for dinner again, are we? They smell. I won't eat them."

"All the more for the rest of us then," Nora said.

"All we ever eat is fish. Fish, fish, fish."

"Ella Grace Cunningham."

"How about if you help me gather some mussels?" Owen asked Annie.

"You already have them," Annie said.

"I meant shellfish." He smiled. "Your cove has the best, if your mother doesn't mind sharing."

"Not at all," Nora said.

Annie took off at a run, Owen close behind. Nora wished she could have accompanied them, but she had Ella to deal with.

Ella shook her head at Annie's retreating back. "You should."

"Should what?"

"Mind."

"It's none of your business what I do, young lady."

"Because you're older and wiser? Are you really? Because sometimes you don't seem that wise to me."

Tears came to Nora's eyes. "We're doing the best we can. Me. Your dad." She'd give him that, even if she didn't always believe it, for Ella's sake.

"I thought you hated him. You hate him, don't you? Just say it. Say it!" She threw down the kite and stomped on it.

Nora pulled her to her chest. That bird-thin body thrashing in her arms, as the kite had done, caught in the tree.

"Let me go!" Ella cried. Her elbow hit Nora in the cheekbone.

She felt a sharp pain. "Go ahead," Nora said softly. "Let it out."

They fell into the grass and lay there, unmoving, hearts beating fast. Their eyes met, and for a moment, Nora thought Ella would let herself be held, that they could cry together at last.

But it wasn't to be, not that day. Ella scrambled to her feet and ran.

"El!"

She didn't stop, heels pounding, feet flying, away, away.

Nora cast one last glance in the direction her daughter had gone, into the copse. Much as she wanted to, she would not follow. She would let her come home when she was ready.

Chapter Eighteen

Maire caught the end of the drama. She'd been heading over to pay a visit when she heard the raised voices. She'd often wondered how it would have been to have daughters of her own. While she would have liked to think her relationship with Jamie had been perfect—grief did that sometimes, allowing people to view their relatives as angels on earth, when nothing could have been further from the truth—she had to admit it hadn't been. There had been struggles. The drugs. The lost jobs. And her too, compounding the problems, not forcing the issue early, when they could have gotten him into treatment. That was why he'd been living at home, rather than on his own, as he should have been at that age. Working for his father, because he was the only person who would hire him.

They'd fought that night, the last time she'd seen him before he and Joe shipped out. The beginning of lobster season.

"It was only beer," Jamie had said.

"That's all it takes."

"I know what I'm doing. It's my life."

"Is it? Is that why you're still here?"

"Do you want me gone?"

"That's not what I meant—"

She didn't shout. She rarely shouted. She didn't like confrontation, kept everything in. Maybe that was why she'd had headaches, terrible ones, bits of light all around her like falling stars, ever since she was a girl.

That gray morning when her boys pulled away from the dock, Jamie had his shoulders hunched against her, his resentment palpable, she and Joe exchanging well-practiced looks of blame. Yes, blame, because she'd expected too much, and he too little.

She'd never told anyone this. She'd pretended everything was fine. What good would it have done to say otherwise? She said Joe needed the assistance. That he shouldn't go out on his own, not at his age, with his heart. Which was true. But it was more complicated than that, as things often were. Jamie the helpful son, yes, but needy too.

How might her life have been different, if she had been different? Another man. Another fate. Another child. Another chance.

No one knew this about her. She concealed it beneath a placid face, seemingly content, accepting. The face that reassured expectant mothers, helped bring babies into the world. The face that encouraged her niece. That deceived. Oh, yes, she had deceived too.

She hadn't told Nora everything. Hadn't told her about the last time she'd seen Maeve. Maire had come to the door of the cabin. Maeve was in a state that day, her hair a sooty cloud, her eyes wild.

"What's wrong? Were you fighting?" Maire asked. The arguments between Maeve and Patrick had been escalating lately. Patrick had a job offer in Boston. He hadn't sought it, but Maeve thought he had, going behind her back. Sometimes Maire and her parents could hear them at Cliff House, exchanging glances over the dinner table, saying nothing, her mother getting up to close the sash.

"You'd like that, wouldn't you?"

Maire's heart pounded. There was a part of her that did, that wondered what it would take for Patrick to leave her sister. "What are you talking about?"

"You know, coming over here all the time—"

"You're my sister. I just want to help."

"Do you. Do you really? Or are you looking for spoils?"

"I don't know what you're talking about."

"Yes, you do. It's obvious to everyone."

"What is?"

"That you want him. That you always have."

"That's not true!"

"I'm tired of you mooning after him. He's my husband. Mine!" Maeve gave her a shove.

Maire pushed her back. "If he's yours, what are you so worried about?"

"I'm not worried. You're no competition to me. You never have been. I'm just sick of dealing with your envy. Find yourself your own man, why don't you? Oh, that's right. You can't."

"Damn you, Maeve. Damn you to hell."

Young Nora in the background, crying at the sound of the raised voices.

Maire turned and fled. She'd done it. She'd cursed her only sister. She wasn't sorry for it, not then, not until Maeve disappeared, and Maire realized the power words could have.

The present. She was in the present. The here and now, though it too had changed. A gull landed in the center of the road. It stared at Maire with a beady eye, a snap of the beak, then away it flew in a frenzied blur of white, bleeding into the clouds. White flashes, everywhere, exploding over the house, the trees.

What's wrong with my eyes?

She couldn't see—

A searing pain in her head.

The meadow tilted. The trees growing out of the sky, their roots in the clouds, dirt raining down, burying her. The smell of earth, filling her lungs. She couldn't move. She could only watch the world spin, grass blades whirring, clouds tearing apart along fraying seams.

"Nora!" she cried, as she had, all those years ago, searching, searching.

Now she was the one who needed to be found.

Footsteps? Blood rushing. A tide—

"Aunt Maire. Maire, can you hear me?"

Nora's face, above her, looking down. Her mouth a gash. Skin white. Everything white—

"My head hurts. I can't seem to . . ." she murmured. She couldn't move. Why couldn't she move? Frozen. The white—

"I'll get help—"

"Hold my hand. Hold—" As Maire had said to the women giving birth. As she had said to Maeve when she was about to deliver.

This daughter. Nora. Nora must be the one to break the pattern, to restore what was lost. If only there had been more time . . .

"Maire."

A roar in her ears. The sea. Her blood. One and the same.

Beginnings and endings. How simple it was. Clear as water, cupped in the hand.

Polly screeched into the driveway at the sound of the shouting, the van heaving, mail spilling across the seat. Nora saw her out of the corner of her eye as she ran into the house to call for help, the girls with her, sobbing. Owen in the grass, holding Maire's hand. *It's going to be all right.* But it wasn't, it wasn't.

The doctor? Out fishing that day. Maire, his backup. Maire, who could fix anything, anyone, but herself. By the time the helicopter arrived from the mainland, she was gone. How could she be there one moment, seemingly fine? How could she? It didn't make sense. None of it made sense.

The days passed in a haze of disbelief. Nora could barely concentrate, but arrangements had to be made. The director of the small funeral home, Mr. Dunn of Dunn & Sons, did his best to be helpful, leading her through the process. She'd been through this before with her father, the dizzying array of choices in stone, lettering, sentiments, style. This time, there wasn't as much to do. Maire had everything in place, as if she knew what was coming, a space ready next to her husband, Joe, the island granite awaiting the inscription on its right side: "Maire Katherine Flaherty. September 30, 1951–August 15, 2012." Polly took time off work, watching the girls while Nora did what needed to be done. Thankfully, she wasn't gone long. She didn't like to leave them, particularly now, but she thought it best not to bring them along. She could hardly focus on the road as she drove back to the cottage after the appointment. Her head ached behind her eyes with the pressure of unshed tears. They came upon her suddenly, in the shower, especially, the grief welling up in racking sobs.

"I don't understand it," Polly said quietly when Nora returned to the cottage, the girls on the deck, dangling pieces of string for the cats to play with. "She did all the right things. She never even dyed her hair or used nail polish or wore makeup. She ate organic from the very beginning. She exercised. She had friends. She went to church. Everything a person is supposed to do to stay healthy and live a full life."

Nora squeezed her hand. They'd been over this before. They couldn't stop talking about it, couldn't believe it had happened. "How are they doing?" She gestured toward the girls.

"Well enough. I don't think it's really sunk in yet. It hasn't for any of us, has it? I opened up the windows of Maire's bedroom, to let her soul go free. I hope that's all right. It's an island custom. I'll close them again before I go, so the damp doesn't get in during the night."

Nora nodded.

Polly gave her a hug. "We'll get through this. We'll get through it together."

Owen tapped at the living room window after the girls had gone to bed. Nora had waited up in front of the dying fire, unable to sleep, hoping he'd come. She brought blankets out to the deck and they sat there together, under the stars. The night was clear and still. It was hardly ever still like that. It was as if everything were suspended, as if the very universe had paused to mourn, only the sound of the waves breaking the silence.

"I was just getting to know her," Nora said. "I meant to go over there that morning. I should have. I shouldn't have waited. Maybe I could have gotten help sooner if I had—"

"You couldn't have known what was going to happen."

"I wish I'd told her how I felt. She was like a second mother to me. I never said— I was so caught up in my own problems."

"There was no way you could have sensed what was going on. She never said anything about her symptoms, other than the dizzy spells, and only then, because they were noticeable to the rest of us. She lived more for others than herself. That was how she was."

"Do you think she knew something was wrong?"

He sighed. "Maybe. It's hard to say."

"There were all those notes on the refrigerator. Reminders everywhere. I thought she was being ultra-organized, but—"

"None of that matters anymore, Nora. All I know is that she was happy having you here. She told me these were some of the best days of her life. That's what we should try to focus on, not the things that can't be changed." Words to comfort them both. She knew he missed her too.

Would he leave, now that Maire was gone? She rested her head against his shoulder. She couldn't bear any additional losses, not now. "Life is fragile, isn't it?"

"Yes," he said. "It is."

She stayed with him until the night grew colder and the present reasserted itself, until it was time to go inside, alone, closing the door softly behind her.

Ella woke up screaming.

Nora jerked awake. She'd dozed off, the bedside lamp still burning, her book splayed open beside her where she'd left off reading. She threw back the covers and hurried into the room to find Ella cowering under the bedcovers, nearly hysterical, Annie awake too, but calm.

"I saw her." Ella pointed to the window, the curtain rippling in the breeze, a hole in the fabric letting in the night.

"Saw who, honey?" Nora put her arms around her. Ella couldn't seem to stop trembling. Nora had never seen her like this before.

"Aunt Maire. I heard Mrs. Clennon say she'd left the windows open at Cliff House so that she could get out, and she got out, didn't she? She's there, like the other ghosts, trying to get in."

"She was making sure we're all right," Annie said, as if it were the most reasonable thing in the world. "You don't have to be afraid."

"You didn't see her. She was gone by the time you woke up."

"Maybe you weren't really awake. Maybe you were having a bad dream. Aunt Maire would never hurt us, ghost or not."

306 · HEATHER BARBIERI

"You didn't see. Your eyes were closed."

"How do you know? It was dark. The only reason you could see Aunt Maire was because her skin was so white."

Ella shuddered. "Stop saying things like that."

"Well, it was," Annie insisted. "That's what happens when you're dead, doesn't it? Being dead isn't the end. It's another beginning."

"That's enough, sweetie," Nora told her.

"I'm trying to help."

"Well, you're not, are you?" Ella glared at her. "You're making it worse." She turned to Nora. "Can I sleep with you tonight, Mom?"

"Me too," Annie chimed in.

"Of course you can." Nora brought them into her room, an arm around each slender shoulder.

"She was there," Ella murmured, still shaky. "Why was she there?"

Nora kissed the top of her head. "Sometimes dreams can seem real." Her own certainly did.

"I told you. It wasn't a dream."

Nora searched for the right thing to say. "We all have a life force in us, don't we?" she said finally. "Maybe that energy radiates outward after we die, touching those we love."

"Aunt Maire loved us?"

"Oh, yes. Very much."

In the days to come, they would see Maire in the jay perched on the post, in the bees gathering nectar from the wildflowers, heads bowed in the wind, as if in grief. They would see her everywhere.

"I don't want you to die, Mama." Annie nestled closer, the bedding in drifts around them.

"I'm right here," Nora said. She couldn't promise more than that. "I'm right here."

The day of the funeral arrived, clear and blue. The little church was filled with people wearing Maire's favorite color. It had been Annie's idea. "She wouldn't want everyone wearing black, would she?" Annie said. "Black is a sad color."

"Black isn't a color," Ella said. "It's the absence of light."

"Yes, blue," Nora said. "It's what she would have wanted."

And so they wore it, every shade, like the flowers, the sea, the sky. Blue as far as the eye could see, surrounding them. Blue on which Maire could sail into the great beyond, into whatever came next.

Nora and the girls sat in the front pew, Polly alongside, Owen standing at the back, near the entrance. Reilly Neale was there, wiping his eyes with a handkerchief,

Polly's father, Gerry, beside him. A Scanlon or two in attendance. Alison, of course. Maggie there too, her eyes fierce. *You,* she mouthed the word, or so Nora thought. She couldn't be sure. She turned away, her heart beating fast. She couldn't take another confrontation, not this day, of all days. She hoped Alison's father would take Maggie home directly after the service. Alison had said he would.

Nora kept her gaze toward the front of the church, the smell of incense heavy in the air. The sad-eyed saints—she supposed that could have been the name of a band or a team, and tears came to her eyes, because it was the sort of thought she might have shared with Maire—bearing witness to another passing. Father Ray saying the mass. Such a lovely voice he had, singing Maire to heaven, or wherever it was she had gone. Out there.

They took communion. They blessed themselves. Each other. Maire. Her spirit. Remembered all that was good in her.

Polly got up to speak. Polly, who knew Maire best.

"How do you talk about your dearest friend? How do you talk about someone who has been there through everything? Who has known you best in the world? Who loves you, no matter what?"

Her voice shook, then she composed herself.

"There are so many stories I could tell. Yes, Da, I see you smiling over there. You knew the trouble we could get into. But I'll keep it simple. I'll start at the very beginning, when we first saw each other. I was five years old, Maire six. So long ago. And yet in some ways, it seems like yesterday. Time is like that, isn't it? The best friendships too. Maire is one of my first memories. I use the present tense, because memory is something that never leaves us. Memories are something we can hold on to, when other things are gone.

"I first met her at dance class. I couldn't get one of the steps. The teacher gave up on me in frustration. Can't say I blamed her. I've never been known for my grace. I started to cry. Some of the girls jeered at me. But Maire told them to stop and took my hand. 'Don't listen to them,' she said. 'I'll show you what to do.' She stayed after class and worked with me the rest of the afternoon until I got it right.

"Family and friends were everything to her. This island, the sea, were everything to her. She brought out the best in us, didn't she? Our babies, our very selves . . ."

Nora's attention drifted. Nothing seemed real, except the weight of the girls against her, their heads resting against her shoulders.

"Can we go?" Ella asked, tugging at her sleeve, as she had as a small child. "I want to go."

"I know." Nora stroked her hair. "It's almost over."

The service, yes, but not everything that would come after.

They headed up the aisle, past those who whispered about her being in it for the land, thanks to the Connellys or their source, she supposed; others who said she looked like Maire and Maeve, meeting her eyes with sympathy, pressing her hand. And Malcolm in the last row, rising to meet her in his black suit, perfectly fitted, as if he were going to trial. The sight of him brought her up short. She caught Owen's eye. His face still as he took in the scene, his eyes locking on Malcolm before he abruptly turned and left the church.

Malcolm stepped in front of her before she could catch up to Owen.

"What are you doing here?" she asked. When had he slipped in? He was always slipping in and out of her life. And now, of all times.

"I heard—"

She didn't have to ask how. Ella. "You shouldn't have come. This is a family matter."

"Yes, he should. He should be here, with us," Ella said. She didn't seem surprised to see him.

"I am family," he reminded Nora.

No, she thought. The island was her place, with her people, not his.

"I still care. How can you think I wouldn't care?" he asked.

She didn't answer him. Couldn't answer him. She sensed eyes on her, curious. About her. About him. She, who seemed to have a habit of creating drama wherever she went, so like her mother.

I don't want you to care! And yet there was a part of her that did. That part that was still tied to him, that couldn't let go.

They filed outside, where a small group of mourners gathered. The graveside ceremony passed in a blur. The shovel chinked as it struck the soil, the grit murmuring as it tumbled onto the coffin. The white birch trees showered leaves into the burial site, as if to make their own offerings. Father Ray recited the words, his eyes shining. The sea rumbled in the distance. That was where Maire should have been, on a boat set adrift on the current. Not there, among the bodiless graves of her family—her sister, her husband and son, never found. Memorials only. She wasn't there anymore anyway. None of them were, their spirits flown.

Nora crossed herself, bowed her head. There was some solace in prayer. Some small solace.

Polly took the girls by the hand and walked them toward the gathering in the parish hall. "Time for some cake."

"Would Aunt Maire want us to have cake?" Annie asked.

"Yes, definitely, especially if it's chocolate."

Malcolm took Nora by the elbow as they left the graveyard. "Take a few days," he said.

"How magnanimous you are this morning," she replied, shrugging him off.

"I only meant, there's no hurry about the papers."

"You're bringing that up now? Leave it to you to make everything sound like a deliberation, circumstances be damned."

"That's a gross generalization. All I'm saying is that when this is over, I hope you'll consider coming home."

"To what?"

His voice caught. "Boston. I didn't mean—"

Hedging as usual. "Of course you didn't. And even if you had, I wouldn't have agreed. I can't believe you're making this about you."

"I still love you. It's possible to love more than one person at a time. Just because we're separated doesn't mean I don't care about you."

"No, you just get to pick and choose how you do."

They fell silent, markers of the dead all around them. Something between them dying too.

Malcolm strode off in the direction of his car, parked outside the gate. She heard the beep of the alarm, and a muttered oath as he noticed something amiss—a fresh scratch on the finish, perhaps. He was particular about such things. She didn't bother to investigate. Whatever it was, it was his problem. He slammed the door, revved the engine, and drove off, taking the corner too fast. The curl of dust in his wake soon dissipated to nothing.

The murmur of voices flowed toward her from the parish hall. Voices speaking of Maire, of memories, of grief. Mourners in their Sunday best. She took a deep breath. It was time to go in.

"How are you holding up?" Alison came up to her right away, casting a glance outside. "Is he gone?"

Nora made sure the girls were out of earshot before answering. "Yes."

"What was he doing here?"

"Making his case."

"For what?"

"For being in our life. My life. He wants to be supportive, at least when it suits him."

"How big of him."

"He's not a terrible person, but he's not necessarily the right person for me anymore."

"It sounds like you're reaching a decision."

She took a deep breath. "I'm getting there. Everything's so jumbled right now. I'm still in a state of shock."

"I know. I keep thinking Maire is going to walk through that door and tell us to stop crying."

"Yes, she'd want us to laugh, wouldn't she? Or at least do something productive."

"And dance. Before Joe died, she was quite the dancer. Did she ever show you her trophies?"

Nora shook her head. She must have kept them in a cabinet. She suspected there was much Maire hadn't told her. They'd been making up for lost time, until time became lost itself.

"It happened so fast. I don't understand," Alison said.

Nora motioned her to a secluded table near a window that looked out on the churchyard. Two crows perched on the adjacent stones like scruffy undertakers, and swallows spiraled upward, breaking into song, another ascension, then gone. There, across from a still life of an abandoned teacup and crumpled napkins, Nora shared what Dr. Keane had told her. That there wouldn't have been anything they could have done. The dizzy spells, Maire's memory less sharp than it once was; she who never forgot a name or a face, making countless lists, not only for organization but to help her remember. Nora hadn't realized these were symptoms of something greater, symptoms that must have spurred her to contact Nora in the first place, because there wasn't much time left, to bestow the legacy, to share what she knew of the past. Her condition, cerebral amyloidosis—a series of protein buildups in the brain that triggered memory loss, increasingly debilitating strokes, and eventual death—had no means of prevention, no treatment, only an inexorable decline.

"She would never have wanted to live like that," Nora said.

"No one would."

"So it was for the best."

"A blessing."

Though it didn't seem like a blessing, not to those who were left.

They went home to the cottage and shed their funeral clothes. Nora, the pencil skirt and blouse she'd brought along in case there was an occasion to dress up, never expecting this; the blue scarf they'd found among Maire's things; the heels that pinched her toes after hours of standing. Everything zipped, buttoned, the clothes, her emotions, as she focused on others, the girls, Maire's friends, looking after everyone, as Maire would have done.

Now, she felt herself becoming undone. She had to get out of the house. Everything was pressing on her. The strap of a bathing suit dangled from the dresser drawer; she'd pawed through the contents earlier that day, searching for the right lingerie. She hadn't worn the suit yet, as she had the rest, because it had been one of Malcolm's favorites and less practical for serious swimming. But the others were still damp, hanging on the line outside, and so she put it on.

"Where are you going?" Ella asked as Nora passed through the room.

"To the beach, for a swim."

They didn't ask if they could come along. They were absorbed in a game of concentration, the cards arranged in a neat rectangle.

Nora grabbed a fresh towel and headed toward the bluff. She hesitated—should she see if Owen was home?—but she didn't have the energy for an argument, feeling forced to explain Malcolm's presence yet again. She needed to feel the ocean surrounding her, supporting her. Never mind that the clouds were sullen, threatening thunder, the blue that graced the funeral gone, the air humid and close.

The path was imprinted with her daughters' footsteps, a record of their movements to and from Glass Beach, Nora's too, soon to include this latest, solitary journey. She wouldn't put a toe in the water first. It would be all or nothing. She stood on the diving rock, the one from which Malcolm had made a rather spectacular somersault during his initial stay, the girls his adoring audience. She raised her arms overhead, held her breath, and plunged; no time for second thoughts.

As she knifed into the water, the cold took her breath away, enveloping her. And it was there, at the point of impact, that she cried out with every ounce of her being, the fish darting away from the roaring creature in their midst, a rush of bubbles rising, until she broke the surface, dripping with seawater, with tears and rivulets. She rolled over on her back, floating in the current, gazing up at the leaden sky. A drop of rain fell, another, and then the sky broke open. The torrent drove her up the beach with its stinging fury, along the muddied path, until she reached the doorway, where she leaned against the frame, listening to the sounds of her daughters within, remembering, matching, the perfect pairs. Deep breaths now. Slow, easy. There was air. Shells on the deck. Pieces of sea glass. A bird feather. The lost and found. She would collect herself. And then she could go in.

Chapter Nineteen

Nora and the girls checked the bees. The gaillardia and helianthus had come into bloom, exuberant yellows and reds, the other flowers in the garden fading, past their prime. The orchard fruit continued to ripen, green giving way to purple and scarlet. The plums would be ready soon. The garden flourished, even if its gardener was no longer there to tend it. They would have to do the best they could, in her stead.

"Do they know she's gone?" Annie asked, nodding toward the bees. The girls were fascinated by the insects' movements. They knew how to move among them with calm assurance. Maire had trained them well.

Ella blew smoke into a hive, the guard bees zooming outward to investigate before being lulled into a drowsy complacency. The girls had given each box a name, as if they were kingdoms: Floris, Narnia, and Petalline.

"I'm not sure," Nora said. Maire said bees had been known to flee after their keeper had passed away. She hoped these would stay.

"Maybe they'll leave too," Ella said. "They're hers, you know, not ours."

"Now they belong to us," Nora said. "It all does." The cottage, the point, Cliff House.

"A summer place of our own," Annie said.

Or perhaps something more. Nora could choose to stay, to build a life on the island. There was so much to sort out. She took a deep breath. She must maintain focus, like the bees, intent on their purpose. They thrummed from flower to flower, pouches brimming with yellow pollen, industrious, subdued. Nora and the girls would gather the honey if they stayed into September, or returned for a long weekend. She didn't know what the future would bring. What place the island would have in their lives.

They moved on to the next task, picking green beans and armfuls of sunflowers for bouquets, the basket—one of those Maire used to carry, the handle worn from the constant, sure guidance of her gloved hands—overflowing with a bounty Maire would never see.

From the dock below came the tapping of the hammer, the clanging of rigging. Day and night, Owen worked, unceasing. Nora hadn't seen him since after the funeral, neither of them willing to make the first move.

"I'm getting hungry," Annie said as she lugged a basket of tomatoes to the porch.

"Why don't you two head to the cottage and make some sandwiches for lunch? I'll be there in a minute. El, you can supervise."

"What kind?"

"Whatever you want."

She watched them disappearing into the woods, their movements nimble as fawns, then took the path to the overlook. If he wouldn't come to her, she would go to him. There Owen was on the deck, putting on a last coat of varnish, his work nearly done. Maire had left him the boat, as she'd intended.

She called out a greeting.

He squinted against the light, and perhaps against her too. "I'm not in a mood for games."

His tone took her aback, and she found herself bristling. "I had no intention of asking you to play."

"That's right. You already have a fourth."

"I'm not following you."

He picked up a hammer and began to pound at a loose nail, speaking between blows. "I saw him at the funeral."

"I know. You left before I could explain."

"You don't have to explain anything."

"I didn't invite him."

"So you keep saying, and yet he keeps showing up, doesn't he?"

"He's gone, not that it's any of your business."

"I never said it was." He went into the pilot's house and closed the door. She could see his outline, moving around the interior, behind the glass.

She would not go down there. She would not pursue it, pursue him. She didn't need this right now. She was done with all that. Done.

Nora's mood worsened when she returned to the cottage and saw that Ella had left the dirty cups and plates on the table. It was her turn to do the dishes. "Do you expect the dishes to wash themselves?" she asked.

"What's wrong with you?"

"Nothing. I'm tired of the mess."

"Some vacation. Otherwise known as prison camp."

"I'll have to arrange a comprehensive work detail for you, to make it more authentic."

"Ha-ha," Ella said. "Can we go into town today? I want to see Dad."

Nora looked up at the ceiling. *Give me strength.*

"You said something at the funeral to make him leave again, didn't you, after he'd come all that way to be with us?"

"In case you hadn't noticed, he does what he wants," Nora said. "And don't you dare call him again. I'm tired of you calling him without permission."

"Why do I need permission to talk to my own father?" Ella took the cell phone off the counter and stared at Nora, defiant.

"Put that down."

She bolted from the cottage, toward the bluffs, Nora in pursuit. "I'm calling him. I'm calling him right now," Ella shouted. "And there's nothing you can do about it." She veered toward the promontory, poised on the precipice, as if she might hurl herself off it to spite Nora.

"Get back from there," Nora said.

"No." Ella was stabbing the keys. "I'm telling him—"

"What? What are you going to tell him?"

There was nothing Ella could say that would force Malcolm to do what she wanted; didn't she understand that by now? Nora grabbed her by the elbow with one hand and disarmed her of the cell with the other. She threw the phone down onto the rocks. There was a jarring crunch as its casing shattered.

"What the hell, Mom?"

"It's my phone," Nora snapped back. "I decided we don't need it anymore. It's more trouble than it's worth."

"You're more trouble than you're worth. I hate you!" She turned and ran back to the cottage.

Nora didn't have the energy to go after her. She slumped against a rock as the door slammed in the distance. "I don't blame you, honey," she said softly. "I don't blame you at all."

They met Polly and Alison at Cliff House later that afternoon. Everything was as Maire left it, the possessions, the mementos of a life, without the one person to whom they meant the most. Nora fingered a picture on the mantel. She hadn't taken any photos with Maire. A deep ache lodged in the same place that contained the other losses, an ache that wouldn't completely subside. There was no balm for it, not even time. It didn't heal all wounds. It just made them more bearable.

"One thing at a time," Polly said as she brewed tea, perhaps sensing Nora's mood.

"It seems odd to sit here without her," Nora said.

"It seems odd to do everything without her. Molly Creehan will be having her baby on the mainland now. She's due in a month."

"She was in the shop the other day," Alison said. "She was beside herself."

"She touched so many lives, did our Maire."

"She's not really gone," Annie said as she drank cranberry juice from a teacup.

"What do you mean?" Polly asked.

"I see her sometimes. She's there, watching. It's like she wants to say something, but she can't."

"I do too," Polly said quietly. "Funny, isn't it? Perhaps the line between the living and the dead isn't as clear as we think."

"Stop talking about it," Ella said to Annie. "I told you not to talk about it."

"El." Nora frowned. "Please."

Alison put on a pair of rubber gloves and picked up a sponge. "So, where did you want to start?"

"I suppose with the fridge." Nora saw Maire's lists in a different light now. The details of names and birth dates, addresses, things to do, written in Maire's even, flowing script, her voice reflected in the phrasing. There would be no more notes. No more appointments to be kept. Had the stories she'd told Nora about Maeve been part of her confusion too? It was difficult to know what to believe. "I'm afraid some of the food might be going bad."

"Not the honey. It won't start sugaring for at least a year," Polly said.

It was hard to imagine life a year from then. So much had changed in the past few weeks.

"Will you be staying on?" Alison asked.

"No," Ella said, adamant.

Nora shook her head gently. They could talk about it later.

"There are always the summers," Polly said.

Yes, the summers, past and present. A wind chime sounded on the deck, a fragment of melody, a half-completed thought, ringing in the air, dissipating.

Nora looked around the room. "Let's deal with the cleaning to start out with. Otherwise, we'll leave it as it is for now. There's no hurry."

"No, of course there isn't," Polly agreed.

Because no one lived there anymore.

Ella ducked outside, the others seemingly unaware. She marched past the fountains of switchgrass and the arthritic pine, past the lark's nest and the snarl of dinghy nets and floats, those hollow plastic globes that were supposed to keep things afloat, cracked at the seams, worthless. She glanced behind her. Annie hadn't followed, for once. Annie, who always followed, a little sister, a little conscience. Ella didn't need her now. She would only complicate things. She couldn't be relied upon to play her part, do what had to be done.

The fishing shack was as ramshackle as ever, not meant for full-time living, only for storing tackle and lines. Who could live in such a place? Who would want to? A curl of smoke rose from the chimney in a question mark, as if asking what she was doing there. She told herself she didn't believe in fairy tales, in magic, and yet there was an eerie atmosphere that made her shiver. She squared her shoulders. This was no time for doubts.

She rapped on the door. No answer. Maybe he'd stepped out. He hadn't been at the dock. She nearly lost her nerve, ran back the way she'd come, when the door opened, as if of its own accord, and he appeared, this man who had paid too much attention to her mother, and she knew what she must do.

"We're going home," she said.

"Your mother—" His eyes swept over the field behind her, as if for some sign of Nora.

"She sent me to tell you. She said it's easier this way. That you'd understand." Her delivery was flawless. Her father would be proud. Perhaps she'd take acting lessons in Boston that fall. "You understand, don't you?" She made her eyes sad, so that he would know that, in the end, she sympathized with him.

"Yes."

She knew he wouldn't inquire further. That he didn't dare. She felt a thrill of triumph when she saw the regret in his eyes. Triumph, and a flicker of doubt too, though she didn't let it show. The pleasure of hurting him wasn't as satisfying as she thought it would be. Though hurting him was beside the point. The point was to get home, to her father.

They would return to Boston.

And Owen would go back to wherever he was from.

Nora went through boxes in the attic. Annie was studying the charts. "The marks have moved," she said. "More seals are on Little Burke."

"I think those marks were already there, honey," Nora said. "The map is mildewed. We might have to get rid of it."

"No!" Annie said. "We have to keep it. No matter how old it gets. . . . Aunt Maire said the magic is everywhere, within us too. All we have to do is find it."

"She did, did she?" Her confused mind, braiding together their past with myths, true or invented. Would they ever know which was which?

So many family heirlooms, carefully preserved. Maire, the conservator. What else had she kept? Hidden? Things of Maeve's too? There were porcelain dolls from the sisters' childhood. Pull toys. A top. "Look, it spins," Annie said. "Like the compass. Is the compass broken? It spins at weird times."

"I don't know," Nora said. Its erratic movements had unnerved her to the point that she'd stuck it in the nightstand drawer. "I'm not sure how it works."

"But you said Grandpa showed you."

"His compass wasn't like that one. Maybe something got into the works." It didn't seem to play by the same rules.

At the bottom of a steamer trunk, filled with dresses from the 1950s and '60s—the fabrics were gorgeous, if slightly yellowed from storage; they looked as if they hadn't been touched for years—she found a leather-bound journal. A journal, locked, without a key. "Private" embossed on the front cover. Could something more be written there, something Maire hadn't said, from a time her mind was clear? Nora slid it into the bag of cleaning supplies, vinegar and orange oil among them, substances to remove tarnish, to dust, to restore, to bring things to light.

Nora had her own journals, kept in a box in the far corner of the storage room in the house on Oak Street, behind the girls' outgrown rocking horse and crib. The toys and baby furniture she and Malcolm had held onto, because the girls may have outgrown them but they didn't want to let them go; a tie to the past, to the heart of their childhood. Nora stopped to consider: Did she want her daughters to read her journals someday, for that sort of evidence to remain? Her mistakes, joys, sorrows, complaints, observations, over things that seemed insignificant now? (She'd stopped when the girls were born. There wasn't time for her own thoughts, much less to write them down.)

Private. Maire was gone now. Nora couldn't speak to her, request permission. There would be no more conversations, searching or mundane. She could only gather what she could from what was left behind— including this journal, part of her inheritance, after all. Maire had left her everything except the boat.

"Did you find something?" Annie asked.

"Aunt Maire kept everything, didn't she?" Nora evaded the question.

"The attic is like a big treasure chest."

The journal most of all.

Nora would decide whether to read it later, when eyes weren't upon her.

Ella was neatening the deck when Nora and Annie came downstairs. "I didn't realize you were so handy with a broom," Nora said. "You wield it quite professionally."

"I'm good at cleaning up messes."

"Perhaps you'd like to tackle the cottage next." They couldn't keep ahead of the incessant sand.

"Whatever you say," Ella said calmly. Thank goodness her mood seemed to have improved.

Polly called to them from the kitchen. "It's all boxed up. Do you want help carrying the provisions to the cottage?"

"We'll take what we can manage for now," Nora replied. "You and Alison should have the others. It's what Maire would have wanted."

"Are you sure you don't want us to stay? We don't have to go into town, if you need us," Alison said.

"We'll be all right."

Polly's gaze flickered toward the point, where the smoke continued to curl from the chimney. "I forgot you have Owen."

Alison shot her a smile with a hint of mischief. Perhaps she guessed what had been going on.

Nora didn't think to ask Ella what she'd been doing during that missing hour, an hour that could not have been taken up entirely with the tidying of the deck—or whatever else she was sweeping away.

Chapter Twenty

After the girls had gone to sleep, Nora settled beside the fire and cut the strap that secured the journal. The brittle leather yielded easily to her scissors, and yet she hesitated before opening the cover. A shower of petals dropped from the vase of late-season daylilies on the table. Maire had given her the bouquet of unopened buds before she died, and they were beginning to wither. A sign? Perhaps.

The words floated up from the paper as she skimmed the entries. She heard her aunt's voice, as if she were there in the room, the language simple, yet vivid.

Thought Da would have been pleased with my marks this term. I showed him the paper. But all he talked about was Maeve. How she'll be the Queen of the

Fleet this year. How she'll ride the float through town and everyone will clap and cheer. When he saw my face, he said I would be too, in another year or two. But I know I won't. I'm not that sort of girl. The sort of girl everyone admires. Everyone votes for . . .

Fought with Maeve today. With hairbrushes. I drew blood for once. M. told Mam she'd hit her head. There are some things we'll never tell on each other for. It will make a scar when it heals. Something for her to remember me by. . . .

Cried in my room today. Johnny B. heard I liked him and treated me like I had leprosy. Meanness to cover the embarrassment. Having a crush. I'd never thought about the weight of that word. How it can harm the person who has it. Maeve heard me and made me tell her what was wrong. I can never keep anything from her for long. She said she'd blacken his eye if I wanted her to. I've never seen her so angry. It's all right for her to make me cry, but whenever anyone else does, she gets protective. I told her not to punch him, but I felt a little better, knowing that she would have come to my defense.

Maeve took center stage at the dance again, the girls jealous because the boys couldn't take their eyes off her, giving her the candy and flowers intended for their dates.

No one ever looks at me that way. I wonder if anyone ever will.

Da towed a man into port today. His sailboat was battered in the storm. Mast broken and everything. Da says he's lucky to be alive. He's staying in the fishing shack for a while. Da seems to like him. I do too.

He's staying. I don't know for how long. Sometimes, I sneak down into the meadow and hide, watching him. Maeve caught me at it and made fun, threatening to tell.

I saw them. Him and Maeve. Through the window. Why does she have to get everything? Everything she wants?

Nora skipped ahead, another year or two. Maire hadn't been the most prolific writer.

Maeve went into labor. Mam gone. Had to help her on my own. She didn't want anyone else there. I thought I knew what to do. The baby came out blue. Patrick there, holding her. The cord around the baby's neck. Maeve screamed and cried until she didn't have any strength left. She lay there, not speaking, looking at me with vacant eyes. I think she blames me. I blame myself. I can't help but think things would have turned out differently if Mam had been there. . . . A little cross in the churchyard, marking the grave. I've never seen a coffin that small. Patrick made it with his own hands.

The pages went blank for a time, then a final entry:

I knew something would happen eventually. It was bound to, given her nature. Wanderlust. A perfect word. I didn't know she'd take Nora with her. A child. What business did she have, taking a child out there? But maybe she hadn't meant to go far . . . I'd never seen Patrick so distraught. He'd always been steady. That was one of the things that drew me to him.

We found Nora on the beach at Little Burke. I helped take care of her as I always had. The fantasy I'd dreamed of seemed to be coming true—that it would be the three of us, our own little family, as it should have been from the beginning, because I was the one who'd seen him first. He should have been mine.

I stayed later at the cottage that night. A week ago, it was. I haven't been able to bring myself to write about it until today. Even now, I hesitate to do so, because I'm not sure I want to commit it to the page. To admit my part in it.

We'd had ale with dinner. I'd brought the jug on purpose, from Da's stores. After I tucked Nora in bed, I went into the kitchen. Patrick was waiting for me, and I for him. He was nearly trembling, with desire I thought, hungry for signs of affection, of need. He pulled me to him roughly, and his kiss wasn't like anything I'd imagined. It was hard, angry.

"Is that what you want?" he asked. "Is it?"

I didn't know what to say to him. I started to cry. He didn't have any sympathy for me. It hadn't happened this way in my dreams. I'll never forget the look on his face. The look of utter revulsion, as if he might be sick.

"You're not her. You could never be her."

He didn't want me. He never had.

The next day, we found he'd taken Nora and gone.

What have I done?

Nora closed the book with a snap and pressed it to her chest. She needed to go through the photo album again. Perhaps there was something she'd overlooked.

She hurried along the path, the flashlight's beam swaying wildly over the ragged fields, the narrow band of dirt and sand marking the way ahead. She glanced back at the cottage. She couldn't leave the girls for long. They were safe enough there—there'd been no further trouble from Maggie Scanlon or the Connellys— but she didn't want them to wake and wonder where she was.

But as she drew closer to Cliff House, she found her feet taking another path, toward the point, toward Owen.

The night was full of shadows, the shack dark. That didn't surprise her. He might have gone to bed early; most fishermen did. The bass were running.

She knocked.

He didn't answer. The silence made her uneasy. Even the seals were quiet that night. The seals, which were never quiet. She tried again, knuckles stinging. She turned the knob. She hoped nothing was wrong. He had always been there when she needed him. "Owen?" Her voice was too loud in the room, his name echoing. She lit the kerosene lamp by the door. His bag— the one Maire had given him, the one that used to be Jamie's—was gone.

The landscape listed around her as she ran to Cliff House, as if everything had slipped its moorings. He wasn't there either. A door opened, but it was only a draft. She checked the dock, where the fishing boat had been tied. It wasn't there.

A twig snapped behind her.

Nora whirled around, shining the flashlight in Ella's face. "Jesus, El, you need to stop sneaking up on people like that."

"He's gone." Her daughter's eyes were hard as stones.

"How do you know that? What did you do?"

"What did I do? What did I do?" she cried. "You mean what did you do? Leaving Dad, bringing us here, going off to see *him*."

"What did you say to Owen?"

"I told him we were leaving for Boston."

"Why would you do such a thing?"

"Because it was the only way you'd go back."

"Go back? I brought us here to get away from the scandal."

"And Dad. To get away from Dad."

"He hurt us."

"He hurt you. That's why you started talking to Owen, wasn't it? Because you needed someone to like you?"

"He was Aunt Maire's guest. She was the one who—"

"You were too! You more than anyone—"

"And so you lied to him? He couldn't have believed you."

"I'm not stupid. I didn't put it as a message from me. I said you told me to tell him. That it would be easier that way. I must have been convincing, because it worked. Maybe he didn't like you as much as you thought. Maybe he has someone waiting for him too."

Nora grabbed her by the shoulders and shook her. "You had no right."

Ella pushed her away. "I had every right—and you know it."

"I can't let him think—"

"He already does. And what does it matter anyway? It's time for us to leave. We don't belong here."

"Get back home. Now."

"That's exactly where I'm going." Ella stormed up the path.

Who knew how much of a head start Owen had had, how far out to sea he was by now. No ships' lights shone in the distance. The water was flat, expressionless, beneath a wan sliver of moon. How could Nora get in touch with him? Let him know it was a mistake, that she wasn't ready for him to go? She had felt more alive with him in those few weeks than she had in years. Maybe it was the newness of him, the lack of real life intruding with its problems, its conflicts. Maybe it was never meant to be more than an interlude. Still, she wished she could talk to him, hear his voice. She could tell Polly what had happened, see if she could summon him on the ship's radio. She nearly did, racing into the kitchen of Cliff House, picking up the phone receiver, dialing her number, then hanging up. Second thoughts again.

After all, he wouldn't have left if he hadn't wanted to. He'd had a choice. Perhaps the news had only made it easier for him to go.

Chapter Twenty-One

Nora took the girls into town the next day, thinking a change of scene might do them good. They'd agreed to meet Alison and Polly for fish and chips that afternoon at Sloane's before the latest dustup, and Nora didn't want to have to get into the reasons for cancelling. Besides, she didn't relish the thought of being trapped with Ella in the cottage the entire day.

The fish came wrapped in newspaper, tails still on. It was the best Nora had ever tasted. She'd never had such a craving for seafood as she did on the island. Ella and Annie went over to play foosball in the corner after they'd finished their meal. The women lingered over cups of coffee.

"Has he gone? Owen?" Polly asked. "The harbormaster said he saw a boat go by yesterday evening."

"It looks like it. I don't know."

"Owen didn't say? I'm sorry. I thought he would have."

"Maybe it was time," Nora said. "He made it clear that his life is at sea."

"That's not how it looked to me," Alison said.

"Looks can be deceiving." She'd had time to think about the consequences of asking Polly to try to locate him, how desperate she'd look.

"It could have been too painful for him, losing Maire," Polly said. "She was like a mother to him."

Nora nodded. To her too.

"Any news from that husband of yours?" Alison asked.

Nora shook her head.

"Ghost lines," Polly said.

"Meaning?"

"Abandoned fishing lines," Polly explained. "Things get caught in them. Like a snare. They can be rather treacherous."

She was obviously talking about more than the lines themselves. So many things had turned treacherous on the island and the surrounding sea, below the surface.

"There's something I've been meaning to mention," Nora said. "I found a journal in Maire's things, from when she was young. I have to confess I read it. I'm not sure I should have—"

"Well, it's part of your inheritance," Alison said. "If she hadn't wanted it to be read, she would have destroyed it. My guess is either she couldn't let go of the memories, or she wanted someone to know about her life. To have her say."

"Did you know she was in love with my father?" Nora asked Polly.

Alison raised her eyebrows. This was clearly news to her.

Polly thought for a moment. "Well, she was the first to meet him. She was down on the docks that day, waiting for her father's boat to come in. She was only a teenager, too young for anything serious as far as your father was concerned. After your grandfather offered him the fishing shack—it was in better shape back then—while his boat was being repaired, she'd drop by to see him, hanging on his every word. Used to drive me crazy. I couldn't see it. He seemed too old for her, and he wasn't my type. Too levelheaded, at least in most ways. I liked the bad boys back then, before I found my Fergus."

"And then?" Alison asked.

"And then Maeve returned. She'd been helping your grandmother with a delivery up-island. A complicated birth, it was. The last she attended. Maeve didn't have the gift or interest in the profession. Maire did. They were competitive with each other over so many things. That's the way it can be for sisters, can't it, loving and resenting each other by turns? One look at Maeve, and it was as if he'd been put under a spell. Maire didn't have a chance. She was too young, and Maeve was too beautiful."

"Maire must have been devastated," Alison said.

"Yes, I suppose. You know how strong your feelings are at that age. She cried, sure, and then, after a while, she pushed it all down. She was practical that way. I knew the sadness was there, but I'm not sure others did. She could appear so steady, even then. But what else would she have done? Maeve and Patrick got married that spring. Maire was the maid of honor."

"There was a mention in the journal of a miscarriage. Was my mother pregnant before she had me?" Nora asked.

"Yes." Polly fell silent.

"There was something else, wasn't there?"

"I'm not sure I should say."

"I'm tired of secrets, aren't you?"

Polly sighed. "The marriage was somewhat rushed, because Maeve was pregnant. There were some doubts as to whom the father was. But when it came to Maeve, there were always doubts. I'm not sure if your father was aware or not. He didn't mix much with the islanders, perhaps because he was reserved. A couple of weeks before the wedding, Maeve had a miscarriage. Maire was there. Your grandmother was off-island. Not many people knew what was going on—Maeve wasn't showing enough to give anything away—and those who did thought they might not get married after all, since it happened before the ceremony."

"Including Maire?" Alison asked.

"Yes. Her and Maeve's relationship became more strained after that, each sister blaming the other. There was nothing that could have been done. But the incident called up other things that had come between them—that they'd allowed to come between them. The suspicions, the accusations of entrapment, among the worst of it."

"Did my mother truly take my father away from Maire?" Nora asked.

"He was never hers to have. Maeve and Patrick belonged together. Or at least he thought so."

A couple of flannel-clad fishermen entered Sloane's and sat down at the counter. "Surprised to hear you put out to sea again so quickly, after the boat went down," said one with a gaff-hook scar on his cheek.

"Couldn't stay away—and there's child support to pay," said the other, his skin ruddy and freckled, curly red hair springing out from beneath a grease-stained hat. He must have worked in the engine room.

"Odd how it happened," his friend mused. "I never thought anything could sink the *Owen Kavanagh*."

Nora and the women exchanged surprised glances. "Excuse me," Nora said. "I'm sorry to interrupt, but the *Owen Kavanagh* is a boat?"

"Yes. Or was."

"Was it named after the owner?" Polly asked.

"The owner's grandfather."

"Was anyone missing?" Nora asked.

"All hands were accounted for, thank God. Went down in that gale a few weeks back. We were doing fine until we hauled up a seal in the net. Don't know how he got in there. Sneaky bastard, one of the biggest I've ever seen. After the fish, I suppose. Fought so hard he pulled the boat to starboard. We tried to cut the net, but it kept swinging wide. Then all it took was a wave to send us over. Why do you ask?"

"Just glad to hear you're okay," Nora said.

"Us too!" He raised a glass. "Here's to clear sailing."

Nora turned to Polly and Alison. "A strange coincidence, isn't it?"

"Strange indeed," they agreed.

Now that Owen was gone, Nora supposed she would never have the opportunity to ask him why he'd taken the name of a downed boat, or if it were truly his own.

Maggie Scanlon stood across the street, staring at Nora, as the group exited Sloane's. She waited for a car to pass, then headed toward them.

"Mom, it's that lady again," Annie said with alarm.

Polly seemed to make a quick assessment of the scene and directed the girls into the bakery next door. "How about a treat for the road?" she asked.

"Mom, are you coming?" Ella asked.

"In a minute."

"Let me handle this," Alison said, stepping between Nora and her grandmother.

"No," Nora said. "It's all right."

"If you're sure—" Alison moved to the side, but remained poised to intervene, if necessary.

"Why are you still here?" Maggie asked Nora. She wore the same clothes as the day Nora had first seen her. Her pants were held up with a safety pin, the fabric covered in stains.

"I live here," Nora reminded her.

"It's all your fault." Maggie rocked on her heels, chin to her chest. Her hair hung in greasy strands.

"What is?"

"He was only a boy."

"Who?"

Maggie's words came out in a rush. "One among many to you, maybe. Nial. He was my date to the dance. You already had Rory Gleason but one wasn't enough for you, was it? You had to have every boy in the room. Me standing there, like a fool. No one to dance with. No one to talk to. You had all the flowers. You had all the men, even the chaperones couldn't take their eyes off you. No one could. You went out to the rocks, to drink and carry on. You promising kisses to anyone who could catch you. Into the water you waded, in your dress, them after you. 'The water's fine,' you said. But it wasn't. It wasn't. Nial went out too far. It was too cold. You knew he wasn't a strong swimmer—no one could swim like you. There were so many boys in the water—you were the only girl—that no one noticed he was gone, not until the next morning, after the sun had risen and they'd sobered up. He washed up later on the beach, his skin blue as the sea." She began to sob. "You didn't come to the service. You didn't even care."

"I don't know what she's talking about," Alison told Nora quietly as Maggie stared into the distance, continuing to rock back and forth. "It's the dementia at work again."

Nora nodded. They'd never know the truth, not for certain. Her mother wasn't there to ask.

"Come on then, Gran." Alison put a hand on Nora's shoulder, before she took Maggie's arm. "It's time to go home."

That evening, Nora met Polly at Cliff House to go through the closets. "I wouldn't be surprised if they contained a skeleton or two, after this afternoon."

Polly shook her head. "Maggie mixed it up. Nial tried swimming to the outer rocks on a dare. He didn't make it. Maeve wasn't there. She didn't have anything to do with his death."

"But Maggie thinks she did. That my mother took him from her. Was she really that manipulative?"

"She didn't mean to be. She had that effect on people, is all."

They sorted through Maire's things—the practical wardrobe of jeans and shirts, only a skirt or two for church; the shoes on the rack flat-soled, one pair of heels, dating to the 1980s.

Polly went through the drawers of the wooden jewelry box on the vanity. "I gave this to her for her tenth birthday." She pulled out a charm bracelet. "I can't believe she kept it."

"You should have it," Nora said. "And anything else you want."

"Things won't bring her back, but I might wear it, to remember her." She fastened it on her wrist with Nora's help, wiping away a tear.

Polly removed another box from a vanity drawer.

"This must have been Maeve's," Polly said.

There was a slip of paper inside. "For Nora," written in Maire's hand. She'd labeled everything throughout the house. *For Polly. For Ella. For Annie.*

"She knew something was wrong, didn't she?" Nora asked.

"She must have." Polly handed Nora the box.

A necklace with a single pearl. "Your father gave that to Maeve for their first anniversary, I think," Polly said. "They came into town for dinner to celebrate. I was bussing tables at the time."

A malachite ring. "From your grandfather's family," Polly said.

A dried corsage.

"From the dance?" Nora asked.

"A dance."

And Nora had an idea.

After Polly left, Nora sat there in the living room, cradling the corsage in her lap, the rose brown, no hint of pink in the petals, the corsage Maggie thought she should have had. Dust motes drifted in the air. A lace curtain overlooking the water stirred listlessly, perhaps an invisible guest admiring the view. It was as if the house were stuck in time. The clock had stopped. No need to wind it now. She was inclined to leave everything as it was, a museum to what had been. She couldn't bring herself to consider the logistics of selling or rearranging, dividing up possessions and property. And yet she knew the time was coming when such decisions would have to be made. To stay, to leave. To prolong the separation or set the divorce proceedings in motion. Search for Owen or let him go. Perhaps it was too late for that. She suspected it was.

The answering machine clicked on. A male voice—Jamie's, probably; Maire had apparently never changed it—announced, "*We're not here right now. Please leave a message after the tone, and we'll get back to you as soon as we can.*"

The cassette hissed, mimicking the insistent noise of the wind pushing leaves and sand across the deck. Nora didn't pick up the receiver. No one would be calling her, not there. The tape continued to spool. Why didn't someone speak? Were they imagining Maire's musical greeting, "Halloo"? Missing the sound of her voice, as Nora did?

She got up. Maybe she should answer. Maybe someone hadn't heard the news—

As she drew closer, she saw the cord dangling loose. It wasn't plugged into the wall. It hung in the air, disconnected. The tape advanced until there was nothing left. Then it clicked, rewound, and started again. There must have been a battery inside, a backup that was malfunctioning—

Her heart pounded. It was the only sound she heard, that and the tape, making that noise. "What are you trying to tell me?" she asked, her voice ringing in the room, the living room, in which she was the only living thing, little ironies everywhere.

The shadows lengthened as the sun flared, low in the sky. Night would be coming soon. A chill crept down her spine. She didn't want to be at Cliff House when darkness fell.

Chapter Twenty-Two

The following day Nora headed toward Portakinney, on the coast road that wound along the cliffs. They were steeper here than at Cliff House, a guardrail the only protection against a plunge onto rocks below. A dirty-winged gull flew directly in front of the windshield, startling her with its agitated wing beats and cries. She was nervous about what lay ahead as it was, but she'd already made the call and said she was coming. She couldn't turn back now. She could put this one thing right—or try to.

She'd spoken to Alison's father, Liam Scanlon, the night before, asked if she could visit Maggie, and why.

"You don't have to do that," he'd assured her. "I'm sorry she's been bothering you. She was never like this before."

"It's the least I can do. Maybe it will help put her mind at rest."

"It's not your problem. Whatever it was, is in the past."

"For her, it doesn't seem to be."

"No, it doesn't," he agreed, a weariness in his voice. "It's funny the things she fixates on. The other day she got worked up about the rain. The rain—it's not as if there's anything that can be done about that. She thought it was attacking her. I don't know how much longer we can care for her here, but I can't bear to send her away. She's my mother, after all."

"I can't imagine what it must be like for you."

"I wish we couldn't, either. But life doesn't always present us with the easiest path, her especially, poor woman."

No, Nora thought, it didn't.

He gave her directions: "Go a half mile north of the village, take the third right, inland. Look for a cottage at the top of the hill, behind the wooden gate."

Nora stopped for a cup of coffee at Joe to Go—even the island had an espresso stand—not so much for a caffeine fix but because she was procrastinating. She stole a look at her face in the rearview mirror, wiping a stray flake of mascara from beneath her eye. She glanced at her watch. She didn't want to be too early.

She sat there for a moment in her parking space, watching the world of Portakinney, such as it was, pass by. Cis McClure gave her a nod as he muscled a cask through the front door of the bar. Dec Connelly ambled past, looking right at her. She froze as their eyes met. But he didn't appear to recognize her. He was just a kid, really, early twenties at most. She could see that now, in the light of day.

She took one last sip of coffee before setting out, leaving the town behind. Close-set dwellings gave way to rolling fields and headlands, a flock of sheep or the occasional cow ambling over the grass. Ten minutes later she passed a stocky brown horse, which regarded her with a woeful expression as it nibbled at the oats in its paddock, then a pile of broken glass by the side of the road, where someone must have either thrown a bottle or crashed into the low retaining wall that ran along the length of the property.

She took the appointed turn, the butterflies in her stomach multiplying. Up the incline she went, through a stand of glowering pines, then onward through more open country, bypassing an oak tree, a tire swing suspended on the lowest bough, the sky visible through the ring. The house stood beyond. She pulled up to the entrance and killed the engine. The house was similar to the cottage at Glass Beach, but larger, the door painted kelly green, echoing the color of the moss growing on the roof. Fishing nets were draped along the fence line of an enclosed garden, where green tomatoes and beans hung on the vine, yellow nasturtiums brightening the scene. A truck was parked to the right, the front bumper mangled where Maggie must have gone headfirst into the ditch, Alison's Capri alongside. Nora was glad she was there.

The curtains stirred. Alison waved from the window. She opened the door and came out to greet her. "Welcome to Casa Scanlon."

"It's lovely." The views of the rugged north coast were stunning.

"Are you sure you want to do this?" Alison asked as they walked up the path.

Nora nodded.

Liam and his wife, Rita, stepped out onto the porch. He was a bear of a man with scarred fisherman's hands and graying hair shaved close; his wife, dark-haired and slender. "Come in, come in." They motioned her inside.

Rita excused herself to retrieve a tray from the kitchen. Nora sat down on a blue velvet chair that made her think of Maire; Alison and Liam on a gray couch with lace panels draped over the arms, opposite. An oil painting of the dockyards was displayed over the mantel.

"Ma made that," Liam said. "Maybe that's where our Ali gets her artistic ability."

"Does your mother still paint?" Nora asked.

He shook his head. "She ends up frustrated— punched her fist through the canvas of a landscape we tried to get her to work on. 'That's what I see,' she said. 'That's what I see!'"

"Or there was that time she painted herself," Alison said.

"Don't remind me. Red paint. I thought she was bleeding to death." He shook his head. "Her cackling away like a creature in a horror film. At least she had a sense of humor that day."

Rita brought out a tray with a pot of tea, cups, and biscuits. "Would you like something to drink?"

Nora nodded, casting a glance around the room as she took a sip from the cup, burning her tongue. Maggie was nowhere in sight.

"I'm glad to have the chance to meet you," Liam said. "Normally, I'd be off fishing with the boys if I hadn't hurt my back last week."

"I'm glad too."

"Ali has talked so much about you," Rita said.

"Good things, I hope." Nora smiled.

"The very best. We don't get many visitors here, not like some of the other islands."

There was an awkward pause, during which Nora heard coughing from behind a door at the end of the hallway off the main room. "Maybe I should see her, before I lose my nerve."

"Of course," Liam said.

"I hope I don't upset her."

She noticed the shadows under his eyes, registering to some small degree the toll the illness was taking on the family.

Alison led the way. "She's been quiet today. That's a good sign." She pushed open the door.

Maggie sat in a chair by the window, staring at the distant ocean. The sky was bleached the palest shade of blue.

"She can sit like that for hours, sometimes," Alison whispered. "She doesn't move at all."

The walls of Maggie's room were a warm white, the faded quilt patched together from swatches of green florals and ginghams. Two throw pillows, embroidered with sprays of roses, lay on the bed, a well-loved, mildewed white rabbit, missing an eye, perhaps from Maggie's childhood, in the center. There were photos on a bulletin board, fastened with tape rather than pins, Nora supposed, to lessen the chance of Maggie hurting herself. The picture frames on the light pine desk—of Maggie and her husband, her children when they were young, her grandchildren—had no glass. It was a simple yet warm room, timeless in its way; the room of a child or an old woman, depending upon the day.

"Gran, someone is here to see you." Alison touched Maggie's shoulder.

Maggie looked up at her, eyes clouded with suspicion. "Who are you?"

"It's Alison, Gran."

Maggie stared at her, uncomprehending, before turning back to the window with a dismissive grunt.

"Sometimes it's like this," Alison told Nora matter-of-factly. "Don't take it personally. I'll give it another try." She touched Maggie's shoulder again. "Gran, you have a visitor."

"Hello, Maggie." Nora took a deep breath and stepped forward. She pulled a box from her purse. Inside was the corsage.

Maggie squinted at her for a moment, then widened her eyes. "You've come to see me," Maggie said. "You never come to see me."

"I have a present for you." Nora handed her the box.

"A present?" She cradled it in her palm.

"Something that should have been given to you a long time ago," Nora explained.

Maggie opened the package.

"For me," Maggie said, eyes brimming with tears. "For me."

The Scanlons invited her to stay for dinner, but she'd told Polly she'd be back in time for her to return to town for her bridge night. She promised to visit with the girls another time. Even the sky seemed particularly benevolent that evening as she drove down-island, washed, as it was, with a warm glow. Swallows swooped ahead, as if leading the way. The boats steamed into the harbor after a long day's work, beeping their horns in greeting, the lights of Portakinney flicking on as dusk approached.

She zoomed along the cliffs, the windows down, wind in her hair, the tang of salt, as always, in the air. She passed the turnoff to the church and the berry fields, then, eventually, Cliff House. She felt a pang of sadness at the thought of her aunt, no longer there.

She parked next to Polly's red mail van. Inside, she found her and the girls wrapping up an intense game of gin rummy. "Ella is quite the card shark," Polly said as Ella lay down her cards in triumph yet again.

"One more round?" Ella asked.

"Not on your life. I hope I have better luck with bridge tonight." She played in a league in town. Maire

did too, or used to. "I'll have to scoot, or I'll be late."
She promised to teach Ella how to play another day.

Nora walked Polly to her car.

"How did it go?" Polly asked.

"Better than I expected."

"I'm glad to hear that. The past can't be undone,
but that doesn't mean we can't try to make things
better."

"Thank you for watching the girls."

"Any time. Don't hesitate to ask. They're lovely. I
hope you'll consider me an honorary auntie," she said,
biting her lip, perhaps thinking of Maire.

"Always." Nora gave her a hug. "Good luck tonight."

"I'll need it. It's not the same without Maire." She'd
had to find another partner, but no one could take
Maire's place.

Polly had made a pot of chicken soup and biscuits
for dinner. Nora was grateful for the extra help. She
was exhausted after the long afternoon and didn't feel
like cooking. She dished up the food and motioned the
girls to the table. "Soup's on."

"What's the green stuff?" Ella asked, wrinkling her
nose.

"Seaweed, probably. It's good for you," Annie said.

"It's kale," Nora said, "from Maire's garden. You
don't mind kale."

"I mind a lot of things."

"Where did you go again?" Annie asked Nora.

"To try to straighten things out with Maggie Scanlon."

"Did you?"

"I think so."

"What about straightening things out with Dad?" Ella asked.

Not that again. Nora made an effort to keep her voice even. "We're working on it."

"It doesn't seem like it."

Walk away, Nora told herself. She didn't want to argue with Ella. She got up from the table.

"Where are you going?" Ella asked.

"To get a sweater. I'm cold." A headache pulsed at her temples. Then she spotted the suitcase—Ella's case, fully packed, outside the bedroom door. She hadn't noticed it before. "What's this?" she asked.

"For when we're going," Ella said. "We are going, aren't we?"

"We're not going anywhere. By the time I come out of this room, I expect to see that bag—and its contents—back where they belong."

"Where they belong, huh? That would be in Boston."

"You know what I mean."

Nora slammed the bedroom door. She hadn't meant to. Well, maybe she had. She sat down in front of the mirror. She'd looked different, transformed, when Owen was there. Because she'd been desired. Because she'd been seen. Now she looked tense and dull. Make your own happiness, she admonished herself. Keep it together.

And she had been happy. There, on the island. With or without Owen, whoever he was, whatever he was. Surely, it wasn't possible . . .

She'd caught her mother sitting there, like this, when she thought no one was looking, a haunted expression on her face.

"Is something wrong, Mama?" she'd asked.

What had been the nature of Maeve's unhappiness? Nora couldn't be sure.

She opened the door. She'd heard movement outside. The case was still there, taunting her. "El, I told you—" When she turned to confront her, she saw pages curling in the fireplace: the separation papers, too late to save them from the flames. "What do you think you're doing?"

"Now you'll have to go back to Boston."

"No, I won't. I don't need your father's papers. I'll be filing my own." She paused, letting the news sink in. "You, however, are going to go straight to your room."

Chapter Twenty-Three

The book of fairy tales fell to the floor, waking Annie in the middle of the night. She'd been reading it under the bedcovers and had fallen asleep. An imprint from one of the embossed letters was tattooed on her hand, a Gothic *A*, from where she had pressed her weight against it, dreaming. She traced the shape with her fingers. It was as if the book had begun to spell her name. As she reached down to retrieve the collection, she saw Ella climbing out the window. Their eyes met, a telegraphed question in the silence. *Are you coming?* Annie put on her coat and boots. She brought Siggy too. He'd already been left behind once.

As they entered the darkened world outside the cottage, moonlight shone on the water in a long, glimmering streak, lighting the way. Down the path they went, to the beach, always to the beach.

Ella tugged the coracle across the sand. "Are you still the first mate?"

"Yes. Why are you moving the boat?"

"Because we're going home."

"But you've hardly packed anything."

"We need to travel light. Mom will bring the rest, once she comes to Boston."

Annie got in. What else could she do? She wished Ronan were there, so that she could say good-bye. Or had he already moved on, like Owen, the two of them together at last? In any case, she couldn't let Ella go alone. Ella didn't know the ocean like she did. They paddled to the mouth of the cove. The seals were nowhere in sight. Perhaps they were sleeping; perhaps they'd left for better fishing grounds. She and Ella had never been out this far before, not alone. The porch light of the cottage was growing smaller by the second. "Did you leave a note?" she asked.

"Why would I do that?"

"So she won't worry. She's going to worry."

"She doesn't care about us. She only cares about herself."

"That's not true."

The boat seemed to move of its own volition, the waves taking control.

"You have to paddle harder," Ella said. "Veer left. South."

"To the horse platitudes?"

Ella laughed. "It's horse latitudes. You should consider getting a degree in malapropisms when you go to college."

"Maybe I will," Annie said with a touch of pride. "I brought this." She handed her the compass.

"You little thief," Ella said with admiration. "Well done."

Onward they went, into the night. Annie didn't know how much time had elapsed. It passed slowly in the channel, the currents holding them back. It was as if the island didn't want to let them go. Ella said they couldn't give up—no matter how much their hands blistered and their arms ached. She'd told Annie what they'd do when they made landfall in Boston: borrow a sailor's or dock-worker's phone, call their father's number, and tell him to come get them. He would be surprised and proud of their accomplishment. He would see how much they loved him, the lengths to which they'd go. He would take them out to dinner, Chinese, their favorite, and they would read their fortunes, which would predict only good things, and they would say whatever they wanted and have the worst table manners ever, because their mother wouldn't be there to correct them.

"What about Mama?" Annie asked.

"What about her?"

The water turned black and viscous as oil, muttering to itself as it slapped at the boat, slaps that rocked them sideways, the waves rising.

"A storm is coming," Annie said. "Remember what Reilly said? That the sea is unpredictable. The weather can change in an instant. You can smell it on the wind."

"The only thing I smell is you."

A wave came out of nowhere, swamping the boat. "Bail!" Ella cried. They used two plastic buckets in which Maire had once gathered honey, to no avail. The coracle climbed up the side of a wave, crested, slid down another, each more precipitous than the last. The waves rose higher. A sea serpent, Annie thought, lashing its tail. The roar grew louder; they could barely hear each other.

"We have to meet the waves head-on, otherwise we'll capsize," Ella shouted.

The ocean altered its tactics, coming at them with sneaker waves, rogues, front- and broadside assaults, and then a spiral. Annie felt it first. "We're going down the drain," she said.

"No!"

"The sea's not listening. It gets to decide." Annie almost liked that her sister wasn't going to get her way for once, that there was something bigger than her, than all of them. Than their father and mother and the difficulties they'd been through. The whirlpool pulled the girls into a canyon of water. She wondered where it would end. How long she would be able to watch before it engulfed them. It was the most magnificent thing she had ever seen, a city of water, towers all around. She blew on the shell, as Ronan had told her. It was the only thing she could do. Someday had arrived.

A chute opened up ahead, sending them into the air, the coracle flipping. Ella screamed as they hit the water, blackness all around. Up. Which way was up? If Annie had gills, she could live there, beneath the waves; she could make the ocean her home. Then she felt, rather than heard, the boat come down over-head, and she swam toward it, that dark shape against the darker night. She surfaced, sputtering, one hand on the rope. Ella. Where was Ella? She glimpsed the orange life jacket, her sister floating. She pulled her toward the upside-down boat, slapped her hard across the face. "Wake up! Wake up!" Ella didn't stir. She put her face next to hers. Yes, she was alive. She was breathing.

Ella blinked and stared about her with uncompre-hending eyes. "Where's the boat?"

"Here. It's upside down. You have to hold on to the side." There were two rings on the front, for the rope, once used to tie it up.

"We'll get hypothermia. The water's cold. We won't last."

"Remember the story we read with Mama, about the man whose boat sank, and he floated in the ocean for days? He stayed warm by the power of his thoughts, like the monks in Tibet, who meditate in the snow." Her teacher, Ms. Kelly, had told the class about them.

"The time for playing pretend is over. Don't you understand? We could die." Ella's teeth chattered.

"Do you feel that?"

"I can't feel anything. I'm going numb."

"It's the current. It's carrying us somewhere. Fast."

"That somewhere better be land. I'm sleepy. I'm taking a nap."

"No. Stay awake. You have to stay awake." Annie shook her.

Ella closed her eyes, the waves rocking, rocking.

How would their story end? It was as if they were within the pages of the book of fairy tales, living the very words they'd been reading. Would their mother pick up the collection and find them there—the scene illustrated in color plates? The old-fashioned words describing their ordeal, telling how Annie was doing her best to be brave and strong, though she was only seven? Especially in the sea that dwarfed anyone and anything that dared sail upon it.

They hadn't asked permission. Was that the problem? Ella should have known better than to trespass upon the waves.

"I'm sorry," Annie whispered. "We should have asked first. We didn't mean any harm. Please protect us. You have it within your power to keep us safe."

She was tired, so tired. She fought against sleep, eyelids fluttering, open, closed, the sea a seesaw, seasaw. She smiled at the pun. She'd have to tell Ella . . .

It was as if she were sliding under the waves.

Stay awake, she told herself.

Someone had to. Someone had to watch over them, to make sure nothing bad happened. To keep the sea monsters at bay—she knew they were out there, gnashing their teeth, sharpening their claws. How could they not be, when two small girls had entered their territory? Two small girls, seasoned quite nicely by the salt of the sea.

But there were good creatures too, weren't there? The good and the bad and the in-between, in the ocean, as on land. If there was anything Annie had learned in the past few weeks, it was that—in Boston and here on the island too.

Stay—

Then she too lost consciousness, the ocean claiming her at last.

Chapter Twenty-Four

It began with a speck, a grain of sand, on Nora's arm. She brushed at her skin, whole parts of her sloughing away—fingers, hands, limbs. She was losing shape and form, disintegrating, a woman made of sand. She tried to scream, but she had no mouth, no voice. The wind carried her away. She was borne skyward over the ocean, scattering across the beach, the waves. There would be nothing left of her. The girls, playing far below, out of reach—

She opened her eyes with a start. Eyes gritty from sleep, as if filled with the sand from her dreams. She rolled out of bed and stumbled into the bathroom. Her eyes were red and puffy. She reached for the glycerin drops in the medicine cabinet. There, that was better, though the raw feeling remained.

It was uncharacteristically quiet in the cottage that morning. The girls, early risers, were generally up by then, playing, plotting, arguing. Though Ella had started to sleep in, as adolescents often did. Nora felt daunted at the prospect of a teenage Ella, the challenges that next stage would bring. Joys too. There would be joys, if she had anything to do with it.

She puttered in the kitchen. The fridge and pantry held ingredients for coffeecake—frozen blueberries from Maire's freezer, buttermilk, eggs, flour. She poured and mixed, a meditative quality to her movements. She would begin the day from this centered, nurturing place. The scent of baking filled the cottage. She glanced at the clock: 10:30 a.m. She'd take a peek, check on them, as she had when they were babies. She turned the knob, winced at the click—she didn't want to wake them if they were still resting. She smiled as she pictured Ella, sprawled with her face half in the pillow, Annie with her hands folded over her chest, like Snow White. Their faces peaceful, innocent in sleep.

Instead, there was the open window, the empty beds. They must already be adventuring. It was kind of them to let her sleep; even Ella, demanding Ella, had her considerate moments. The coffeecake would be ready soon. She set out to call them to breakfast. Or maybe they'd already had cereal? No, there were no bowls in the sink or on the drain board. It didn't appear they'd eaten anything that morning—which was the first detail that gave her pause. A pause in which the scene gradually went still. Everything was in its place—the path, the trees, the beach, the house—except the girls weren't there. Nora tried to be logical. Where would they have gone? She checked the woods, the meadow, Maire's. She hardly felt the ground beneath her feet, the wind in her face, the absence of sensation, of her daughters, intensifying. She looped through another field, down along the bluff to the beach.

No girls.

No coracle either.

The sea lapped at the shore, delicate and knowing as a cat. The sea that went on and on as far as the eye could see, not a boat, not a person in sight.

She ran to Reilly Neale's, falling and skinning her knee, rising, running again. She couldn't feel her legs beneath her. She beat on his door with both fists. "Mr. Neale? Mr. Neale, are you there?"

He shuffled to the door, the dog barking. He wore a moth-eaten sweater, his hair a white-wisped nest, as if he'd just run his hands through it or gotten out of bed.

"Have you seen them? Have you seen the girls?" she asked.

"No, I—" He tugged at the sleeves of his holey cardigan.

"The coracle is gone."

He seemed to understand the source of her panic now. "The tide might have taken it," he said. "When did they go?"

"I'm not sure. Sometime during the night?" She'd slept hard, dreamless, for once.

"During the storm?"

"Storm?"

"Didn't you hear it? Wasn't as bad as some—winter brings far worse—but rough enough for this time of year. The quick and dirty type. No time to be on the water, especially for the young, though there's no saying they took the coracle in the first place. The sea came high up the beach yesterday. There's been a surge lately."

"I didn't hear a thing." She felt dazed.

He patted her arm. "You can't watch them twenty-four hours a day, especially that Ella. No stopping her when her mind is made up, is there? If they did set out, they're probably close by, at the Mermaid Cave or one of the coves. They're smart, capable girls. We'll call Polly from Maire's. Darn me for not having a phone. She'll get the word out. Don't worry. We'll find them. Chances are, they're hiding, having a good laugh."

Nora ran ahead and phoned Polly, who broadcast the alert. *"All hands, two young children lost at sea."* She closed the post office for the day to man the radio. It was usually one of the men they searched for, never little girls, not since Nora herself went missing that long-ago summer. The bells rang in the church, in the harbor, summoning the fishermen to duty.

Reilly limped in behind her and made tea in Maire's kitchen.

"Now what do we do?" Nora paced the length of the living room before sitting down at the table, jiggling her leg.

Reilly gave her a cup of tea, a slice of lemon and spoonful of honey on the side. "We wait."

Nora had no boat. She must stay there and hope for news. Good news.

They regarded each other across the table, the former fisherman and the politician's wife. They were a team now. The minutes ticked by without a word. It would take time. She knew that. Outside, the mist gathered. "The weather is turning," Nora said, not against them, she hoped. She closed her eyes, asking for the strength to get through this one day, and whatever would follow.

Time passed. She tried not to look at her watch, to mark the passing minutes. Reilly told her stories, tall fishing tales, Irish versions of Jonah and the whale, to keep her mind off things, until a ship's horn sounded from the dock.

They hadn't expected a boat to come to Cliff House, but it appeared one had—her uncle's, Owen motioning them aboard. Reilly went first.

"You're here—" Nora nearly threw her arms around him in relief. She only held herself in check because Reilly was there.

"I came as soon as I heard," he said.

She fought back tears. It was too much, seeing him again at such a time.

"And a good thing too," Reilly interjected. "We should get moving. Visibility is getting worse by the minute."

Owen took the wheel, his eyes on the waves ahead. He wore one of Jamie's sweaters, jeans, boots, and a rain jacket. "There's another slicker over there, if you want it. You're not exactly dressed for heading to sea." He noted her bloodied jeans. "And bandages in the cabinet."

"They could be anyplace by now—"

"We'll find them."

She wanted to believe him. She'd never wanted to believe anything more in her life. "I thought you'd gone."

"I thought you had too." He steered the boat past the breakwater.

"That's what Ella wanted, not me. Did you believe her?"

"I didn't know what to believe."

"No, I suppose you didn't." She paused. "I heard a curious story in town about the wreck of the *Owen Kavanagh*."

He regarded her steadily, as if waiting for her to draw her own conclusions.

She thought of that night, the ocean, the story Polly told, and that of the sailors.

"You can't mean—"

"Perhaps you called me," he said, a glint in his eye. "That first night you arrived on the island."

Her tears in the sea. "You can't expect me to believe that."

"Believe what you want. It's what we choose to believe that shapes us."

"It's sounding mighty philosophical in here." Reilly rejoined them, stamping his feet.

"Do you think Ella is trying to get back to Boston?" Owen asked.

"She wouldn't be so foolish," Nora said, their unfinished conversation hanging between them. It would have to wait for another time. "The coracle is hardly fit to sail, certainly not that far, not by children."

"Depends on how badly she wanted to go home."

"Boston, you say?" Reilly said. "That must have been why she was asking me about navigation. I thought her interest had been academic, not practical."

"When was that?" Nora asked.

"A few days ago. I'm sorry. I didn't realize what she was up to."

"None of us did."

They lapsed into silence as the vessel headed into the open water. They could search for hours, days, weeks, without a trace. The girls were gone. Like Maire's husband and son. Like Nora's mother.

A voice came on the radio. One of the fishermen. *"Possible debris found. South of the Teeth. Searching for survivors."*

"There are always boards floating about after storms," Reilly assured her.

"The water's too cold," Nora said as if he hadn't spoken. And the Teeth too formidable, wave-lashed, and narrow for anyone to get a handhold. How would the girls survive? She couldn't stop shivering. Reilly put Owen's coat over her shoulders, and still she couldn't get warm, the adrenaline, the mist, the thought of her daughters out there, somewhere, alone, too much for her. "When can you get us there?" she asked Owen.

"In about half an hour if the conditions are good," he said. "But the current splits in two, something like a maritime fork in the road. One goes south, where the wreckage was found, the other, which isn't consistent, north, toward Little Burke."

"Yes—I hadn't thought of that," Reilly agreed.

Nora stared at them. "But the others said—"

"I know what they said," Owen replied. "There are plenty of boats due south and none to the north. They'll let us know if they find something definite. In the meantime, we might as well try this."

Reilly nodded. "He's right. It's worth a shot."

Little Burke. It was an island. A place the girls could find shelter, as she had, once upon a time.

Annie was awake now, wasn't she? Swimming in and out of consciousness. She'd thought she heard Ronan. *You'll be all right. You'll see. I told you I knew where to find you.* She could get her breath now. Air. Land. Her skin felt tight, itchy. Her hair stiff. Sea salt. The sound of waves against the shore. She still felt the movement, though they were no longer afloat. A cabin. No, a shack. You could see the night through it in places, and yet it was dry inside. There was a fire. She didn't feel the cold anymore. The smell of smoke, seaweed, the beach at low tide. Siggy at her side. He'd made it. So had Ella.

There was a woman with long silver hair. She tucked something around them. A blanket? Annie couldn't be sure. "You're safe now," she said. She had the Burke's Island lilt, but something else too. Annie wanted her to keep talking, but she turned away and sat by the fire. Ella didn't stir, sleeping deeply, as if she were under a spell, but Annie drifted somewhere between enchantment and reality, though she couldn't speak or move. The woman looked away. *Who are you?* Annie wanted to ask, but she couldn't form the words. "It's time to sleep, little one," the woman said, drawing closer again, stroking her cheek. The warmth, her words, her touch, too much to resist. Annie closed her eyes and dreamed.

"**Is this** the area where the current would have taken them?" Nora asked. There'd been no sign of the coracle. She was beginning to doubt the plan. The mist grew more impenetrable.

"It matches the charts, but the islands don't always follow them," Reilly said.

Her eyes ached from the constant effort of peering into the fog. They had to get to the girls—and soon. "Can't you go any faster?" she called to Owen.

"I've pushed the engine to its limit as it is." As if in agreement, it ground to a halt.

"Oh, God, no. Can you fix it?" Nora didn't attempt to keep the panic from her voice.

"I don't know." He went below with Reilly. She could hear them hammering, swearing.

She paced above, listening to the occasional conversation on the radio, the latest alluding to another possible storm brewing in the south, churning up the coast. "They say there's another storm coming," she yelled down the steps.

Reilly ascended, his breathing labored as he hoisted himself back onto the pilot house. "Yes."

"You don't seem surprised."

"I heard it earlier, when you were on deck." She'd popped outside at intervals, monitoring the water for evidence of debris. "There was no use in worrying you further—"

"All the more reason to move quickly."

"Storms like that often lose energy. There's a good chance it won't even make it this far."

"But there's also a chance it will—and that's a chance I'm not willing to take."

"I thought there was life left in the old engine," Owen said when he joined them a few minutes later, wiping his hands on a rag. "But it's given out. According to my calculations, we're not that far from shore. We could radio for help. Someone will come. They'd be able to get closer; they'd probably have a dinghy for landing." Joe's boat didn't have one, at least not anymore.

"It's as if the island doesn't want us to draw any nearer. It makes its own rules," Reilly mused.

"And I make mine," Nora said. "How far are we from shore?" She shed her shoes and coat. She was tired of waiting. She knew what she had to do. She wouldn't let Owen stop her.

"It could be a mile or more. Wait a minute. What are you up to?" Owen asked.

"I'm going in," she said.

"That's not a good idea."

"There's no alternative. You know there isn't."

"I'll go with you."

"No, you should stay here." Her gaze shifted to Reilly, who was listening to the radio. "In case one of the boats comes."

"They will. The *Mary Grace* is en route. If you'd wait a little longer—"

"There might not be time. I can't take the risk."

"Aren't you taking a greater one?"

"No." Not when it came to her children.

"If anything were to happen to you—"

She didn't hear the rest of the sentence. She dove. The water closed over her, chill as ever. She was used to it by now, but she knew she needed to move fast. A seal shot past her, bound for shore. She stroked hard, head down, in its wake. Her breath, her motion, her choice. No struggle, just forward momentum. The seal surfacing, submerging, the mist swirling. She treaded water, saltwater stinging her eyes, the boat no longer in sight. The seal bobbed nearby; its head suddenly appeared human, with long silver hair. Was she seeing things?

A rip current pulled her away. She swam parallel, hoping it would relent. If it didn't, she might be carried out to sea. Her arms and legs felt leaden. She couldn't let them fail her now. Perhaps this was what she'd been training for, not that other race with its starting guns and ribboned medals, but this—to reach the shore, to find her daughters. The thought of them spurred her onward when she didn't think she could go any farther. Stroke. Breathe. Her arms flailed, her legs dangled beneath the surface, lower, lower still. If she could only make it to the beach, feel land beneath her feet once more.

Nora wriggled her toes in the sand. It was the summer her mother disappeared. She'd followed her down to the shore, life jacket in hand. She knew her mother was taking the coracle. She'd seen her do it before. "Where are you going?"

Maeve stood knee-deep in the water, preparing to launch. "On a little trip. I'll be back soon."

"I want to come."

"You're not old enough."

"I am. I am." She crossed her arms over her chest. "If you don't let me, I'll tell."

Maeve laughed. "Who said it was a secret?"

"No one." But if it wasn't, why didn't she tell anyone? Why did she vanish for hours at a time?

Maeve thought for a moment. "Come on, then."

"What about Daddy?" Nora asked.

"There's only room for two. We won't go far. Does he know you're here?"

"No." She wanted to be part of her mother's secret, whatever it was. She wanted to find out. "Where are we going?"

"Around the bend."

Off they went, across the cove, into the ocean.

"Look, Mamai," Nora called, *mamai* the Gaelic word for mommy, "I'm flying." Over the waves. Nora spread her arms and closed her eyes.

The fishing boats were farther afield, mere dots on the eastern horizon. They'd gone out early that morning, as always. Nora and her mother were the only ones on that part of the ocean. Nora thought of it as their kingdom, the paddle her mother's scepter, ruler of all that lay below. Onward they went, to places Nora hadn't been before. They sailed around sea stacks and through arches, to a hidden cave.

Her mother tied the boat to a rock. "Wait here." She went inside.

Nora sat in the boat, counting the waves. She could never count them all. They kept coming and coming.

A short time later, her mother returned with a package, wrapped in oilcloth and tied with string.

"What's that? Is it treasure? Is it a surprise?"

"You'll see, someday." She began paddling again.

Nora didn't want to wait until someday. She wanted to know now. She pulled away an edge of the wrapping when her mother wasn't looking. She still couldn't see what was inside. It was odd. It felt like fur.

"Nora!" Her mother snatched the package away. "You mustn't touch things that don't belong to you."

"What happens if I do?"

Her mother didn't reply. She seemed worried now. The weather was changing, and they needed to get back to Glass Beach.

The fur reminded Nora of the story in the book of fairy tales her mother read to her. "Are you one of them?"

Maeve didn't answer. The waves rose around them, peaks of liquid glass. They swept the vessel into the channel. The sun dimmed, the clouds advancing, the wind blustering. Maeve stroked hard up one face, then another. She was strong. She could do anything. She would keep them safe. That's what Nora told herself, though she crouched in the bottom of the coracle, frightened.

The boat flipped, as if an invisible hand had turned it over and tipped them into the ocean. Nora fought against the water; it slapped her in the face. She glimpsed the boat continuing on its way, like a riderless horse, before the waves closed in on them again.

She felt her mother's arm around her. The package floated from Maeve's grasp. She couldn't hold on to them both. "You can swim, remember?"

She could, but never so far.

"Pretend you're a fish, a fish in the sea."

"I can't. I'm just a girl."

"Try. You have to try—"

Maeve's voice grew fainter, her breathing labored. She was bleeding. Nora saw the blood, seeping down her arm, staining both of them red. "You're hurt—"

"Don't worry. I'll be fine." She pushed Nora up on a rock ledge.

Where were they? Everything was too far away. The boats. The shore. Nora began to cry.

Maeve hugged her. "Hush now, hush." She hummed a lullaby, her grip on Nora, and the rock itself, weakening. Nora didn't know what to do.

"I'm sorry I peeked inside the package, Mamai. It's all my fault."

"It's not, love. It's mine, for not making the choice."

"What choice?"

A seal appeared, then another.

"You need to help her," Nora said. "She's hurt. You can help. I know you can."

"Hold on. Don't ever let go." Her mother slid into the sea, the seals too.

"Mamai! Mamai!"

Her mother didn't answer. She was gone.

Be strong. *Swim. You know the way.* Maeve's voice again. Nora thought she was losing her mind, falling through time. Then she heard seals barking nearby. Land had to be close. The current lessened, her strength too. There was nothing else for it; she had to make a hard break for shore. Her lungs felt as if they might burst.

She was all motion now, memory. She sensed the tide with her, carrying her in on the crest of a wave. She scraped her legs against a rock, kicked with everything she had left. The sea spat her out onshore, the seals sliding off the rocks into the water. She struggled to stand, her legs so wobbly they gave out the first time. She'd crawl if she had to. She pulled herself up on the granite boulders lining the bank, sensation slowly returning.

"I'm here," she shouted. "I'm here." There was a trail, heading upward. A trail she would take.

Granite, sand, pebble, that was all Little Burke was, chosen by seals and birds for its natural ledges, leading up and up, to a stone plateau. Tide pools flourished along the shoreline, shadow boxes filled with delicate starfish and anemones, in shades of orange and green, rocks slick with seaweed, barnacles, and mussels. The beach was littered with sea glass, shells, floats, a single glove, a shoe, a cobalt blue bottle—the treasures, the debris, of those who lived or spent time by the ocean.

The island's stones held its history, of creatures large and small, the living and the dead—of the earth reshaping itself, this place too, the waves that never stopped, would never be still.

The way was far from clear. The path seemed to peter out, then started again a short distance ahead. She needed to be alert to find the way. Her feet were numb from the cold, bleeding from barnacle cuts. She felt the pain only mildly, as if it belonged to someone else.

She heard the blast of the ship's horn in the distance, Owen letting her know he was there. She imagined the seals circling the boat, as if to tell him she'd landed safely, that she'd finally come home—and she had. She understood that now. That this was part of a journey begun years ago, left incomplete, the site of her abandonment, of beginnings and ends. The island had been waiting for her. Everything circles back on itself in the end, she thought. Everything is connected. The geography of the land, of the soul. The edge of a curtain had lifted, and she glimpsed what lay beyond, if only for a moment, and yet that moment was enough to comprehend, in part, her mother's sacrifice.

"Ella! Annie!" She called for her daughters, for minutes, for hours, it seemed, though it couldn't have been that long. Her voice grew raspy. Shapes loomed in the mist, shifting, undefined, no sign of the girls yet.

Mama?

The word so faint she might have imagined it, an echo of her own voice ringing back to her, across the years.

Ella. Annie.

They needed her. She would not let go, would not slip away. Perhaps her mother hadn't had a choice. Nora did, and the power of that knowledge propelled her forward.

"Mama? Is that you?"

She set off in the direction of the voices, half blind with tears, down the stony slope to that isolated beach and its ruin of a fishing shack, withered gray boards standing the test of time, yet enough to provide shelter. Her girls, sandy and scraped but whole, even Siggy, in Annie's arms.

"Mama, you wouldn't believe what happened."

"You wouldn't believe where we've been."

"What we've seen."

Oh, but she did, she did.

They launched themselves at her and she held them fast, and in that embrace, borne of love and relief, she saw herself, a little girl, her mother's daughter, clinging to the rocks for dear life as Maeve slid into the water. *Don't let go.* She had saved Nora the only way she'd known how.

"I knew you'd come," Ella said.

Time bends, end on end.

A bird soaring. A whale breaching. A seal diving, surfacing.

This. This is what mattered.

To feel your children in your arms. To feel the life flowing within you, within them, in the sky and the sea and a tiny island in the middle of nowhere.

Nora presses her cheek to their temples, her girls, her lovely girls, feels their pulses thrumming with the rhythm of life.

Their life. Together.

This.

This is the place.

Acknowledgments

With affection to those who've helped me on the journey to writing this book, especially Kyle Lindskog, Jeannie Berwick, and Marcellina Tylee; the Dorans—my dad, Robert, who has always encouraged me to follow my own path, sisters, Robbi Anderson and Tessa Effland, and aunt, Letty Pericin; the Barbieri clan, especially Kay and Jannie; Carol Carlson; Bob and Paula Rohr; Robin Jones and Leona DeRocco, for their love of books and carpooling assistance at a crucial time; Sara Nickerson, stalwart reader and friend; Kit Bakke; Maria Semple; Seattle7 Writers; and the Fiction Writers' Co-op. My agent, Emma Sweeney, her assistant, Suzanne Rindell, and my editor, Jennifer Barth, for their support and belief in this project. And most of all, to my dear family, Mark, Sian, Connor, and Sera. You are everything to me.

About the Author

The author of two previous novels, *The Lace Makers of Glenmara* and *Snow in July*, Heather Barbieri has won international prizes for her short fiction. She lives in Seattle with her family.